Dear Reader,

Firstly may I thank you for all your letters and the questionnaires you have returned? If you haven't yet completed a questionnaire, we'd be delighted if you could fill in the form at the back of this book and let us have it back. It is only by hearing from you that we can continue to provide the type of *Scarlet* books you want to read.

Perhaps you'd like to know how we go about finding four new books for you each month? Well, when we decided to launch *Scarlet* we 'advertised' for authors through writers' organizations, magazines, literary agents and so on. As a result, we are delighted to have been inundated with manuscripts – particularly from the UK and North America. Now, of course, some of these books have to be returned to their authors because they just aren't right for *your* list. But others, submitted either by authors who've already had books published or by brand new writers, are exactly what we know readers are looking for. Sometimes, the book is almost perfect when it arrives on my desk, but usually we enjoy working closely with the author to give their book that essential, final polish.

What you'll notice over the coming months are more books from authors who've already appeared in *Scarlet*. Do let me know, won't you, if there's a particular author we've featured who *you'd* like to see again? See you next month and, in the meantime, thank you for continuing to be a *Scarlet* woman.

Best wishes,

Sally Cooper

SALLY COOPER,
Editor-in-Chief – *Scarlet*

About the Author

Sally Steward has been hooked on writing since her teacher let her get away with a scam: Sally made up a story for a book report, including imaginary author, publisher and publication date and her teacher pretended to be deceived and gave her an 'A'!

In order to support her 'habit', Sally has worked as a secretary, real estate agent, administrative assistant and so on. In addition, she sold true confession stories to pay off debts. She gave this up when the bills were paid and her sources of material dwindled as her friends figured out what was going on and stopped telling her their secrets! Sally now writes full-time and has had five books published, including this her first *Scarlet* novel.

Sally is married and lives in Missouri, USA, with her husband Max, a very large cat, Leo, and a very small dog, Cricket. Other than writing Sally claims her interests are: 'drinking Coca Cola, eating chocolate and reading *MAD* magazine!'

Other **Scarlet** *titles available this month:*

CARIBBEAN FLAME by Maxine Barry
WIVES, FRIENDS AND LOVERS by Jean Saunders
THE MARRIAGE SOLUTION by Julie Garratt

SALLY STEWARD

UNDERCOVER LOVER

Enquiries to:
Robinson Publishing Ltd
7 Kensington Church Court
London W8 4SP

First published in the UK by Scarlet, 1996

A copy of the British Library Cataloguing in
Publication data is available from the British Library

ISBN 1-85487-499-3

Printed and bound in the EC

10 9 8 7 6 5 4 3 2 1

To Cheryal Ainsworth Southerland
for never being too busy or too soundly
asleep to answer my questions about
Oklahoma City and for being my friend
for twenty years

CHAPTER 1

Allison Prescott dashed down the alley, elbowing her way past the onlookers and other reporters, up to the police tape surrounding the murder scene. With a quick look behind her to be sure Rick Holmes was following with the video camera, she leaned over the tape and thrust her mike toward the nearest police officer.

'We believe it's the same as the other four,' the man was saying in answer to someone else's question. 'A head injury from a blunt instrument, probably between midnight and four or five this morning.'

'Who found the body?' Allison asked.

'A clerical worker on the tenth floor.' He pointed upward. 'She came in early and opened the blinds in her boss's office.'

'Do you have any suspects?' another reporter called out.

'No suspects at this time. We're working on the case and expect to solve it soon.'

3

'Do you have an i.d. on the victim?' Allison, keeping her eyes fixed on the officer, avoided the sheet-covered mound. She hadn't been doing this long enough to be able to view crime scenes dispassionately.

'No identification yet. He appears to be another street person.'

A big man in a dark suit pushed his way through the crowd, lifted the tape and slid under.

'Detective Raney, do you have any new leads on this case?' Allison demanded.

He glared at her, then slowly scanned the group of media people, his contempt for them obvious. 'The department has several leads we're currently working. However, I'm not at liberty to discuss them with the press at this time.' He turned his back, raised the sheet from the body and muttered a phrase that wouldn't be allowed on television.

Talking to the other officers, he ignored the questions hurled at him from the media.

'The public has a right to know!' Allison finally called in frustration.

Raney aimed a glare in her direction that would have had her skulking away six months ago. Now she returned the glare and stood her ground.

'The public has a right to have this murderer caught and punished, and that's what I'm trying to do.' He knelt beside the body, again excluding the reporters.

Allison gritted her teeth in frustration. Along with the others from the local newspapers, radio and television stations, she would hang around for the duration. Most of the police work consisted of boring minutiae, but they stayed, waiting for the one significant item that would make their story unique.

A tall, shabbily dressed man shuffled up to the scene and stood beside Allison. Though she didn't want to look at him, couldn't deal with such a close-up view of the frightening specter of poverty, a specter already crowding the edges of her life, nevertheless, her gaze was drawn to him with a morbid fascination.

His head and face seemed to consist mainly of one huge mass of curly, light brown hair. His eyes and nose were barely discernible. His nondescript clothing was worn and faded but, she noted, clean. A brown plaid shirt-jacket hung loosely from his lanky frame, and his tan slacks ended a good two inches above his ankles.

'Who you got there?' he called to the officers.

She cringed inwardly, feeling sorry for the man as she anticipated the officers' annoyed responses.

But Detective Raney lunged over to the tape – almost eagerly, Allison thought – and raised it for the tall man to pass under. 'You know this fellow? Take a look.'

The stranger knelt beside Raney and peered at the body from all angles. Because of the detective's out-of-character action toward the bum, Allison studied him as intently as he studied the corpse.

No, she corrected herself, her interest growing. Not just because of Raney's actions. There was something about the stranger – an intensity, a sense of purpose – something that drew her attention. In spite of his appearance, he didn't have the beaten-down demeanor she usually saw in the homeless.

'I've seen him around.' The man spoke so quietly his words were barely audible. Even so, Allison heard the frustrated anger in his tone.

He stood and turned to leave, and as he did so, his gaze met hers for a fraction of a second. He immediately ducked his mop of hair and began to push through the group, ignoring the questions directed at him by the media.

'How long have you been on the streets?'

'What do you know about the killings?'

For once, Allison had no questions. Her mind raced, adding up the evidence that was really no more than intuition – except for the man's eyes. They had been a clear hazel, alert, intelligent and blazing. And he'd hidden them from her immediately, as if he feared she'd notice . . . what?

Sidling up to Rick, she whispered, 'Stay on him as long as you can.'

Rick gave her a quick, questioning look, but did as she requested.

'What do you make of him?' she asked when the man had disappeared from sight and Rick finally lowered his camera.

'Nothing.' Rick shrugged. 'What do you make of him? You're the one who wanted his picture.'

'I don't know. Something. I make something of him. He was acting strangely.'

'Scared.' Rick adjusted his equipment and peered around for something more interesting to shoot.

'No,' Allison disagreed. 'That's not it. He wasn't frightened. He was angry. I saw it in his eyes.'

'Yeah, a lot of them are mad at the world.'

'Damn it, that's not what I mean. Did you really look at him? He's different from the rest of them.'

'Different how? He looked the same to me. You think we have enough footage of the scene?'

'Just different. Stronger, younger, more intent, I don't know. For one thing, his eyes weren't cloudy or confused. They were clear and bright. And did you see the confident way he pushed through the crowd? Not to mention the way he kept his head down and hid his face. Not that there was much left to hide. I swear it looks like his hair and beard are permed. You don't see a lot of homeless people who spend money on permanents.'

Rick put his free arm around Allison's shoulders. 'Could it be that you're getting so desperate for your big break, you're starting to fantasize?'

Allison poked him playfully in the ribs. 'Mind your mouth, or when I do get that big break, I'll get myself a nicer cameraman. Come on. We might as well do something constructive.' She positioned herself for her standup that would later introduce the story.

'We're here at the scene of the latest brutal slaying of one of Oklahoma City's street people.'

Allison completed her lead-in, then paused and looked over the morbidly curious hanging around the scene and the unconcerned hurrying to work. No story there.

Across the street she noticed an unwashed, be-whiskered man hanging onto a light post, watching the proceedings.

'Over there,' she whispered to Rick, motioning with her head, unwilling to let any of the other media persons share in her find. She moved cautiously in his direction, still talking as though this were all part of the prepared script.

'Did you know any of the victims?' she demanded, thrusting the microphone toward the man as soon as she was within range.

He wrapped his ragged sweater more closely around his frail body though the early autumn morning was pleasantly warm, then stared at Allison uncomprehendingly for a moment. Suddenly his rheumy eyes blazed. He smiled, exposing toothless gums. 'You want a drink, pretty lady?' He extended a green bottle toward Allison.

'Uh, no. Thanks anyway.'

Then she saw the tall, hairy one again. A few feet away he lounged against an office building, watching her from clear, knowing eyes. He wasn't bent over now, and she'd been right; he appeared strong and healthy in spite of a lanky frame.

'Over there,' she instructed Rick, making a bee-line for the man.

When he saw her coming, he cursed and ran into the nearest alley. Undaunted, Allison ran after him, but his stride was strong with none of the shuffling steps he'd used earlier. He easily outdistanced her.

'Bill!' the older man called, almost knocking her down as he shambled after his friend. 'Don't leave Dealey! I got a bottle. Don't leave Dealey.'

'Allison, get back here! Are you crazy?' Rick's voice called from behind her.

The tall man ran around a corner, but by the time Allison got there, he'd disappeared. 'Damn!' she swore, looking around her. He could have gone into any one of half a dozen back doors.

Dealey shuffled up beside her, looked around, then with a heavy sigh, tilted his bottle to his lips and drank deeply.

'Where did he go?' Allison asked, though she had little hope the man could . . . or would . . . answer her question.

Dealey lowered his bottle and wandered off, aimless and silent.

Allison watched him for a moment, feeling his despair like a chunk of lead in her own gut. With a sigh that echoed the old man's, she turned away to start back and found Rick coming up behind her, lugging his camera, panting and scowling.

'What on earth do you think you're doing, following a couple of bums back here where they could hit you over the head and take that nice watch and, hell, who knows what else?'

'Well, it didn't happen. Want me to carry the camera back?'

'No, I don't want you to carry the camera back.' He shook his head. 'Damn it, Allison, you've got to stop taking such crazy chances. Last week you almost got shot in that shoot-out. When you kept badgering that stockbroker who's accused of fraud, he almost punched you out. No story's worth your life.'

'Come on, let's finish up,' Allison said, ignoring Rick's familiar tirade. She'd do whatever was necessary to get the story. If she didn't manage to succeed, she wouldn't have a life.

Back at the scene, she pasted a professional smile on her face, repositioned herself in front of the camera and went back to her prepared script.

In the five months she'd been a reporter for

Channel 7, Allison hadn't exactly become a threat to Barbara Walters, and today didn't seem likely to improve matters.

'Relax,' Rick told her when they finally wrapped it up. 'It's a good piece.'

Allison kicked at the curb as they headed back toward the K-SVN van. 'It's an adequate piece. I haven't got one lousy thing the other stations don't have.'

'They don't have your gorgeous face and sexy voice,' Rick replied, storing the camera and climbing into the driver's seat.

Allison slammed her door. 'Well, you're right on one count. They don't have my face. They have faces without these crevasses creeping in around their eyes.'

Maybe she should have accepted Douglas's offer of a free face lift as part of the divorce settlement. Starting a career in television at thirty-four was a frightening experience when everyone else seemed to be twenty-two going on nineteen.

'You're the only woman I know who inspects her face every morning with a magnifying glass,' Rick protested. 'That damn ex-husband of yours with his cosmetic-surgery propaganda has got you paranoid. Trust me, no one but you can see those imaginary wrinkles.'

'Nevertheless, you can't deny that thirty-four is old for a female reporter, especially a beginner.'

'You'll make it,' he assured her, but she noticed he didn't deny her assertion.

As the van wheeled around a corner, Allison spotted the two homeless men again, the tall one evidently comforting the older man.

'Rick – '

'No. They're not going to talk to you.'

'We only tried once.' She injected a pleading note into her voice. Looking over at the cameraman, however, she knew it wasn't going to work.

Short and skinny with glasses and carrot-colored hair, Rick didn't look at all like the dictatorial, self-appointed guardian he was. But she couldn't complain too much. If not for him, she wouldn't have this job.

'We need an in-depth story on the homeless,' she mused, staring out the window at the streets that would come alive with them after dark.

'We had one.'

'Hah! You call the drivel Tracy the Twit came up with an in-depth story?'

'I don't have to. The manager does.' Rick pulled the van into the station parking lot. 'Come on. I'll help you edit.'

'Hold it!' Allison exclaimed. 'Back up. Right there. Now freeze it.'

'Your suspicious man?' Rick asked, adjusting the film they were editing.

'Right there in the corner of the frame. I tell you, there's a story there. Look at him, look closely, get a magnifying glass. Don't you see what I'm talking about? His posture, his bearing – '

'His eyes, I know.' Rick frowned and shook his head. 'It's probably only the power of suggestion, but I do kind of see what you're talking about.'

'All right!' Allison exclaimed. 'So when do we hit the streets, partner?'

'What are you going to do? Prowl around until you find this guy? Consort with the winos? You're nuts, Allison. I suspected it in college, and now I know for sure.' He pressed a button to start the film moving again.

'We do an in-depth on the homeless, like I said earlier, and eventually we're sure to run into this man – Bill, that older guy called him.'

'And if we don't?'

'Then I'll admit I was overly zealous, not to mention overly old for this profession in general. I'll give it up and get a job screwing nuts into bolts on an assembly line somewhere.'

'Bolts into nuts,' Rick corrected.

'That, too. I'll need at least a couple of jobs.'

Rick leaned over to give her a quick hug. 'I know it must cost you an arm and two legs with Douglas hauling you into court every few months on some trumped-up custody charge. I'll do whatever I can to help . . . even though I still think you're crazy.'

'Thanks, Rick. You're a real friend.' She returned the hug and started out.

'Hey,' he called after her, 'if this guy turns out to be the killer, maybe we could sic him on Douglas.'

She laughed. 'Hold that thought.'

'This is so cool, Mom,' Megan enthused as Allison's face appeared on the television screen in front of them. 'All the other kids are, like, so jealous.' She squirmed deeper into the huge armchair, skinny legs draped over the side.

'You just like getting to stay up until ten o'clock,' Allison teased.

But secretly she was thrilled that her twelve-year-old daughter approved of her new career. She needed some kind of a draw to compete with Douglas's financial bribes in his efforts to woo their daughter away from her, the tactics he employed in between the recurring court sessions.

Douglas could – and would – keep taking her to court forever, and as long as she could afford lawyer's fees, she could get his cases against her dismissed. But she didn't have his resources. She shuddered, unwilling to think about what might happen. Megan was her whole world. She couldn't lose her – especially to as lousy a father as Douglas! If only she had more time to become a success, if only she were twenty instead of thirty-four . . . if only Douglas hadn't fallen in love – or lust – with

14

his twenty-one-year-old nurse.

She set her jaw determinedly. She couldn't change the past, but she could – and would – see that the future was different from the present.

She scowled at her own image on the television screen. From her vantage point on the sofa, no more than three feet away, she searched for the telltale lines she knew were there or at least would soon be there. She did photograph well, she admitted to herself. High cheekbones from some Indian ancestor made her rather ordinary face appear striking on camera. Her brown hair, glossy from heredity and expensive hair preparations over the years, swung sleek and natural around her face. Not glamorous, but presentable, she decided.

'I wish Dad hadn't taken the big screen TV,' Megan complained.

'I dunno. If we had the big screen, we could see all my wrinkles.'

'Get a face lift. Dad said he'd still do it for you.'

Allison groaned. As the daughter of a plastic surgeon, Megan classed face lifts with hand washings, a necessary evil but no big deal. Any woman over thirty should have a couple. If Douglas got her unconscious and a knife in his hand, he'd probably slit her throat rather than take out her wrinkles.

'Who's the cool dude?' Megan pointed, focusing Allison's gaze from her own image to the man leaning against the office building in the background. 'He looks like a rock star or something.'

'Or something,' Allison replied, intrigued that Megan had picked up on qualities that set the strange man apart from the other homeless. 'He's a street person.'

'A bum? No way. I think he's somebody famous, hiding out, you know.'

If Allison had harbored any doubts about tracking down the man, they took wing and disappeared forever. Kids saw things with a clarity adults lost as they grew up. This really could be the big story she'd been waiting for.

She permitted herself a tiny smile and a brief fantasy. How nice it would be when she became a well-known television personality, when Douglas and Bonnie couldn't turn on that big screen set without seeing her five-foot face smiling at them. Then let him take her to court every week. She'd hire his own lawyer out from under him. Let him offer Megan a fur coat for Christmas and she'd tell him she had three at home.

The first thing they'd do would be to move from this terminal tenement into a house where everything worked, a house that wouldn't allow Douglas to claim she wasn't providing a decent residence for his daughter. The irony of that, of course, was that Douglas had provided this house and stuck her with it in the divorce.

This time, she vowed, she'd be the one to provide

their residence, their lifestyle, their freedom from Douglas's harassment, and if she owned it all, no one would take it from her – not the material things or her peace of mind . . . or her daughter.

'Is that all?' Megan asked, startling her out of her reverie.

Allison focused her attention on the television and noted that a local tax issue was being discussed. 'That's all of my story. I did another one on recycling, but I don't know if they'll run it tonight,' she said.

'I want to see that cool dude again. If I could check him out a little closer, I bet I could tell who he is.'

'We'll see,' Allison replied, a standard parental evasion; in fact, she was considering the idea. She needed a photograph of him, something she could have blown up for closer scrutiny.

Megan was right, she reflected, still seeing the man in her mind's eye. He did sort of look like one of those long-haired rock stars. But his movements were more like an athlete – not a muscle-bound football player but the sinuous sexuality of a swimmer or a skater.

Allison caught herself up short and shivered, appalled as she felt a thrill of attraction to this bearded bum. That's sick! she chided herself.

The louder sounds of a commercial jarred into her thoughts.

'All right,' she said, 'show's over. Upstairs to bed.'

'Aw, Mom,' Megan protested routinely.

'I'm going to watch the weather, then come up myself. Give me a kiss.'

'Aw, Mom,' she said again, but embraced her mother before bouncing upstairs.

All too soon, Allison thought, watching her, she's going to decide she's too old for goodnight kisses from her mother. It seemed she was fighting time at every turn.

At least maybe she was getting a handle on one aspect of her life. Tomorrow she'd get right on this new project, track down this man, find out who he was, see if she had lucked into a big story. She was certainly overdue for a little luck of the good variety.

The next afternoon, as soon as the office workers had time to clear out, Allison pulled into a parking lot on the southern outskirts of the downtown area. The victims had, according to her charts, all been found in this general vicinity.

The hour was late enough for the rush of office workers to have cleared out yet still early enough to enjoy a couple of hours of daylight. She wouldn't want to be in the area after dark.

She took a basket of sandwiches from the car and started down the street, stopping when she spotted a likely prospect leaning against a building.

'Hi. I'm Allison Prescott. Would you like a sandwich?' she offered, unsure of the proper etiquette.

'What's the catch?' the man asked, eyeing her warily.

'No catch. I'd just like to talk to you. I'm a reporter for Channel 7.'

Even though her blue jeans and sweatshirt were old and faded, Allison sensed that she didn't quite fit in. Obviously the man didn't trust her. He took a final puff from a half-inch-long cigarette, tossed it to the sidewalk, snatched the proffered sandwich and ran away.

Allison suppressed an urge to swear. She hefted the basket and continued down the street.

Okay, she decided, we go to Plan B. Enter one of the shelters and try to make contact. Surely the manager wouldn't run her off if she was contributing food. The nearest one, New Hope, was small and only a few months old. It seemed her most likely prospect.

Though she'd read about it and even seen a glimpse of it on the story Tracy had done, she was surprised at how small and old the building was. Her tiny house, the bane of her existence, looked like a palace in comparison.

She opened the heavy wooden door. Scattered about on homemade wooden benches, twenty or thirty people sat eating or talking. At the front of the room, faded purple satin covered a low altar with a makeshift pulpit behind it. Beside the pulpit stood an equally rough table presided over by a huge man, bald except for a few wispy strands of white hair. As he passed out plates of food, he delivered fiery religious exhortations that matched his blazing blue eyes, but conflicted with his wide, unwavering smile.

'Come in, friend,' he said, when he saw Allison hesitating at the door. 'Come and share what we have, though you don't look as if you bring only hunger. If you have food in that basket, you're doubly welcome.'

'Well, uh, yes, yes, as a matter of fact, I do.' She strode boldly toward the front. This could be the 'in' she was looking for.

'These seem fresh,' the man said, lifting a plastic-wrapped sandwich from the basket Allison set on the table.

'I made them a couple of hours ago.' Up close the man was even bigger than he'd seemed. He reminded her of an elderly wrestler who'd dropped too much acid in the sixties.

His clothes weren't much better than the others'. They were clean, but the sleeves of his faded blue shirt ended a good inch above his wrists, and the buttons strained over his barrel chest.

Smiling at her, he continued to hand out food as

more people straggled up. 'Many of the restaurants let me have their leftovers when they close, so my friends are accustomed to stale sandwiches.'

'I'm not from a restaurant. I'm a reporter from Channel 7.' The man's pale eyes frosted, but his smile remained intact. 'I'd like to do a really in-depth story on the plight of the homeless,' she continued. 'Let those people sitting down to dinner in warm houses know what's going on around them. The publicity would probably help you get more restaurants to contribute to your cause.'

The man seemed to consider for a moment. 'And how can I help you?'

'I don't know exactly,' Allison replied honestly. 'I'd just like to talk to some of these people, get to know them, get a real feel for what's going on here.'

The answer seemed to satisfy him. He nodded slowly.

'Maybe you could even introduce me to some of your friends. They don't seem to trust me. By the way, I'm Allison Prescott.' She extended a hand.

'Reverend Samuel Pollock,' he replied, wrapping his massive paw around hers and shaking gently.

With the reverend's blessing, Allison found the people dining in the small shelter a little more accessible. They didn't run from her, but most were still reluctant to talk. She didn't push, having already decided her best route was to move in slowly, allow them to become accustomed to her, let down their guard, and give her a real story.

Pretending she was at one of Douglas's parties, she moved from one to another, chatting, looking for interests they might have, memorizing their faces and names, as any good hostess or reporter would. However, to her disappointment, the strange man she'd seen the day before, 'Bill', wasn't there.

Then, just as she was preparing to leave, Bill and the older man, Dealey, came in together. Instinctively she took a step backward. She was off to one side where the light was dim, so she was pretty sure they hadn't seen her. She'd have time to observe the situation and decide on a plan of action.

Dealey went to the front and got a sandwich, but Bill settled onto a bench midway down and began talking to a group of four men and one woman. Allison moved nearer, carefully staying between him and the door so he couldn't run away from her again.

She was more than ever convinced that here was a story. Seeing him in the midst of these people highlighted the subtle differences she'd noticed before. His hair, though shaggy, was clean. His voice was stronger with none of the uncertain tones she'd noticed in the others. White, even teeth flashed in and out of his beard as he talked.

She took a seat directly behind him. 'Hello, Bill,' she greeted him and was rewarded with a surprised but pleased expression as he whirled around and saw her. Instantly, though, that expression changed to one of anger.

Brad Malone had been concentrating on his work, on playing the role of Bill, the street person, on eliciting information without seeming to. So entrenched was he in this other world that he felt a momentary thrill when he first saw the familiar features and bright brown eyes smiling at him.

But immediately he remembered why the face was familiar. His first impulse was to run away from her again, but the set of her jaw told him that would only solidify her determination.

'Hello,' he finally said, nodding to her, then dismissing her by turning back to the people with whom he'd been discussing the recently deceased Hank.

'You know her?' Mike asked.

'She's a reporter,' Brad said quietly.

'Yeah,' Kay agreed with a sneer, clutching her canvas bag tightly. 'She told us. Doing a story on us homeless.'

A slim hand with shiny, white-tipped nails suddenly appeared between Kay and him.

'Allison Prescott with Channel 7. Can I ask you a few questions, Bill? Reverend Pollock said it would be all right.'

He stared at the hand, resenting and admiring its smooth perfection. With a sigh of resignation, he stood and shook it. It felt every bit as soft as it looked, but her grip was firm, distressingly so.

'How about I walk you back to your car while we talk?' he offered.

He'd feed her his cover story and get rid of her.

CHAPTER 2

*N*ice, Brad had to admit, watching the curves in the tight blue jeans as the woman preceded him out the door. Under other circumstances . . . but these weren't other circumstances.

As they strolled down the empty sidewalk into the crisp fall evening, she began digging around in the large canvas bag she carried. It had some sort of logo on it. Probably a designer bag to go with the designer jeans and fancy painted sweatshirt. It was worse than he'd thought. She was not only a reporter but a status-conscious reporter with more money than brains – or ethics.

'Do you mind if I tape our conversation, Bill?' she asked, pulling out a small recorder.

'Yes, I mind.'

To his surprise, she returned the recorder to its hiding place without a protest. 'No problem,' she said. 'I have a good memory. So, how long have you been on the streets?'

'I've been here a couple of weeks.' Better not tell her any lies she could catch him in.

'And before that?'

Brad started to speak, closed his mouth, cleared his throat and started again. 'Houston,' he said, having a hard time getting out the lie.

Lying was a necessary part of his job, but suddenly it wasn't easy. She was a reporter, a muckraker, and he usually had no trouble telling them whatever he felt they needed to hear. But this vulture had smooth, shiny hair he wanted to touch and big, liquid brown eyes that looked up at him trustingly.

He clenched his jaw. Trusting that she'd worm a story out of him, he reminded himself. He shoved his hands into his pockets as though to trap them and assure they couldn't fulfill his illogical desires to touch her. He started walking faster, staring straight ahead at the empty streets with their deserted buildings, keeping his field of vision away from her.

'I worked in the oilfields for a couple of years up here in Ok City,' he said, his words clipped and rapid, echoing his footsteps. 'Then I went to Houston and worked as a roughneck on offshore drilling rigs. When the oil crunch hit, I couldn't get work. I finally decided if I had to be on the streets, I'd rather be on these streets. So I came home.'

Even to his own ears, the story sounded rehearsed, as though he were reading from cue cards. Damn! What was the matter with him?

He stole a glance at her as she kept pace beside him. She was watching him, head tilted slightly; her eyes, the color and sheen of his mother's walnut table, were alight with doubts and questions. He slowed, shrugged and made an effort to sound casual. 'That's all there is to it. This life isn't so bad, really. The preacher hands out food – '

'Which you weren't eating,' she pointed out.

Brad stumbled, almost falling, as they stepped off a curb. Damn nosy woman. 'I ate earlier,' he said.

'What did you eat?' she demanded.

Brad flung his arms into the air in exasperation and said the first thing that came into his head. 'Dog food.'

She didn't bat a long, dark eyelash. Her expression didn't change, but he knew she didn't believe him, wasn't buying any of it.

'What kind?' she asked.

He stopped on the corner and turned to face her. 'Where is your car?' he demanded. They were getting pretty far away from the mission.

'In a parking lot back there,' she replied, waving a slender hand with a slim gold wrist watch in the direction from which they had just come.

'Why are we walking away from your car?' he demanded. 'I thought we had a deal. I'd talk to you on the way to your car.'

She smiled and started across the street. 'That was your suggestion. I made no deal.'

He lunged after her, grabbing her shoulder to halt her. Betraying no hint of agitation she turned, gazing up at him, waiting calmly for his next move. Beneath his hand her shoulder felt fragile, and she smelled like a field of summer flowers.

He jerked his hand back as though from a live wire. They'd warned him that undercover work could do strange things to a cop's head, but he didn't remember them mentioning anything like this.

'Well, we're making a deal now,' he growled. 'Either we head on back to your car or I don't answer any more questions.'

'Okay,' she agreed, sounding a little breathless, but he refused to look at her, to see why she sounded that way. His mind had better sense than his body.

'Come on,' he ordered, stalking off. She's the enemy, he reminded himself. And even if she wasn't, Miss Name Brand would surely freak out totally if an unwashed, undesirable street person tried to become friendly.

'What kind of dog food?' she asked as they strode along.

'What?' Brad asked in astonishment, then remembered the lie he'd told her. 'The store brand,' he replied. 'I didn't get much money from panhandling today, and I have to save some of it for wine to keep me warm tonight.' That should shut her up and send her scurrying away.

'Where will you stay tonight?' she queried, off on a new tack. She wasn't easily discouraged.

'Some of us stay in the mission,' he replied evasively.

'Do you?'

'I like being outside in good weather. Where did you say your car is?'

'I didn't. We're going back to the mission, anyway. I have to pick up my basket. Can you show me some of the places you sleep?'

'No,' he answered, deliberately leering at her. 'You might come back in the middle of the night and attack me.'

Her expression clouded, and for just a moment he thought he'd gotten to her.

'Have you ever attacked anyone?' she asked, and he realized she was considering the possibility that he might be the killer.

'Not recently,' he snapped. 'Looks like our little talk's over. We're back at New Hope.' And not a moment too soon.

'Are you coming in?'

'No. I have to do my wine shopping and find a warm bridge to sleep under.'

'Good night, then. And thanks for the help.' She gave him a smile so warm it made him leery. She was up to something.

He watched her enter the mission, then he turned and walked away, making a wide circle of the area as he headed for his parking garage.

If he hadn't already been suspicious of the woman, if he'd been less a veteran of the streets, he might not have noticed the white Volvo that passed him once then came back around again and parked up the street from him. He might never have seen Allison Prescott trying to be unobtrusive as she photographed him from inside the car.

Silently he ran through an impressive litany of four-letter words while he continued to stroll toward the car, making a determined effort to appear unconcerned. When he was still several feet away, she turned to face forward, and he heard the starter crank. The engine failed to catch, and she ground it some more.

Brad smiled as he reached the car and smelled gas fumes. Flooded. She wasn't going anywhere for a few minutes, long enough for him to make his presence felt.

He tapped on her window, feeling a small surge of gratification when she jumped.

'Need some help?' he asked as she lowered the window a scant inch.

'No. Thanks anyway.' For the first time, she'd lost her composure. She sounded nervous and looked guilty, her gaze darting everywhere except to the 35-mm camera lying on her bag in the passenger seat. Why, he wondered, had a television reporter been taking a photograph, and why was she acting so guilty about it? He didn't like the feel of this situation.

'Better wait a few minutes,' he advised. 'Smells like you flooded the engine.'

'Thank you.' She nodded, making an obvious struggle to regain her composure. The lady was tough. He could almost admire her. Almost.

He strolled on down the street and around the corner before he stopped and kicked the side of a building. Damn! Damn all nosy reporters. They'd always been the bane of his existence, but now more than ever when he had to avoid publicity or risk blowing the whole case.

He strode onward, making a wider circle than usual around his goal to be sure he'd lost her.

All those blasted vultures wanted was a story, preferably a more sensational one than their competitors. They didn't care who they hurt in the process or how badly they jeopardized the progress of an investigation. This broad wouldn't lose a wink of sleep if she blew his cover. Hell, she'd love it! Expose an undercover cop. Scoop the other stations.

Damn her! What could she be planning to do with those pictures? Whatever it was, he was sure he wouldn't like it, sure it wouldn't help the case he was trying to solve.

Well, he had her name and even her license-plate number. Within the hour, he'd have her address, and then he'd get those pictures from her before she had a chance to create problems.

As he turned onto the street where his parking garage was located, he paused and bent over as though to tie his shoe. Actually he checked behind and on all sides for Allison Prescott, for anyone who might be watching. Before he entered the garage, before he got on the elevator to go up to his level, before he climbed in the truck, he surveyed each area carefully.

He'd taken the precaution of switching trucks with his father, and this one looked like it was on its last legs; still he wanted to avoid being seen driving any kind of a vehicle. Occasionally the street people managed to borrow a car or even buy a clunker, but he wanted to draw as little attention to himself as possible.

He crunched the ancient truck into gear, shuddering at the thought that his dad was even now stripping gears and hauling plumbing supplies in the new, 'loaded' truck Brad had driven off the lot only a month ago.

This assignment was in no way his idea of a good time, but he had taken it because it needed to be done, and he'd complete it in spite of Allison Prescott.

* * *

32

Allison clenched her teeth, took a deep breath and turned the car key again, almost sobbing with relief when the engine purred into life. Her hands still shook as she drove down the street at a sedate speed, her earlier manic excitement quelled.

She didn't understand why Bill had made her so nervous. In spite of her logical conclusion that he might be a murderer, she didn't really believe he was. She wasn't frightened of him. But for some reason she didn't feel good about taking his picture, delving into his secrets, his privacy.

Well, those were feelings she'd just have to get over if she intended to succeed. She squared her shoulders and gripped the steering wheel tightly, making an attempt to grip her errant emotions in the same way. She was onto a story she desperately needed, and in order to get that story, she had to ferret out Bill's identity. Photos Rick could enlarge and she could study might be very revealing. She was only acting in a logical manner. Anyway, if he had nothing to hide, there was no harm done. And if he did, well, he deserved to be exposed.

She pulled into the television-station parking garage and walked determinedly inside to the newsroom.

Tracy lifted her blonde head from the copy she was revising. 'Allan doesn't like us to run around in grungies,' she advised.

'Stow it. I'm not on the clock. I'm just looking for

33

Rick.' Allison continued past the girl, around the maze of desks and computers where the rest of the anchor team was working, toward the editing room at the back.

'Good job on that fashion-show story. You gave it a real mature touch,' Tracy called after her.

Allison bit her lip and took the compliment the way it wasn't intended. 'Thanks,' she answered without stopping.

Rick looked up from the tape he was editing as she entered the room. 'Hi, lady. What's up?'

'Keep your voice down. Tracy would love to get her hands on this story.' She scanned the room to be sure they were alone.

Rick leaned back on his stool and shook his head. 'Sometimes I worry about you.'

'I've been out laying the background for that story on the homeless. I'm establishing contact with them, trying to gain their trust. Soon you can go with me and get it on tape. In the meantime . . .' She perched on the stool beside him and extracted her camera from her bag. 'I have in here pictures of Bill, the mystery man, and let me tell you, there is a mystery there.' She rewound the film and removed it.

Scowling, Rick accepted the spool. 'You've been down there talking to those people by yourself?'

'If I go in now with a camera crew, all I'll get is the surface story, the same thing every station

34

around here, including ours, has already done. I start out talking to these people, gaining their trust, and eventually I find out what makes them tick, their real stories.' She popped her camera back into her bag. 'Even the real story on this Bill character. He's lying through his pearly whites, and they're awfully pearly for a street person.'

'I don't know how to break this to you, my dear, but I imagine a lot of these people will lie to you. We're not dealing with members of the First Presbyterian Church.'

Allison laughed. 'Definitely not the First Presbyterian, but Cotton Mather's descendant is doing his best to keep them in line at the New Hope mission. Anyway, back to this Bill. He sounds educated, yet he says he used to be a roughneck. Okay, okay, I know that's possible.' She spread her hands as though to forestall any objections. 'But there's more. He didn't eat the food at the mission. His fingernails aren't dirty. He smells like soap and deodorant. He won't tell me where he sleeps – '

'Where he sleeps? You asked him where he sleeps?'

'Maybe he's the murderer,' she suggested, certain that would pique Rick's interest.

He ran through every swear word she'd ever heard and a few more besides. 'Let's go get a cup of coffee and talk,' he finally said, sliding off his stool.

'Can't. Megan's home alone with only Mrs Parsons next door to check in with. Since I've got Douglas watching my every move, trying to make a case to take her away from me, I can't let her stay there long.' She stood and slid her bag over her shoulder, preparing to leave.

'And that situation is the basis of what we need to talk about.' Rick took her hand in his warm, freckled one. 'We've been friends a lot of years. Our friendship has outlasted one husband and two wives, and I feel closer to you than I ever felt to them.'

'Especially to the husband,' she interjected, trying to stave off the lecture she knew was coming.

Rick ignored her attempt at humor. 'As your friend, I feel I have the right, even the duty to say this to you. You've changed since your divorce. I understand you had to, and it's not all bad. You're developing goals and purposes. On the other hand, after today, you've gone beyond dedication to the job. We're talking obsession here. You seem to think if you can reach the top, that will solve all your problems, from Douglas on down.'

'Bingo,' she replied firmly, then sagged back against the counter, her determination momentarily flagging. 'You know my situation. Douglas took everything . . . not because he wanted it, just because he didn't want me to have it. He can't take Megan legally, but he knows I don't have the money to keep fighting him in court. Eventually . . .' She shook her head. 'But that "eventually" can't happen. Somehow I will get the money to keep on fighting him. Now, can you develop this film for me tonight?'

Rick ran a hand through his bright hair and sighed. 'Yes, I can develop the film. But what I'm saying is, maybe you're counting so heavily on finding a story that will send you to the top that you've – ' he cleared his throat ' – invented or at least magnified some rather obscure circumstances.'

She leaned over to kiss his cheek. 'I love you, Richard Holmes. If I didn't, I wouldn't let you get away with telling me I'm crazy. Just develop the picture and stand by to be catapulted to the top for your involvement in this incredible story.' Pausing at the door, she looked back at him and winked. 'Well, maybe catapulted up one rung of the ladder.'

Rick gave her a worried smile and a thumbs up.

As she drove homeward, a tiny portion of her brain niggled at her that Rick might be right, but her instincts told her differently. Bill was not a bum. There was an undercurrent of excitement about him, something she needed to know about . . . and would.

She pulled into her cracked driveway and, for a moment, considered leaving the Volvo outside for the night rather than have to wrestle with the stubborn garage door. But that wouldn't do. The car might be a few years old, but it was a good one and would have to last her 'until'.

She settled the car in the small, detached garage, crossed the few feet to the house and opened the side door. Putting on a smile for Megan's benefit, she stepped inside. Her smile disappeared, however, as soon as she entered the dining area and the taupe carpet squished.

'Mom, where have you been?' Megan splashed frantically from the kitchen and hurled herself into her mother's arms.

'Working, baby.' Then, because hope springs eternal, 'Did you spill something?'

'Mother!' Megan protested. 'The sink's gushing, and I can't make it quit.'

'Let's go have a look, then,' Allison sighed, laying her bag on the scarred oak table.

Of course, there was no cutoff under the sink. This old house had been nothing but a white elephant since she and Douglas had bought it for rental property five years ago. Just as they were sure everything had been repaired at least once, something else broke.

A year ago when Douglas had, to her astonishment, insisted they were on the verge of bankruptcy, she had agreed to sell their home and move to this place for what she understood would be a temporary stay. For him, it was. Since that time, since the divorce when she was awarded 'the 'residence', things had continued to fall apart.

'Hand me a pair of pliers,' she called from under the sink. The water was spurting from a connection. Maybe, just maybe, she could fix it and save the price of a week's worth of meals that a plumber would charge.

Over the noise of a kitchen drawer being pulled out with resultant rattles, she thought she heard Megan suggesting they call her father.

'Don't even think about calling him if you want to continue to call me "Mother",' Allison grated.

'Mom.' Megan pressed the cold pliers into her wet hand. 'I already called him.'

Allison jerked her head upward directly into the water's path, then out and up to crash against the top of the open cabinet door.

With water trickling down her face, she clasped one hand to the back of her head to stop the blood she felt sure must be gushing.

'Mom, he wants to help. He was really concerned when I told him, and he's on his way over right now.'

The ringing of the doorbell saved Megan's life. It wouldn't do to kill her with Douglas at the front door.

Standing on Allison Prescott's front porch, Brad rang the bell a second time. He'd been a little surprised to learn where she lived. Not that it was a bad neighborhood. In fact, it was very similar to the one where he lived. The houses were small and old, certainly not what he'd expected for Ms Designer Labels/Gold Watch.

When the kid opened the door, he was pretty sure he had the wrong place after all.

'Hey, all right,' she exclaimed. 'Mom's been holding out on me.'

'Excuse me,' he mumbled, backing away.

'Mom, guess who's here,' she called over her shoulder, stepping backward in an invitation for him to enter.

'I think I have the wrong house,' he protested.

'Did he bring a monkey wrench?' a woman shouted from inside the house. 'If I had a monkey wrench, I could break his head and solve at least one problem around here.'

The voice, though loud and angry, still had the smooth, cultured tones belonging to Allison Prescott.

The kid smiled and rolled her eyes. 'Mom,' she called, 'it's not Dad. It's – what's your name?'

'Br . . . ill.' Mom? It was hard to think of that reporter as a mom.

The girl offered a small hand for him to shake. 'I'm Megan.' She turned back into the room. 'It's Brill,' she called, 'the man from your news tape.'

'Bill,' he corrected. Lousy timing, he thought. The ex on his way over, and I'm trying to get in and steal her film.

'You're a rock star, right?' the kid asked.

All things considered, Brad thought maybe he ought to come back another time.

Then a bedraggled female appeared behind the girl. Just went to show what happened to those glamour types when they let down their hair. And this one's hair was definitely down. Soaked, to be precise, and straggling all over her face as she sponged futilely at it with a dish towel.

He took a step backward as an irrational impulse urged him to go inside, take the towel and dry her hair for her. She looked so naive and helpless. Deceptively so, he reminded himself.

'What are you doing here?' she asked, grabbing the child and clutching her protectively.

And then she did look like a mom after all.

'Uh – ' He hesitated, swallowed hard and gathered his thoughts, reminded himself that, present appearances to the contrary, she was the enemy.

'You dropped this,' he said, holding out a rhinestone earring he'd bought thirty minutes ago in preparation for this meeting. 'I thought it might be valuable.'

She studied him for an endless moment, then seemed to relax. 'It's not mine,' she said.

He bounced the earring in his hand, then tucked it into a shirt pocket. 'Oh. Well, I guess I made the trip for nothing.'

She ran a hand through her wet hair and

nodded, her expression uncertain, as though she couldn't decide whether to talk to him, to pursue her story, or go back inside and slam the door in his face.

He took advantage of her hesitation. 'Do you mind if I just sit on your steps and rest for a little while? It was a long walk.' With the ex on his way, she'd likely tell him to leave, but he had a few more scams to run before he gave up tonight. 'Maybe I could have a glass of water?'

'Our water's broken,' Megan supplied.

'Broken?' he repeated.

'Broken,' Allison exclaimed, flinging her arms wide. 'The damned pipe is squirting water all over everything, the carpet's soaked, the kitchen tile's coming loose – do you mind if I get back to my catastrophe?'

'Let me have a look.' He stepped past her into the house.

'Why do you want to look at a mess like that?' she asked, but he was already inside, following the trail of wet carpet.

'I used to be a plumber,' he told her.

'I thought you were a roughneck.'

'I'm multi-skilled. You do have a mess here.' He spotted the canvas bag lying on the dining table, but ignored it, turning into the small kitchen, biding his time.

No cutoff under the sink. He looked up to see her

42

standing over him. 'Where's your water meter?' he asked.

'Out by the sidewalk.' She pointed toward a corner of the yard.

'Any chance you know where the key is?' She probably didn't know what the key was.

'I think it's in the garage.' With Megan following close behind, she led him outside and into the wooden structure that leaned distinctly to the southeast.

As Allison flipped on the bare overhead light bulb, he saw the familiar white Volvo parked in the middle of the garage, sharing the otherwise empty space with an elderly lawn mower that lurked in one corner.

The key to the water meter hung on the wall. It was easy to find. The only other items on the garage wall were a rusty handsaw and a yard rake. Brad took it down, his eyes scanning the rest of the interior. 'Do you have a shop vac?' He could see for himself that the question was pointless.

'No.'

'Dad took it,' Megan supplied.

Still pretty friendly with the ex, he noted. In spite of the fact that she wants to brain him with a monkey wrench, he borrows the shop vac, comes over in emergencies. 'How about tools?' Again he could see the answer for himself, but he asked anyway. Maybe she kept them in the house.

Allison shook her head.

'Well, let's get it shut off and I'll take a look anyway. Maybe it's something simple.'

After he got the water turned off, he crawled under the sink, kneeling in the puddle.

'Get some towels, sweetheart,' he heard Allison say to the girl. 'Let's get started cleaning this up.'

At least she wasn't going to leave it for the maid – though now that he'd seen her house, he doubted that she had a maid. Things were not as they'd seemed.

'Do you have a flashlight?' he asked.

When she slapped one into his hand, he scanned the system of pipes. Though he hadn't actually been a plumber, as the son of one he'd worked on a lot of plumbing, including his own rental properties, and this was about the worst he'd ever seen. The leak was no surprise; the only surprise was that there was just one leak. Copper tubing was bent at sharp angles; fittings, including the faulty one, were heavily caulked to compensate for being the incorrect size – the woman had been royally screwed by whoever did this job.

The doorbell rang again. Probably the ex. Maybe while she was distracted with him, he could get the film. If he had to, he'd take the camera, then figure out how to return it after he'd extracted the film.

He crawled out, squeezing water from his tattered slacks, and listened.

'Daddy! I'm so glad you're here.'

'Hi, Princess. Allison, can't you go a week without some disaster?'

Okay, maybe relations weren't so great with the ex.

'I probably could if I had a brand new half-million-dollar house,' she snarled. Dignified Allison Prescott actually snarled.

'Go upstairs and pack a bag, Princess. You can come stay with Bonnie and me until this mess is cleaned up. I'll get a plumber over here tomorrow. I suppose I'll have to pay for it, as usual.'

'We don't need your help. We can handle things just fine.'

'Oh, yes, you've been great at handling things. You've really taken good care of my daughter. Can't even keep the house in livable condition. She doesn't need to walk on this wet carpet. In a few days, it'll be mildewed. That'll be just fine, too, won't it? Go on, Megan. Grab whatever you want that we don't already have for you at home.'

Brad sighed as he heard soft footsteps going up the stairs. Tough situation for the kid, putting her in the middle like that. Too bad.

'When are you going to stop being so stubborn?' the man demanded when the footsteps were crossing the upstairs floor. 'Why can't you accept defeat gracefully? It's obvious Megan would be better off with me than with you.'

'Douglas, you've taken everything we owned – '

'I owned,' he corrected. 'You never worked a day after Megan was born.'

'You don't call raising a child, keeping your house clean and waiting on you hand and foot "work"?' she demanded, her voice so icy Brad involuntarily shivered.

'No, I certainly do not! Look at you. You can't do anything right. It's obvious you can't support yourself, much less Megan! She told me you even took her to a used clothing store. How low do you have to sink before you turn loose of her?'

Obeying an impulse he didn't understand and felt reasonably sure he'd regret later, Brad stepped out of the kitchen. 'Excuse me, but I'm gonna have to get some parts to fix that pipe. The hardware store's closed now, but my boss said if I couldn't fix it tonight, we'd put you and the little girl up at any hotel you choose.'

Allison looked as surprised as her ex. Her mouth dropped open, but she quickly closed it.

'Who are you?' Douglas demanded indignantly.

Brad moved closer to the ex, deliberately invading his space. The blond man was at least six feet tall, almost as tall as he was, but the ex looked soft. When Douglas leaned slightly backward, Brad smiled, knowing he'd taken control away from the man.

'It's a real honor to do business with someone as

famous as this little lady,' he said. 'Important television reporter, you know.'

Composure regained, Allison walked to the front door and held it open. 'So you can see, Douglas,' she said, 'everything's under control. Good night.'

'I'm not leaving without Megan.' The man turned to face Allison, excluding Brad from the discussion. 'She'll want to go with me. You know she loves to get out of this dump and live a normal life whenever she can.'

Brad slapped him heartily on the back. 'Ah, you know how kids are.' He walked forward, bringing Douglas along with him as though he were a reluctant prisoner. 'They like anything new. She'll get a real charge out of staying in a big hotel. We could do the Waterford. Kids just love room service.'

'I never heard of a plumbing company that puts people up in the Waterford. Who did you say you're with?'

'Ace Plumbing. The boss is a little eccentric. Is that your car out there? What is that? Is that a Mercedes? I've always wanted to see one of those babies up close. Mind if I walk out with you? Maybe I could take it for a spin around the block.'

They were outside and heading down the sidewalk. 'Mmm, boy, I'll bet that baby handles nice! Where'd you say you live, Douglas? Do you need some plumbing work done? Say, is that interior real leather?'

Douglas opened the door and slid in hastily.

Brad loped around to the other side and tugged on the handle of the passenger door. 'Hey, unlock this thing, and I'll go for a ride with you.'

The engine caught, and Douglas gunned it, peeling off down the street.

Brad watched as the cream-colored car drove away, gleaming even in the paleness of the street lamps. The license plate was easy to remember. DR-DOUG. He stored away the information for future use.

CHAPTER 3

Allison stood on the porch watching in amazement as Bill effortlessly maneuvered the man who usually maneuvered her. Bill was in complete control. He exuded unused power and confidence, like a marathon runner taking a leisurely stroll.

Having dispatched the irritant, he sauntered back up the walk and onto the porch. Even with the hair and beard covering most of his face, she couldn't miss his smile.

John Wayne after he conquered the Apaches.

Mel Gibson after wasting the bad guys.

Maybe Megan wasn't so far off on her assumption. Allison didn't think he was a rock star, but maybe an actor studying for a role. He'd certainly switched easily from homeless bum to friendly, eccentric plumber, and finally to a knight in shining armor.

That last designation brought her back to reality with a little jolt. She couldn't deny that she'd thoroughly enjoyed seeing Douglas demolished.

But if Bill could so easily control Douglas, what could he do to her?

Repair her plumbing, she assured herself. It wasn't like he was or ever would be a part of her life and have a chance to control her.

'Come in,' she invited in a firm voice. She was being silly. This man had just done her a tremendous favor. A little hospitality was certainly called for after he'd routed the enemy.

For a moment he gazed at her in silence, his hazel eyes searching her face assessingly, though she had no idea what he was trying to assess. An aura so potent as to be almost palpable seemed to flow from him. He'd definitely forgotten his role as a downtrodden, homeless person. This was a man in charge.

She shivered – from excitement or fear or both.

Then he blinked, dropped his stare to the porch and shrugged, switching roles again.

'Yeah, sure,' he said in answer to her invitation, brushing past her into the house. 'Look, I wasn't kidding about your needing some parts for that mess under the sink. In fact, you need a whole system. The one you've got now sucks.'

'Mom, where's Dad?'

Megan stood at the foot of the stairs, overnight bag in one hand, clothes draped over her arm.

'Something came up. He had to leave,' Allison said.

50

'Without me?' Megan frowned.

'Something very important, sweetheart.' Allison walked over to hug the girl. 'You'll be going over there this weekend. In the meantime, I sure could use your help getting this place cleaned.'

'Dad and Bonnie have a maid to clean,' she grumbled.

'I know.'

'We used to have a maid.'

'But we don't now. So scoot upstairs and put those clothes away before they get wet.'

She turned to see Bill watching her from over by the dining table. He lowered his gaze immediately, but she could have sworn his look was disapproving.

'My ex-husband is a doctor,' she explained. 'Our lifestyle used to be very different. I'm afraid that's all Megan knows. Knew,' she corrected herself with a wry grin. 'And Douglas's constant bribes aren't helping her to adjust.'

He didn't look very sympathetic. 'Yeah, well, I guess I'd better be going,' he said.

'Wait!' Allison ran toward him, catching his arm before he could get out the door. Even in her distracted state she noted, like a good reporter, that his arm was solid, well muscled. He didn't miss many meals.

Making no effort to shake her off, he turned back. His expression told her he wasn't concerned, could leave if and when he wanted to, whether or not she tried to stop him. He was as much in control as he'd been with Douglas.

'Wait for what?' he asked.

Suddenly acutely aware of his arm beneath her fingers, she jerked her hand away.

'You said you were a plumber,' she reminded him. 'Well, I need a plumber, and you need money. So how about if I pay you to fix my sink?' That would accomplish two things at once – take care of her immediate water problem and give her more of a chance to figure out his story.

He crossed his arms and looked past her into empty space. 'You need a good plumber. That's why I had to go to work as a roughneck. I'm not very good.'

She crossed her arms, too, and leaned into his field of vision, refusing to let him evade her. 'That's fine because I can't afford to pay for someone who's very good. Contrary to popular opinion, television reporters don't command enormous salaries. And, as I'm sure you heard a few minutes ago, my share in the divorce settlement didn't cause Douglas to miss any manicures. In fact, I was hoping you might take out some of your pay in home-cooked meals.'

'Hey, Brill, are you staying for dinner?' Megan bounced down the stairs, grimacing as her feet landed on the wet carpet. 'How about I put on some music? Who's your favorite group? Have you done any videos?'

'She thinks you're a rock star,' Allison explained, watching him closely for a response.

He laughed, some of his tenseness disappearing. 'I wish I was. Now those folk make enough money to put your Douglas to shame.' Turning back to Megan, he drawled, 'You got anything by Garth Brooks or the Kentucky Headhunters?'

'Huh?'

'Country music,' Allison explained.

'Right,' he agreed, favoring her with a smile. 'Okay, how about I try to jury-rig this catastrophe and see if we can stop the leak or at least cut it down to a drip? Then you'll have water to get you through the night and you can call a plumber tomorrow.'

While he worked, muttering about various forms of torture he wished upon the original constructor and all those who'd touched it since, Allison threw together a ham, onion and mushroom quiche. Surely when he smelled the tantalizing odors he'd be eager to stay.

For an instant, as she set the oven timer, she questioned her motives in keeping the strange man in her home.

But the answer was obvious, she assured herself. Besides the fact that she owed him for saving her life with the plumbing, he'd be more relaxed, more likely to let down his guard and talk after a good meal.

And she did intend for the meal to be part of his

pay. She wouldn't be indebted to anyone, not even to a bum – or whoever Bill might be.

It took every ounce of Brad's willpower to leave Allison's house while she was trying to bribe him to stay with a large piece of steaming quiche. He hadn't eaten anything since early morning, and his stomach was growling loudly in protest as he forced himself out the door, guarding the bulge in his coat pocket.

Mouth watering, he walked as fast as he dared to his car parked around the corner and headed for the nearest fast-food place that had a drive-through since he couldn't afford to be seen inside a restaurant.

Why these places were called 'fast food' was beyond him, he thought as he waited impatiently for his order. When he finally had his two bacon cheeseburgers, large fries and chocolate shake, he pulled over to the farthest, darkest corner of the lot and began to wolf down the food. Even as his stomach filled, though, he could still remember the smell of that quiche and the disappointed look on Allison's face when he'd adamantly refused to stay – disappointed because she couldn't get a story out of him, he reminded himself.

She really wasn't as bad as she'd originally seemed, though. She had her own problems with that sleazy ex-husband and that cute but spoiled daughter. And he had to give her credit, she was trying to make it – and all on her own. He'd had to literally run out of the house to avoid her trying to write him a check since she was out of cash. Understanding her situation, he could almost forgive her some of her pushiness, could almost admire her.

He finished his last fry, wadded the greasy papers into the sack, scanned the area to be sure no one was watching and pulled Allison's camera from his pocket. He'd open it, expose the film, go back to her house on the pretext of using the bathroom and dump the camera somewhere obvious. She'd just think she or Megan had misplaced it, and the film had been a bad roll.

There was no film in the camera.

He punched the car seat and cursed Allison Prescott for the immoral, money-hungry, deceitful reporter she was.

Gunning the engine, he screeched back to her street, parked down the block and charged up to the house.

Her face when she opened the door was so guileless, and she seemed so genuinely pleased to see him, he had to remind himself of the reality of the situation. They were playing games here, and she was winning.

'I need to use your restroom,' he growled, 'and I'll be back tomorrow night to fix your damned pipes if you'll buy the parts before I get here. I'll make you a list.' One way or the other, he would get back inside and find that film.

She smiled, exposing perfect teeth that had probably paid for some orthodontist's swimming pool. 'Thank you,' she said quietly, her doe eyes large. 'The bathroom's upstairs, first door on the left.'

The next morning Brad sidled in a back door of the local police station. Head down, he slouched along the hall to a small office, trying to look like a vagrant for the benefit of the uniformed officers as well as the clerical staff. Being undercover meant hiding from everybody, especially since most of them knew him from his regular duties as a detective.

'Hey, good looking,' Steve Raney greeted, closing the door behind him.

'Up yours,' Brad replied, slumping into the wooden chair and taking the cup of coffee his partner offered. 'Say what you like about my appearance, but I ran into a kid yesterday who thinks I'm a rock star.'

'Yeah, I can see that. You do look kind of drugged out.'

That was probably true, Brad thought. He hadn't slept much that night. 'Man, I'm too old for this sort of assignment. I need a hair cut, a clean suit and my old job.'

Steve leaned back and propped his feet on the

small table. 'Keep complaining, and I'll volunteer you for 24-hour-a-day duty. How'd you like to sleep on the streets?'

'Very funny. Since it's highly unlikely any of these homeless people are members of organized crime or major drug lords, eight hours a day is about the limit you'll be able to stick me with. And believe me, that's more than enough.' He sighed heavily. 'Tell me someone with a big chunk of rusty iron came in and confessed this morning, and you'll make my day.'

'Well, we had a little old lady about four foot eight and eighty pounds, and the same man who confesses to everything from robberies to suicides. Oh, yeah, and a really suspicious dog with no alibi. He may be our first lead.'

Brad paused with his cup of coffee halfway to his mouth. 'You're a sick man, Raney.'

'It comes with the territory.'

'So you're telling me we have exactly zero.'

Steve scowled and nodded. 'Nothing. All the lab reports are back, and we have exactly nothing. It's identical to the others . . . found within a four-block radius of the others, killed God knows where, body moved, then laid out in the alley, hands crossed like in a coffin. He had the usual head wound from a blunt instrument, traces of rust in the wound. Either we have somebody ten feet tall, or the victims are sitting down facing him.'

'Or her,' Brad interjected. 'Women can be vicious, too.'

'Or her, but it would have to be an awfully strong woman. At any rate, it's apparently someone they trust. We got a lot of dirt under the fingernails, but no skin. No sign of a struggle. They just sit there while someone bashes in their heads.'

Brad sipped his coffee. 'I haven't turned up anything either. The people are starting to talk to me, but they don't know anything. They're scared, and they're staying together more, which is good for their safety. But as far as a common link between the victims . . .'

He shook his head, pulled a small notepad from his pocket and tossed it to Steve. 'Seems everybody liked this last guy, this Hank, no enemies. He wasn't a druggie. He drank every chance he got, though. So we've got, what?' He consulted the file in front of him. 'Three alkies, one of whom was a druggie, one was a mental case, one was liked by all, then we have one druggie who didn't drink, and one man everybody hated for a total of three men and two women — it just doesn't make any sense.' He slapped the table. 'Damn it! Where's the common denominator?'

Steve leafed through the pages of Brad's notebook. 'If you can decipher this chicken scratching, let's go over it together and look for the pattern. There has to be one. There always is. We just have to find it.'

Brad nodded, and for the next hour they discussed and dissected bits and pieces of conversations and observations that might or might not mean anything.

As Brad started to leave, he paused at the door. 'Oh, one more thing. This blasted television reporter has been hanging around, looking for a story, and she took my picture. I thought I ought to go over there tonight and try to get it back.'

Steve's large forehead wrinkled. 'You toss this information out like it's nothing important, but you're willing to risk blowing your cover to get it back? What do you think she's going to do with this picture?'

Brad shrugged elaborately. 'I dunno. I think she's suspicious that I'm not what I seem. Maybe she thinks I'm a cop. Maybe she even thinks I'm the murderer. The thing is, she's divorced and broke and has this kid, and she's desperate for a story.'

'If you're asking my opinion, I'd say stay as far away from her as you can. Screw the picture. With that hair and beard, your own mother wouldn't recognize you.'

Brad nodded, remembering a week ago when he'd walked into his mother's kitchen unannounced and she'd reached for the iron skillet. 'You're probably right. But you see, this lady's got a leak in her kitchen and can't afford a plumber, and I thought I might use that for an excuse to go over and fix it and try to find the picture.'

Brad didn't have to look at Steve's disbelieving expression to know his words weren't coming out quite right.

'Hey, man, you got a thing for this broad?'

'Countess Dracula? Are you kidding?'

Allison pulled to one side of the garage, leaving just enough room for Rick to park his compact car beside hers since he stubbornly, irrationally insisted that if he left it on the street, Bill would see it and wouldn't come in.

'Cleanest garage I've ever seen,' Rick marveled.

'I told you, Douglas even took the dust in the vacuum cleaner bag.'

Rick closed up behind them as they went out, and Allison looked toward the open side door of the house. 'Megan's home. We're trying to dry out the carpet.'

Rick paused at the doorway and leaned over, pressing the dampness. 'It'll never work. You're ruining your carpet and maybe your floor as well. You need to get this up and outside.'

'And pay a carpet layer to put it back? No, somehow we have to get it dry. Maybe we could set the hairdryer to blow on it all night.'

Rick studied his fingers, then took out a handkerchief and pressed the carpet with it. 'I think you're right about one thing. There's no point in paying someone to work with this stuff. Either it's awfully dirty, or the dye's coming out.' He showed her the stain on the white cotton.

Allison groaned. 'When we squeezed the water out of the towels last night, I just thought it was dirt. I guess I shouldn't be surprised. This was the cheapest carpet Douglas could get. We were going to rent out this place, and he said renters would only ruin it anyway.'

'Uncle Rick!' Megan flew across the room and into Rick's arms. 'I'm really glad you're here. This really cool dude is coming over to see Mom. His name is Brill – '

'Bill.'

'Mom, that's too ordinary. Maybe it was Bill before he changed it. Anyway, he's somebody famous. We just can't figure out who.'

Rick peered questioningly at Allison over the top of his glasses.

She shrugged. 'Uncle Rick knows all about the mystery man. That's why he invited himself over.'

She raised an eyebrow in Rick's direction at her reference to how, when she'd told him Bill had been to her house and was coming back, Rick had insisted on being there. She had tried to dissuade him, explaining that Bill would be more likely to talk to her alone than if a stranger were around. He

argued that this man might very well be the murderer, and she was putting both her life and
Megan's in danger. The appeal to her motherhood
had won out, but she still resented his presence.

'So you think this guy's famous, huh?' Rick
asked, walking into the house arm in arm with
Megan.

'Definitely. I have an instinct for these things.'

'Somewhere between the ages of eleven and
twelve, my daughter became an expert on everything,' Allison supplied, dropping her purse onto
the table beside her canvas bag.

Checking under the sink, she found that the
bucket Bill had left to catch drips was full.

'Megan, I thought you were going to empty this.'

'I forgot,' Megan called from the living room.
'I've got this great new video game, Uncle Rick. Let
me show you how to play.'

Allison gritted her teeth, reminding herself that
Megan was only a child and unaccustomed to any
responsibility. Determinedly, she dragged out the
bucket and emptied then replaced it.

A quick survey of the freezer yielded a package of
pork chops which she set in the microwave to
defrost.

When the chops were stuffed and cooking, sweet
potatoes were baking and a salad made, Allison
plopped into one of the dining-table chairs and
took from her purse the pictures Rick had devel-

oped for her. Studying them intently, she looked for some answers in the flat images, but found none.

She dragged her canvas bag toward her and peered in, searching for the tape recorder that had bits of muffled conversation from the day before when she'd left New Hope with Bill. When he'd protested her recording their conversation, she'd secretly kept the recorder running inside the bag. It was there along with her notepads, pencils and odds and ends, but – she dug some more – her camera was missing.

'Rick, did I leave my camera at the station yesterday when I gave you that film?'

'I don't think so. Drat! That was my last man! You made me lose my last man.'

' "Drat?" ' Allison repeated, sliding the pictures back inside her address book in the side pocket of her purse, then gathering up both bags. 'Now there's a four-letter word I didn't know you knew.' She tugged Rick's red hair and Megan's blonde as she passed behind them, careful not to obstruct their view of the television screen.

'Mom, you left your camera on my dresser,' Megan informed her. 'All right! I get a bonus man.'

'I left it on your dresser? I won't by any chance find it contains a new roll of film with pictures of your friends, will I?'

But Megan's attention was focused on shooting down space creatures.

The camera was, indeed, on the corner of Megan's dresser, just inside her door. Strangely, however, it still contained no film. Allison dropped it into her bag with a shrug. Perhaps Megan had given up when she discovered it was empty rather than buying her own film.

Crossing the hallway into her bedroom, she tossed her bags on the bed, went back downstairs and picked up a magazine but found herself too edgy to read. No, she had to admit, the correct term was 'excited', not 'edgy'.

Understandable, though. She'd always loved a puzzle, and Bill was not only a possibly great story, but he was also an intriguing puzzle. Again she thought of the ease with which he'd dispatched Douglas, of his refusal to accept food or money – and the inexplicable fact that, in spite of his outward appearance, she was drawn to him, not repulsed.

An hour later the chops were getting dry, Rick was skilled enough to beat Megan at the video game half the time, and the drip under the sink was gaining in force, already filling the bucket again. But there was no sign of Bill.

'It would seem you've been stood up,' Rick declared, appearing around the corner of the kitchen as Allison dumped the water. 'Can we eat?'

She rubbed the back of her neck and restrained an irrational impulse to snap at her friend. 'I suppose we might as well. You don't by any chance know what to do with all that stuff Bill told me to get at the hardware store?'

'I'll buy a book, and we'll muddle through.' He peered at the leak as Allison replaced the bucket. 'What the hell, we can't hurt it any.'

'I heard you say the "h" word,' Megan crooned, coming to stand beside Rick. 'I'm hungry, too, Mom. Let's eat. Brill probably got tied up with a long rehearsal or something and didn't have our phone number so he couldn't call us.'

He had no trouble finding our address, Allison thought, but elected to allow Megan to believe what she wanted.

The doorbell rang.

Allison felt her spirits rise.

'It's him,' Megan exclaimed, rushing for the door with Allison and Rick close behind.

When the door opened and Brad saw the strange man with Allison and Megan, he regretted his decision to come over in defiance of his partner's advice, in defiance of his own instincts. He'd fought with himself all day, finally admitting defeat at the last possible moment and charging over here.

The pleased, almost feverish look on Allison's face and the mouth-watering smells coming from the kitchen gave him more reason for concern. They made him feel too good about being there.

'You don't know how glad we are to see you,' the small red-headed man said, extending a freckled hand. 'Rick Holmes. Cameraman for Channel 7.'

Since he'd already run off the ex-husband, this must be the boyfriend. That thought brought a curious disappointment, something he didn't quite understand and chose to ignore. He shook Rick's hand. 'Bill. Unemployed roughneck, plumber, take your choice.'

'Come on in,' Megan invited, taking his arm with no regard for his shabby clothes. 'If we don't eat right now, I'm going to pass out. How come you're so late?'

'Show ran overtime,' he said with a wink, allowing himself to be led across the room.

She smiled happily. 'You got here just in time. Mom and Uncle Rick were going to totally wreck the plumbing.'

Uncle Rick? Her brother? Not much family resemblance, but he felt an odd wave of relief nevertheless. Not that he had any reason to be relieved. Dealing with a brother would be just as worrisome as dealing with a boyfriend, maybe worse.

He accepted the chair Megan indicated.

'My daughter means we were going to find a book and fix the sink ourselves,' Allison explained, setting a platter of steaming pork chops on the table.

Remembering that Allison had requested he take part of his pay in meals, he hesitated to tell her he'd eaten pizza earlier in the evening. If he refused the food, she might feel further obligated to him. Besides, it smelled awfully good. He could probably force himself to make a reasonable showing.

Megan plopped down in the chair next to him. 'Do you like pork chops?'

'Love 'em.'

'Think they're worth backstage passes to your next show?'

'Megan!' Allison exclaimed. 'I can't believe you're so rude.'

Megan shrugged unrepentantly. 'Dad says you have to go after what you want. Isn't that what you're doing at work?'

'Within limits,' she replied through gritted teeth.

Brad smiled at the exchange, but it served to remind him once again that he had to be on his toes. Allison was going after what she wanted . . . a story about him. He chewed a piece of pork chop . . . very tasty pork chop. What would Raney say if he told him he'd sold out for a piece of meat?

'So, Bill,' Rick said, 'how long have you been out of work?'

'Oh, months. Several months. A long time. Not much call for roughnecks. Not like it used to be.'

'But Allison tells me you're a plumber. There's always a call for that.'

'Rick, you're not any better than Megan,' Allison complained. 'Neither one of you has any manners.'

Brad found that amusing since Allison herself

had been asking him much more personal questions the day before.

Sometime later when his plate contained nothing but a bone and his stomach had expanded a notch on his worn belt, he was glad he hadn't refused to eat. Maybe he could take out all his pay in meals. He gave himself a mental shake to remind himself that wasn't possible since he wouldn't be coming back.

'Well,' he said, scooting his chair away from the table, 'that was delicious. Shall we get on with the repairs before or after we do the dishes?'

'Before,' Allison declared. 'The leak's getting worse by the minute.'

'I was afraid of that,' Brad mumbled, and realized he was glad he'd come in spite of everything. She desperately needed his help.

'I'll get the parts and tools out of Allison's car,' Rick volunteered, heading out the door.

'He seems like a really nice guy,' Brad said, surprised to find himself envying – okay, just a little, irrationally, jealous of – the closeness he and Allison shared. 'I know you said he isn't your brother, but he might as well be!'

'Rick's pretty great, all right. I don't know what I'd have done without him on more than one occasion.'

'But,' Megan pointed out, coming up beside him, 'Uncle Rick can't fix our plumbing. I think it's so cool that you can. What else do you do?'

Brad kept his attention trained on Megan. He didn't dare look at Allison. She'd be scrutinizing him with X-ray vision, waiting for his answer to that. 'Whatever needs doing, kiddo.' That was certainly the truth!

'I just never knew that rock stars could do so many things. Do you think Sting fixes leaky faucets?'

'Uh . . .' He looked helplessly up at Allison, but she simply arched one perfect eyebrow, amused at his predicament and waiting for his answer.

The door front door opened. 'I think this is everything.' Rick came in with a couple of plastic bags.

Relieved at the distraction, Brad practically ran to take them from him.

A couple of hours later, Brad crawled out from under the sink, mentally exhausted from wrestling with the mangled plumbing but exhilarated with a sense of accomplishment that he'd actually been able to do it. Allison's smile was even more exhilarating.

She stood only inches away in the small kitchen wearing silk slacks the exact color of real cream and a matching blouse, the soft material caressing every graceful curve. She'd been there the whole time he worked, handing him tools, shining a flashlight for him, and now he noted she didn't have a speck of grease on her.

She reached down one hand as if to help him rise. Such a perfect hand, slim with long, tapering fingers and perfect fingernails, and he found himself automatically reaching to touch it.

But then he caught sight of his own grubby, greasy hand. And his brain kicked into gear.

He hoisted himself up and took a step back away from her.

She looked a little confused and stepped back also, as though her own brain might have just kicked into gear, too. As though she realized she'd almost touched a bum, he told himself, lest he himself misunderstood her actions and thought she, too, suffered from hormone dementia.

'The restroom's upstairs,' she whispered, then cleared her throat and spoke more loudly. 'In case you want to wash up.'

He nodded. 'I remember. Thanks.'

'I'll put on some coffee.'

'Good.' Yeah, that would be just great. He could sit around Allison's home some more, bask in her luminous, grateful gaze, watch that immaculate silk cling to every rise and swell of her body. Just great. And he meant that sarcastically and not sarcastically.

Rick and Megan were glued to the television set, playing some game that made a lot of noise. 'Appreciate your help,' Rick said as he passed.

'Don't leave yet. I'm almost through beating

Uncle Rick,' Megan contributed, eyes glued to the screen.

She really was a kind of cute kid, and he had to admit, her fascination with him was pretty damn appealing.

As he approached the bathroom, through the open door of the room directly across from the landing, on a white comforter dotted with pink roses, he saw Allison's purse and canvas bag. Damn! He'd almost forgotten his real purpose in being there.

Reluctantly, he tiptoed into the room, listening carefully for footsteps on the wooden stairs, almost hoping he'd hear them and not have to do this. It seemed such an invasion of the woman's privacy, especially after he'd dined at her table.

But, he reminded himself, the pictures were an invasion of his privacy. A quick look through the canvas bag failed to unearth the roll of film or any pictures. Hating himself for his duplicity, he reached for the purse, then pulled back as he thought he heard a stair creak.

Heart pounding, he moved quickly back to the bathroom. Even though he saw no one coming, he decided to give up the quest. As Steve had said, the risk wasn't worth it. What could she accomplish with pictures that showed mostly hair and beard anyway?

And if he knew that, what was he doing here? The

possible answers to that question frightened him more than the idea of getting caught. He strode downstairs and retrieved his jacket from the hall closet.

'That should last you at least until you get your big break and move to New York,' he said.

Allison appeared in the kitchen doorway, looking up at him with those big eyes again, and he felt an unexpected glow of pleasure that he hadn't invaded her purse.

'Don't you want some hot coffee before you leave? It's chilly out there, and you have a long walk.' Her eyes narrowed. 'Don't you?'

'Yeah, I do. And that's why I'd better get going. It won't get any warmer until morning, you know.'

'I win! Have you been to New York?' Megan asked, bouncing up from the television and coming to his side.

He laughed at the unexpected question . . . at the break in the tension. 'Yeah, I've been there. Have you?'

'No, but Dad and Bonnie are taking me for vacation this summer. She wants to go shopping there.'

He looked back to Allison to see her reaction. Her lips compressed, and she stepped over, placing a possessive hand on Megan's shoulder. 'Bonnie's her . . . her father's new wife.'

'Dad says she's my stepmother, and I should call her Mom, but I don't like to,' Megan explained.

72

'I can understand that,' Brad agreed, 'since you already have a mom. Well – ' He nodded, then extended a hand to Rick who had also risen. 'Nice to have met you. Good to see you again, Megan.'

He accepted her small hand and experienced a flash of the fierce protectiveness he'd seen Allison display toward the girl. She was so naive, could be taken advantage of so easily.

Not that it was any of his concern.

'Good night, Allis.' The nickname slid easily from his lips, and he realized that was the way he'd been thinking of her all evening. Not sophisticated Allison, but wide-eyed Allis. As he took her soft hand in his, more gently this time than when he'd first met her at the shelter, he noticed her palm wasn't perfectly smooth as he'd thought. She had a couple of small, probably new callouses.

'How much do I owe you?' she asked, ending the handshake rather abruptly.

'Owe me? Uh, how about another home-cooked meal?' Which he had no intention of coming over to collect.

'How about another meal and a little cash?' From the pocket of her slacks, she withdrew a folded bill and stuffed it into his jacket pocket.

Her touch was warm but it sent tantalizing shivers throughout his body. He pulled the money out, stared at it, suddenly dry-mouthed, and briefly contemplated putting it back into her slacks.

No, that was far too tantalizing to be a wise idea. He wasn't sure his hand would stop with inserting the money. Already his fingers could almost feel the curve of her hip, the flat tautness of her stomach.

Resolutely, he took a step closer to her, reached for her hand, put the money in her palm and folded her fingers over it.

'How about I come back tomorrow and help you get this carpet up and dried? Then we'll discuss recompense.' No! a voice inside his head screamed. He couldn't have really said that, made plans to return!

He opened his mouth to take back the words, to make an excuse, but none came to him. In fact, his mind had gone into neutral, his sole thought was how Allison looked as she gazed up at him, her full lips parted just enough so he could see a line of shiny white. The fragrance of summer flowers drifted into his senses and, like a closeup in a movie, his vision focused on her lips, only her lips. He could almost feel their softness.

CHAPTER 4

He wouldn't have kissed her, though, not even if Rick hadn't cleared his throat at that moment. Never at any point did he have any intention of kissing her, and that small voice in the back of his head that was accusing him of such intention didn't know what it was talking about.

'Night,' he said and, turning, yanked open the door and fled.

'Allison,' Rick accused, closing the door behind Bill and leaning against it, 'the way you were staring at that bum was . . . I thought you were . . .' He looked at Megan and didn't finish the sentence.

'Get real, Uncle Rick. Do you think I don't watch television or go to the movies? They looked like they were going to lock lips, didn't they?' Megan appeared quite pleased with the idea.

'Kiss an unkempt, probably unwashed street person?' Allison protested, feeling a twinge of guilt as she spoke. Bill might be unkempt, but he'd been immaculately clean – at least, before he undertook to repair her plumbing. And she had seemed to lose her mind for one crazy instant as the impulse to kiss him sizzled dangerously through her head. Not that she was really attracted to him; he'd just caught her at the end of a very trying day. 'You're both letting your imagination run away with you,' she asserted. 'Megan, up to bed with you. Rick, go home.'

Megan hugged her mother and Rick, then charged upstairs.

'That's all he is, you know,' Rick told her, holding her hand as they walked outside to the garage. 'He's not a rock star or actor in hiding, and I doubt very seriously that he's your serial killer. He's just a kind-hearted but lazy bum. Face it, with his skills as a plumber, he could get a job any time he wanted to. If he wanted to.'

'A bum who refers to money as "recompense".' Though she had to admit her brain had fogged a little at some point, probably due to being overly tired, she distinctly remembered his use of the five-dollar word.

'Okay, an educated bum.' Rick raised the door to the garage. 'I don't like the idea of his coming over again tomorrow.'

Allison patted his hand and grinned. 'If you're worried, come by and help. I'm sure we could use an extra pair of hands.'

'You know I'm working tomorrow night.' Rick

hesitated, seemed to consider. 'But maybe I can get out of it.'

'Oh, give me a break! I think I can take care of myself around a "kind-hearted but lazy bum". You said you don't think he's the killer, so what's the big deal?'

'I said I doubted that he was. Anyway, the big deal is – ' He shrugged, shook his head. 'Just try not to get too carried away with this grand scheme of yours, and promise to call me if this guy does anything weird.'

Allison shoved him in the direction of his car. 'Good night, Rick.'

As soon as she crawled into bed that night, she pulled out her pictures. They were good shots. She'd caught not only his physical likeness, but that self-confident tilt of his head, the piercing, knowing glint in his eyes, the air that set him apart from the rest of the street people. The photographs seemed to draw her almost as compellingly as the man himself. But still she found no answers. With that hair and beard, he could be anyone from the president of the United States to Elvis.

A little more investigation was definitely in order. Tomorrow was pretty full, but she could probably squeeze in an hour or two right after lunch – more if she skipped lunch. She was on to something here, and she would find out what. And once that was accomplished, not only would she have a news story, but she'd lose that inexplicable fascination she had with him. She would track Bill down and expose him, and that would solve a lot of problems.

When Allison walked into the station the next morning, everyone in the room stopped what they were doing and looked up briefly, then, identifying the newcomer, returned to their work. An odd occurrence. Usually the president could enter, and no one would notice.

'Allison!' Rick was making his way toward her through the maze. Behind him Tracy glared and slammed her handbag onto the desk.

'Come on,' Rick said, grabbing her arm. 'There's an apartment fire over on Northwest Expressway.'

'The equipment?'

'In the van. Hurry.'

Without comment, she followed him. A fire didn't wait for discussion.

'What's Tracy's problem?' she asked as they pulled out of the parking lot and Rick took the first corner on two wheels.

'Insecurity,' he declared, leaning on the horn, weaving his way through traffic. 'If you'd arrived two seconds later, I'd have been forced to take your blonde twit along.'

'So big deal. An apartment fire doesn't sound like the story of the week.'

'Every story's a big deal right now. There's a new

rumor this morning. If we hadn't left early yester-day, we'd have heard it last night. The old "new management" rumor.'

'The station's being sold?' Allison gasped. Even such a relative novice as she knew that new owners typically made sweeping changes.

'That's the rumor. Get out of the way, you imbecile!' He hit the horn again, sweeping around a Cadillac. 'I hate those people just on principle.'

'Station owners?' Allison braced one hand against the dash as he took another corner.

'No, Cadillac drivers. I hate them because I don't have one. Don't get all upset about an unfounded rumor. It's not the first. And even if it is true, it doesn't necessarily mean you'll lose your job.'

'It doesn't mean I'll keep it, either.'

'In case you haven't noticed, lady, nothing in this life comes with any guarantees. There it is, up ahead. I see the smoke.'

He peeled into the apartment parking lot and screeched to a stop, bouncing Allison against her seat belt.

'Taking Tracy with you today wouldn't have been all bad,' she muttered. 'You'd have aged her fifteen years with your driving, then she'd be older than me.'

Allison tumbled out of the van. Damn, she thought. This rumor business put a new light on everything, or at least a hotter light. Getting a story on Bill and the homeless was even more important now. Maybe she could even find the killer. That would surely improve her job security.

'Ready to roll!' Rick called, and Allison focused her attention on the issue at hand.

Shortly after noon, however, she was striding down Reno Avenue in the direction of the New Hope shelter. She still wore her 'work' clothes – heels and a navy suit trimmed in white. She wouldn't exactly blend in, but it would have to do.

She found the little building sparsely inhabited today. One man lay stretched out on a bench, evidently sleeping, another was eating a sandwich, and two women sat talking. Reverend Pollock was perched on a rear bench, talking earnestly to Dealey.

Etiquette dictated that she neither disturb nor listen to the conversation; however, her reporter instincts had to take precedence over her manners. She quietly took a seat near them and strained her ears to hear.

'My son, you've got to give up the devil's brew. Your whole life has been ruined by this evil concoction. Look at everything Satan has stolen from you.'

Dealey's head was lowered, eyes fixed on the floor, nodding intermittently. However, Allison got the idea he was more comatose than repentant. She eavesdropped for a few more minutes, but the Reverend's monologue consisted primarily of a lot of bombastic rhetoric. Nothing important seemed to be happening there.

She rose quietly and moved across the room to the two women, one of whom she recognized from her last visit.

'Hello, Kay,' she greeted, smiling and extending her hand to the short, gray-haired woman.

At first Kay looked wary, but then broke into a gap-toothed smile and reached out her wrinkled hand. Allison knew that everyone liked having their name remembered, but the woman's obvious delight tugged at her heart.

'How have you been?' she asked, giving herself a mental order to remember this was business.

'Fine, fine.' Kay nodded.

Allison turned to the other woman who, even sitting, towered over Kay by at least a foot. Allison offered her hand to the woman. 'Allison Prescott,' she said.

'Jean.' A large, bony hand shot up to squeeze Allison's in a tight grip. In spite of her faded, ragged clothing, Allison noticed she wore neon-red shoes – apparently a recent prized acquisition, judging from the condition of the shoes and the way Jean swung her leg.

Allison retrieved her hand, wiggled all the fingers

to be sure they still worked, and took a seat in front of the women.

'Did you bring food?' Kay asked.

'No, I'm sorry. I didn't.' In fact, her own stomach was growling from the missed lunch.

Jean and Kay accepted the news without protest, the expression in their eyes becoming only a little deader. Allison reached into her Gucci bag, withdrew a five-dollar bill and four ones and handed them to Kay. The gesture wiped out her cash, but she had food at home. They didn't.

'You can each have a good lunch with that,' she said, and told herself it was a necessary bribe to get them to talk.

The ladies started to rise, and Allison judged Jean to be at least six feet tall with broad, though bony shoulders. She wouldn't have much to fear from the killer.

And could even be the killer. The police hadn't ruled out the possibility of a woman.

'Can we chat a little bit before you go?' Allison requested.

The women exchanged cautious glances and sat back down.

'Whatcha want to know?' Kay asked, obviously impatient to be off. Very likely the women hadn't eaten all day, Allison reminded herself. Nevertheless, she couldn't throw away the opportunity she'd just bought.

'Let's start with how these murders are affecting you two as women. Are you frightened? What are you doing to protect yourselves?'

Kay shrugged. 'We stay together. He just kills people who get off by theirselves.'

'Surely there must be rumors about this person's identity?'

Jean cackled. 'Some say it's the cops, trying to get rid of all of us. Some say it's one of us, wanting less people to share food and stuff with. And some say – ' her faded eyes twinkled ' – it's suicide.'

She and Kay laughed loudly at the macabre joke, and Allison felt compelled to join in.

'What about this Bill you were talking to the other night? He's new around here, isn't he? Any talk that he might be the killer?'

Kay lowered her eyes and blushed, and Allison realized with a start that she probably had a crush on Bill. Well, just because they were homeless didn't mean they'd lost their emotions.

'He's Dealey's friend. Dealey says he's known him for years,' Jean defended. 'Said they used to work together on these big buildings around here.'

The statement took Allison by surprise, and she hesitated for a moment, then decided it probably wasn't significant. Dealey seemed to say a lot of things that made no sense. Bill had claimed to be a former roughneck and plumber, but hadn't mentioned carpentry. But she suspected he was lying.

She filed Jean's information away for future reference.

'Anybody know where he spends his nights?' she continued.

Kay blushed again, then giggled. 'No,' she twittered.

From the corner of her eye, Allison detected movement. She turned to look just as the Reverend settled his bulk on the bench beside her.

Kay and Jean took the opportunity to depart, rising abruptly and promising to spend the nine dollars on food. It hadn't occurred to Allison that they might not. Now she wondered.

'How are you today?' Allison asked, turning her attention to the Reverend.

'It's a great day,' he answered, smiling as usual. 'We can't always feed the body adequately, but food for the soul is abundantly available.'

Commendable, Allison thought, and marveled that the man could keep such an upbeat attitude in the face of so much sorrow.

'I just dropped by to see how things were going and maybe talk to a few more people,' she told him. Even with the stress she was under, it was impossible not to return his smile. 'I'd like to come back again, if it's all right with you. I can't always bring sandwiches, but maybe I could help in other ways.'

'We'll not turn down any offer of assistance. If

84

you have nothing to share but your beautiful smile, we'll welcome that.'

Allison felt warm inside at the idea of helping, then guilty because she had an ulterior motive.

'If you can give of yourself while learning from us and creating your story, we will all benefit,' he continued, as if reading her mind.

That made sense. She wanted it to make sense.

'Tell me your story,' she urged him, genuinely curious. The man might be a little to the left of normal, but she sensed a core of sincerity. He believed in what he did and what he said. 'Where were you before, and how did you end up here?'

He folded his large hands and gazed toward the smoke-stained ceiling. 'I've been to Eden and survived Armageddon. I came here because I was called, because I am needed.'

Definitely a bit to the left.

'What do you know about Dealey's friend, Bill?'

The Reverend's smile dimmed ever so slightly. 'He came from afar.' His gaze returned to her from the ceiling, and he looked profoundly sincere. Too sincere. The man was suspicious of Bill, too. 'He cares for Dealey,' he commented. 'Dealey suffers, though he brings much of it upon himself. His spirit is willing, but his body is weak.'

'Did Bill know any of the people who were murdered?'

'No man can live unto himself. In this world each

soul must reach out to all other souls. We are all one, and we must rejoin with our brothers and sisters to be whole.'

Was the preacher being deliberately obtuse?

'Is that a yes or a no?'

He raised one shaggy eyebrow. 'My child, we all know each other in the spirit.'

It was becoming more and more apparent why no one had done an in-depth study. Getting below the surface wasn't easy.

Nevertheless, when Allison left an hour later, she felt she had made some sort of progress in becoming an established and accepted character in this world of homeless people. She was getting closer to a story – Bill's or the murderer's or both.

The thought again crossed her mind that he might well be the murderer. That would explain a lot.

No, that was impossible. He was too kind and gentle.

But she remembered the solid muscles that had surprised her when she'd clutched his arm.

Absolutely not. Just because he could have didn't mean he would have.

As she slid into her car, she remembered the bone-crushing handshake Jean the Giantess had given her. With her size and strength, she was just as likely a candidate for the murderer as Bill. That was another avenue she should definitely explore.

★ ★ ★

Brad cursed himself all the way to Allison's that evening. If he had any sense at all, he'd go home, go to his parents' house, go out and get drunk – anything but this! But if he'd had any sense, he wouldn't have volunteered to come back and pull up the damned carpet in the first place. She hadn't even asked. He'd just taken leave of his senses and volunteered!

He parked on a different street this time so the neighbors wouldn't become suspicious of his truck.

His actions were sort of understandable, he mused as he walked to her house. He'd taken in enough strays in his life; his mother could attest to that. But the strays didn't usually threaten his career – maybe even his life – by trying to expose him. Nor did they wear a gold watch and drive a Volvo. Allis and the kid – they'd had money once, and they'd find it again. That type always did.

Which was one more reason to avoid her even beyond her profession. He sure didn't want to get emotionally involved. His detective's salary might keep him in beer and blue jeans, but it wouldn't make a dent in Allison Prescott's wine-and-silk budget.

He rounded the corner and saw the cream-colored Mercedes parked in the street again. Mumbling several more expletives, he ordered himself to do an about-face and get out of there. However, his feet continued to march stubbornly forward. Allison's last meeting with the ex could have been disastrous if Brad hadn't intervened.

The door to her house was open, and the voices coming through the screen were restrained but definitely angry.

'You bring her back by seven o'clock on Sunday, just like the divorce decree says,' Allison demanded. Her voice was strong, but Brad thought she sounded close to tears.

'Mo-o-o-m,' Megan protested. 'Dad, maybe you could come by and pick me up Wednesday after school.'

'I could – ' Douglas's oily voice slid through the open door ' – but that's foolish. It would be so much easier if you just stayed over until Wednesday. I could bring her home Thursday night, Allison. You're being unreasonable.'

'Please, Mom. You know how bad I want to go see January Heat. They're my favorite rock group.'

'Wednesday's a school night, anyway,' Allison interrupted. 'Why didn't you get tickets for Friday or Saturday? I'll tell you why. Because that wouldn't have suited your scheming, conniving – '

Brad rang the doorbell, then pushed in without waiting for an invitation. 'Yo, Megan! Hey, Allis. And Dr Doug, isn't it?'

'Brill, make her listen,' Megan pleaded, running to him and taking his arm.

'Hey, Megan, have I got a surprise for you! Some

friends of mine are going to be in town next week-end – have you ever heard of January Heat? – and I thought you might like to go with me.' Damn! That invisible ventriloquist was putting words in his mouth again. He'd never get out of this one!

Megan commenced to bounce up and down like an ecstatic jack-in-the-box. 'Mom, Dad! Did you hear that? Can we go backstage, Brill?'

'I don't know. We'll see.' Maybe he could leave town before next weekend.

Douglas moved toward him menacingly. At least, that's the attitude Brad assumed he was trying to convey. Actually he looked like he might be having hip problems.

'What are you doing back here? More plumbing?'

'Nah. Tonight we're taking out this cheap, soggy carpet.' He shook his head. 'Sure hope the fool that put this trash in didn't pay more than fifty cents a yard.'

Douglas raised one eyebrow and tilted his aristo-cratic nose upward. Brad wondered if he'd had to pay for the job or if plastic surgeons traded out with each other. You do my nose, I do yours. 'I happen to be the fool who put that carpet in,' he declared. 'Do you have any other remarks to contribute to this conversation?'

Brad nodded and tugged at his beard. 'Did you?' he asked.

'Did I what?'

'Pay more than fifty cents a yard?'

'Look, you.' Douglas pointed his finger in Brad's face, not a gesture Brad took well. Brad's fist automatically jerked upward, but Megan's small hands still lingering on his arm reminded him of the circumstances.

'I'll thank you to remember that you're the handyman around here,' Douglas continued, shaking his finger, 'and that doesn't include taking my daughter to concerts or becoming involved in family discussions.'

'Daddy! Brill isn't just a handyman,' Megan protested.

'And I'm the one,' Allison declared, stepping up beside Megan, 'who'll decide who takes my daughter to concerts when she's in my custody.' She stuck her finger in Douglas's face in mockery of his actions. 'And it damned sure won't be you and Bonnie the Bimbo.'

'Mother!'

'Exactly what is this man to you if he isn't "just a handyman"?' The words oozed from Douglas's mouth as he studied Allison closely.

'You gave up the right to ask that six months ago,' she answered.

To her credit, she stood her ground, but Douglas's expression told Brad he had latched onto her angry flush for the wrong reasons.

With a condescending sneer, he looked Brad up

and down. 'I'd have thought a little better of you than that, Allison. But I guess this is the best you can do under the circumstances. Get your things, Megan, and let's go.'

'Let me help you,' Brad interjected, grabbing Megan's overnight bag and clothes from the back of the faded floral print sofa. 'I wouldn't mind having another closeup look at that car of yours, Doug. Not often we handymen types get that close to luxury.'

'You stay away from my car,' Douglas ordered.

'Sunday at seven,' Allison reminded.

'Daddy,' Megan protested. 'Brill won't hurt your car.'

'Maybe I could wax it for you some day, boss,' Brad drawled, following them down the walk.

Douglas turned to glare at him, but Brad kept his face expressionless – an easy task since most of it was hidden by hair anyway.

After tucking Megan and her luggage into the car, Brad stood back and waved. Yes, that was a very easy license plate to remember. He could just pass along the word to keep a lookout in case Dr Doug committed any infractions. And people like him always did.

CHAPTER 5

Allison watched Bill nonchalantly dispose of Douglas for the second time. She thought of Rick's joke about having Bill, should he turn out to be the murderer, put Douglas on his hit list. With a tiny shiver that was a cross between a thrill and fear, she reflected that Bill could easily handle such a task.

'I'm sorry,' she apologized when Bill rejoined her in the house. 'You come to help and end up getting embroiled in a family feud.'

Bill shrugged. 'What's Doug's problem, anyway? Other than bad breeding.'

With a grim bark of laughter, Allison slumped onto the sofa. 'I guess that's about the size of it,' she said. 'He's determined to take Megan away from me.'

'Why?' Bill asked, sinking down beside her.

His nearness had a calming effect on her, and she felt a crazy impulse to touch him, to try to absorb some of his strength. 'Looks to me like you take pretty good care of the kid,' he said when she didn't answer immediately.

'Right now I can't give her the material things he can, but other than that, we do all right. No, it's just the way Douglas is. He has to be in control of everything. When we got a divorce, he already had things set up, his assets hidden, so all I got was this dump and a bare minimum of child support.' Allison took a deep breath to quench the anger she still felt at the injustice.

Bill watched her intently, his hazel eyes widening as if in surprise. She wished he didn't have quite so much hair. She'd have liked to have seen more of his expression.

'With Douglas, it was nothing personal,' she explained. 'It wasn't so much that he didn't want me to have anything; he just wanted it all. But he couldn't take Megan. I fought him on that. So now he's trying other methods. He bribes her with new clothes and trips. He tries to keep her for increasingly longer periods of time. For a few months he had a detective following me to try to make a custody case.'

Bill looked away from her and leaned forward, resting his elbows on his knees and staring across the room. 'So,' he said thoughtfully, 'that's why you're so damned pushy.' He sounded as if he were talking to himself or to the wall he was staring at, rather than to her.

'I wouldn't have called myself pushy, but, yes, providing Megan with her former lifestyle is a motivating factor in my life.' She realized she sounded a little stiff, but she resented his categorization of her as pushy. 'Not that my motives are totally unselfish. I'd like to move out of this dump myself.'

Bill turned to look her directly in the eye. 'I guess your choices are to make a bundle on your own or marry one.' His words were clipped with bitter overtones.

She gasped as if he'd struck her. For a moment she sat gazing at him dumbly, the bile rising in her throat, debating whether she should order him to leave or punch him. Nothing he'd said or done in their brief acquaintance had prepared her for such rudeness.

'I don't have "choices",' she said coldly. 'Losing my daughter isn't an option, nor is selling myself to the highest bidder. The only choice I have is to "make a bundle", as you so succinctly put it. The one with the money is the one in control. And nobody but me is ever going to control my life again.'

Bill started to run a hand through his hair, but the mass of tangled curls stopped it halfway, and, even in the midst of her anger, Allison noted that he apparently wasn't accustomed to dealing with so much hair.

'I'm sorry,' Bill said, disentangling his hand and lowering it to the sofa arm. 'I didn't mean that the way it sounded.'

'Then just how did you mean it?' she challenged.

He shifted uneasily, and the movement surprised her. He'd handled Douglas so expertly, but she was making him uncomfortable. The thought almost brought a smile to her lips – except she was still angry at him for his insulting, hurtful comment.

'I don't know,' he mumbled, talking to the wall again, then he turned back to her and gave her an apologetic half-smile. 'Sometimes my mouth just takes off on its own and leaves my brain far behind. I really am sorry, Allis. I didn't mean to be rude. I guess I've been on the streets too long.'

He was back in character . . . and back in control. And she realized her sensitivity, her emotional rather than intellectual reaction to the situation, might have just cost her an opportunity to probe, to catch him unaware. She'd have to think it through later, but it did seem that the subject of money hit his hot button.

'Well,' he stood, dusting his hands as if disposing of the entire subject, 'I guess we'd better get to work. Where do you want to move this furniture?'

'Out on the porch, I guess, and pray it doesn't rain.' She made a mental note to pay closer attention in the future, to keep a tighter rein on her emotions.

What had appeared to be a minuscule amount of furniture seemed to grow as they lugged it outside.

'This is good stuff,' Bill commented as they maneuvered the sofa through the door. 'It's heavy.

If you get this recovered, you'll have a nice piece for a lot of years.'

They slid it up against the side of the house, and Allison dropped her end with relief. 'You're right about one thing. It certainly is heavy.' She ran a hand over the back and looked wistfully down at the faded flowers, their tinting even fainter in the porch light. 'My parents gave me this when Douglas and I got married. He was still in medical school, and we were so broke.'

'Your folks live here?'

She shook her head. 'Dad's company transferred him to Chicago a couple of years ago. I sometimes think Douglas deliberately waited until they were gone so I'd be entirely alone and easier to defeat.'

'Maybe you could stay with them for a while.'

Allison was suddenly aware that she was standing on her front porch discussing her personal life with a stranger – a street person, a homicidal maniac . . .

'I don't need to stay with them,' she snapped. 'I am perfectly capable of taking care of myself and my daughter.' For one instant she wondered if Bill might be someone Douglas had hired to spy on her. But that was being paranoid. For one thing, Douglas would never have tolerated Bill's behavior from an employee, not even for the sake of duping her.

Bill lifted his hands, palms outward in a gesture of surrender. 'Hey, I was just making a suggestion. No harm intended.'

'Do your parents still live here?' she asked, hoping to trap him.

It almost worked. 'They – ' He caught himself in mid-sentence and started over. 'They're dead. Let's get the television, and we'll be ready to start on the carpet.'

Even though she hadn't learned anything, Allison felt pleased and excited. She'd almost tricked him into saying something he shouldn't. His hesitation confirmed that she was onto something.

With the rooms cleared out, Bill selected a screwdriver from the tools she'd purchased and/ or borrowed from Rick for repairing the sink. Wordlessly he began to pry up the metal strip between the dining area and kitchen.

She watched him for a few minutes then got an old kitchen knife and did the same thing to the one by the side door. 'There's a chicken in the oven, and I'll throw a couple of potatoes in the microwave when we get through here,' she said.

A particularly stubborn section of the strip gave, taking the tip of one fingernail in the process. Biting her lip, she squelched a swear word. Though she couldn't afford to have it sculptured and would have to attempt the repair herself, she wasn't about to bemoan this tragedy in Bill's presence. Not after his insulting comments about money.

'What are you doing?'

She gasped at the nearness of his voice and looked up to see him standing directly behind her, scowling down.

'I'm not sure what the technical term is, but I believe I'm unhooking my carpet.'

'And breaking your fingernails.' He leaned down and grasped her hand, holding up the index finger with its jagged nail.

She jerked her hand back. 'I was planning to cut them all tomorrow, anyway. Short, natural nails are "in" now.'

His beard shifted, and for a brief moment she thought he was going to smile, could see it forming in his eyes. Then he blinked, and it was gone. He turned away with a shrug.

'Up to you,' he said. 'Let's get this obscenity off your floor before the whole thing rots.' He showed her how to lift it away from the nail strips along the wall, then hesitated. 'I wasn't kidding about the poor quality of this junk. You may have to buy new.'

Allison shook her head. 'My budget this week doesn't allow for new carpet,' she said with a wry grin. 'So let's be careful with Douglas's blue-light special here.'

Bill nodded and moved to the other side of the room, but a few minutes later he came back and squatted beside her. 'Any chance the wood under this garbage is in decent condition?'

Allison didn't have to wonder why he was asking. The small amount of carpet she'd loosened was stretched and shredded. 'I don't know. I've never seen the bare floors. When we bought the house, it had green sculptured carpet in it. Douglas had it removed and this stuff installed at the same time.' She rocked back on her heels and sighed. 'Well, I know one way to find out about the flooring. What have we got to lose?'

An hour later the offending carpet lay in pieces in the yard, the furniture was pushed against the walls, and Allison and Bill sat at the far end of the living room ripping up the old padding.

'It's gorgeous,' Allison exclaimed, pulling up a large chunk of the thin material and studying the wood underneath. Where the water had soaked it, the varnish had whitened and would have to be scraped, but over here where it was dry, the finish gleamed smooth and glossy.

'With a little work, it'll be gorgeous,' Bill agreed. 'I'll bring – I think I can borrow a tool to take out these staples, and you're on your way.'

Another slip. He didn't need to borrow any tools. He'd caught himself and added that part to cover up. Homeless people didn't have tools, especially something as specialized as whatever he was going to bring to rip out the staples.

Giddy with the excitement of the approaching discovery of Bill's identity and the salvaging of her floors, Allison snatched up a strip of carpet, shredding it into pieces, throwing them into the air like confetti and laughing.

'I love hardwood floors,' she declared. 'Douglas paid a fortune to have them put in his new house, and I get them for free. A victory! Finally a point for my side.' She tossed a couple of pieces of the padding at Bill.

He laughed, his beard splitting to expose his perfect white teeth. 'I've never seen anybody get so excited over a floor. I think you're a little nuts!' He threw the bits back at her.

'Today the floor, tomorrow the world. What lovely floors. Thank you for discovering them.' She stroked the smooth wood, then rolled over onto her back, looking up at Bill as he balanced on his heels.

He reached one hand and gently pushed her hair back from her face.

Impulsively, she grabbed his hand between both of hers. He resisted, and she turned it loose, but then he leaned toward her.

'Allis,' he said, 'Allis in Wonderland.'

His warm, pepperminty breath touched her first, then his lips, smooth and silky, surrounded by the wiriness of his beard.

Quicksilver surged through her veins. She responded to the increasing urgency of his kiss, clutching at his shoulders as he rolled onto his back, pulling her atop him. A small corner of her mind whispered that she shouldn't be doing this, but she couldn't quite remember why not. He felt so good – hard and strong, soft and gentle – and he made her feel so good. It seemed an eternity since she'd felt anything but pain. This was delicious, and she savored every drop of the pleasure.

His tongue teased her lips, then plunged into her mouth, tantalizing nerve endings she hadn't even known she had. His arms, solid and strong, held her securely, created a warm cocoon, one she didn't want to leave. But she would, she'd make him release her – any time now, in just a little while. She thrust her tongue back against him, let him pull her into his mouth.

Her heart thudded wildly against her chest, against his chest. She was intoxicated, drunk with a wild, leaping euphoria.

He took his lips from hers, and she groaned in protest. But then she felt his mouth on her neck, kissing, nipping, teasing. He slid one hand down her body, stroking the curve of her waist and hip, making her feel sexy, desirable, desiring – feelings she'd almost forgotten. Her breasts seemed to swell, pushing against him, aching for more of the drug that was his touch. Electricity surged through her, finding its center where his hips touched hers.

'Bill,' she whispered, the word a plea though she wasn't sure for what.

His mouth at the base of her throat stopped moving, and his body stiffened. He rolled her to the side and gazed at her for a moment from eyes bright with desire. Then, shaking his head and muttering an expletive, he stood and turned his back to her. She could hear his ragged breathing.

For a moment she lay on the floor, stunned, gasping for air, for control. Slowly the drunkenness of desire ebbed, and her senses returned.

What on earth had she been doing? Making out with a street person? Kissing a derelict? Maybe she had all sorts of reasons to suspect he was something else – maybe even a murderer – but at the moment she only knew for sure what he told her . . . that he was a bum.

Pushing herself to her knees, she rose on shaky legs.

Whoever he was, she couldn't deny how he'd made her feel.

'What do you say we eat before we get back to work on the floor?' he asked, still not looking at her. 'We've got more than a one-night job ahead of us.'

'Yes, good idea,' she agreed, going around him into the kitchen, careful not to get too close, not to touch him again. If she did, she wasn't sure what would happen, whether she would pull away or whether they'd end up back on the floor.

'If I could use your bathroom, I'd like to wash up.'

'Yes, good idea,' Allison repeated, looking at her own soiled hands, aware she sounded like an idiot. But that was appropriate; she felt like one.

When she could hear the water running upstairs, she went to the kitchen sink and squeezed dish-washing liquid onto her hands and arms and rinsed off the dirt. Replacing the bottle under the sink, she noticed the Comet.

With one finger she touched her lips, lips that had kissed a tramp. She ought to scrub them, brush her teeth. But a slight pepperminty taste still lingered, bringing a memory of his kiss. She didn't want to lose that.

She slammed the cabinet door closed, wishing she could slam closed the door to her memory so easily.

When Bill returned from washing up, he acted as though nothing had happened, and that was, she supposed, the way he should act. After all, he was – that is, she was –

She didn't know the end to either of those sentences. Certainly she didn't know what or who he was, and she was no longer sure of her own identity.

When her mantel clock that no longer possessed a mantel struck midnight, Bill stood up and stretched.

'That's it,' he said. 'I turn into a prince any minute now. Let's get your furniture back inside, then we'll finish tomorrow night.'

'Sounds good to me. I'm beat.' Allison stood with him, maintaining an appropriate distance.

They moved everything back inside, leaving it close to the door to make it easier to move back out the next time. Rick's comment about Bill being a lazy bum came back to Allison as Bill carried in the last lamp. Whatever he might be, lazy definitely didn't apply to him. He'd worked extremely hard, and promised to do even more.

And somehow, even if he turned out to be an eccentric millionaire in hiding, she would somehow manage to pay him for it. She wouldn't be indebted to him . . . or anyone else.

'I should be home by eight or eight-thirty tomorrow evening,' she said. 'Saturdays are busy.'

'I'll put it on my calendar,' he promised with a wry grin.

As she walked to the door behind him, she suddenly realized that he had no means of transportation, and downtown was several miles away.

'Oh!' she exclaimed. 'Let me drive you home – uh, downtown or, uh, wherever.'

He stared at her blankly for a minute, then smiled, white teeth dancing in the midst of his beard, the beard that had so recently touched her face.

'No, thanks,' he said. 'I'll be fine.' He reached for the doorknob.

'Really, I insist. I have to get out to go to the store anyway,' she improvised. If he really was homeless, she couldn't let him walk all that way after working himself to a frazzle on her house. And if he wasn't, she wanted to see him squirm out of her offer.

'I have my resources,' he assured her, opening the door and stepping out onto the porch.

'I'll pay for a taxi.'

'No.' He crossed the porch.

'The television station's close to downtown. How about I pick you up at New Hope tomorrow evening?'

He turned halfway down the walk, waved and smiled as though he were enjoying the situation. 'No,' he said. 'We homeless have our pride.' He strolled away.

Curiouser and curiouser, she thought, closing the door. Remembering that the words came from *Alice in Wonderland*, she blushed. Usually she hated the nicknames people bestowed upon her, but it had sounded kind of nice – intimate – when he'd called her 'Allis.'

After pouring herself a glass of wine, she crawled into bed and tried to read a magazine, but the articles about new clothes and diets seemed insipid, failed to hold her attention.

Her address book still lay beside her purse where

105

it had slipped out when she'd tossed the bag onto her bed that evening. She reached down for the book, frowning when she didn't see the protruding edges of Bill's photographs.

She checked the side pockets of her purse. In her recent state of mind, she could have misplaced them. Finally, she dumped the entire contents of her bag onto the bed.

The pictures were gone.

As she looked up, her eyes involuntarily settled on the stairway landing and the bathroom beside it. Her bedroom door had been open, the address book with its protruding pictures lying on the bed in plain sight to anyone coming up the stairs. Bill had been upstairs long enough to – no, that was ridiculous.

She gulped half the glass of wine and lay back against her pillow. On the one hand, she wanted to think Bill took the pictures to bolster her theories about him. But on the other, thinking of him sneaking around in her house, being deceitful, gave her a sad, sinking feeling.

She'd just misplaced the pictures somewhere, maybe even pulled them from her purse accidentally during the day. Rick still had the negatives and could make more prints. No big deal.

Except she wasn't prone to losing things, not important things.

Hating herself, she checked her wallet. She'd

cashed a check on the way home after giving her money to Kay and Jean. The twenty was still there. Relief flooded through her.

Only the pictures were missing.

Then it hit her, and she was amazed she'd missed it before. Some reporter she was to overlook the obvious so easily.

Her camera had been missing, but it had appeared in Megan's room, on the dresser just inside the door.

Bill had come back to her house that first night with a request to use the bathroom. He'd seen the camera in her car, undoubtedly knew she'd been taking pictures of him. So maybe he took the camera from her bag that night, found the film missing, returned the camera – Megan's room was directly across the hall from the bathroom, more easily accessible even than her own bedroom.

He wasn't a thief, she thought with mingled happiness and excitement. The twenty dollars and the replaced camera told her he wasn't a thief.

All he wanted was his pictures. All he wanted was to hide his identity.

She smiled as she lifted her wine glass in a toast. 'I'm coming after you, Bill or Brill or whoever you are.'

A brief cloud appeared on the horizon of her hopes. What if he had a legitimate reason for hiding? What if he was in the witness-protection program? Then she'd have to kill her story. But somehow she didn't think the government relocated people to the streets.

Maybe – abruptly she lowered her wine glass and stopped herself from weaving another fantasy. Maybe she was doing what Rick accused her of. Maybe she wanted him to be somebody else so she'd have a story.

Or maybe she wanted him to be somebody else so she could justify the way she'd felt when he'd kissed her.

CHAPTER 6

'How'd it go last night?' Rick asked as he guided the station's van through the Saturday traffic toward their first assignment of the day, a new art exhibition.

Good question, Allison thought. Just exactly how did it go, kissing a bum?

'Fine,' she answered. 'I have beautiful hardwood floors under that ghastly carpet.'

'That's great!' Rick enthused. 'So how come you sound like it's a catastrophe?'

'I'm just tired. We worked late on the floor.'

'You and Bill?'

'Umm.' She turned to stare out her window, afraid to let Rick see her face, afraid he'd be able to read what had happened.

'You know, I have to admit I've been a little concerned about your situation, so I've done some checking on your suspicious friend, and you may be on to something.'

Allison's head snapped around, and she glared at

him. 'He's a bum, just like you said. He's too lazy to get a job. He's not a rock star or an actor or – '

'Whoa!' Rick said, laughing. 'I'm trying to help. I thought you wanted him to be somebody else.'

He had no idea how badly she wanted Bill to be somebody he wasn't. But this morning, as she'd lain in bed fantasizing again about his identity, she'd forced herself to face reality. Dreaming about becoming rich and returning to the good life was one thing, harmless enough. But making up a larger-than-life story for Bill was no longer harmless. She couldn't go around kissing derelicts and justifying it by making up fairy tales about them – even derelicts who had a phobia about having their picture taken.

'He is what he is, and the discussion is closed.'

Rick whistled through his teeth. 'Have it out again with Douglas?' he guessed.

'As a matter of fact, I did,' Allison replied, glad to have a change of subject supplied. She started to tell him about the confrontation, then realized she'd have to include Bill in the story.

'How much further is this place?' she asked, interrupting herself.

Allison pulled the sheet of paper from the type-writer, read what she'd just written and sighed. Typing had never been her long suit. 'Siamese' was spelled with the 'i' and 'a' transposed every time. Briefly, she considered retyping it, then decided accuracy wasn't important under the circumstances.

She carried the paper across the room and dropped it onto Tracy's desk. 'Cat-show story.' Even if the girl had a working brain cell and was capable of noticing the typos, by the time the words mushed out of her mouth, it wouldn't matter.

'Thanks, Allie,' Tracy replied. 'You always do such a good job on my scripts.'

'Why, uh, thank you,' Allison said, so surprised at the expression of gratitude and the compliment, she didn't even protest the use of the nickname.

As she started back to her desk, however, Tracy's voice stopped her. 'Could you help me write a few more of these?'

Give the girl credit. At least she knew her weak point. If she wanted to impress whatever future owners might be watching, she needed help with the writing. The smart thing would be for Allison to refuse. Why should she help the competition? Tracy had over an hour before the six o'clock news, plenty of time to do her own writing.

'All right,' Allison agreed, wondering why she was slitting her own throat. 'But I need to get out of here fairly early this evening.'

'The kid home this weekend?' Tracy asked, handing her a pile of sheets from the computer.

The question was innocuous enough, but Tracy's

111

tone rankled. She made no bones about the fact that she thought Allison's motherhood was just one more millstone around her aging neck.

'Megan is with her father.' She considered giving the stories back to Tracy. Shoving them in one ear and pulling them out the other would be a nice way to do it.

Tracy studied her for a minute, then asked skeptically, 'Hot date?' – as though the possibility of such an event was inconceivable.

Allison pondered her answer for a minute, finally settled on, 'I'm having some remodeling work done on my house.'

'Hey, Prescott!' the assignments editor bellowed. 'Body on Southwest Third! Just came over the scanner. Could be another homeless.'

'I'm on my way!' Allison exclaimed, tossing the papers back onto Tracy's desk. 'Rick!' She snatched up her bag and darted toward the editing room.

When they arrived on the scene, a crowd was already gathering. However, Allison noted an immediate difference from the other deaths – the location, directly in front of a building rather than in an alley or other secluded spot. As she pushed through to the officers holding back the onlookers, she noticed another difference – paramedics were working on a man, and an oxygen mask covered his face. None of the others had been found alive.

'False alarm,' a uniformed officer was telling the only reporter who had preceded Allison to the scene. 'This man's still breathing, and there's no evidence to suggest any sort of physical violence.'

'What happened to him?' Allison asked, holding her mike toward the policeman.

He crossed his arms and shook his head. 'Too early to say.'

'Who is he?'

'We don't know yet.'

The paramedics loaded the man onto a stretcher, and the officers moved to clear a path to the ambulance. Allison stepped back, checking to be sure Rick was behind her getting it all on film.

As the stretcher passed her, Allison gasped and raised a hand to her mouth as she recognized the pale, wrinkled features. Dealey! Her eyes scanned the area carefully, but there was no sign of Bill. Not surprising. He was probably on his way to her house.

'He takes care of Dealey,' the Reverend had told her, referring to Bill. She wondered guiltily if Dealey's problem had occurred after Bill had left to go to her house. Even if he hoped to hitchhike much of the way, he'd probably left the downtown area early.

Allison was about to suggest to Rick that they return to the station with the material they had, then call the hospital later, when her attention was caught by a big man loping toward the scene. Judging by the warm-ups he wore in place of a suit, Detective Raney had been off duty. She touched Rick's arm and pointed him out just as he pushed through to the uniformed officers.

Several other reporters had arrived, and everyone was clamoring for comments from the man. He held up a hand. 'I'll let you know when I find out.'

Allison edged as close as possible and tried to eavesdrop, but the crowd was noisy. From what she heard, she gathered the preliminary diagnosis was that Dealey had drunk something potentially lethal, probably when he ran out of cheap wine.

She and Rick remained for Raney's official statement, then began gathering their gear to leave.

'Wait,' she whispered as she spotted a familiar figure sprinting up the street. A block away, he slowed down, jammed his hands into his pockets and changed to a slouching stroll.

'I hate to mention this, Allison,' Rick murmured in her ear, 'but your friend, Bill, is exhibiting suspicious behavior.'

'Then don't mention it!' Allison snapped. But she studied his approach carefully, scrutinizing every detail.

The run had been pretty impressive. But she'd really like to hear how he'd planned to get to her house on time unless he had another mode of transportation besides his feet, however fast they might be.

Brad knew something was wrong as he approached. The crowd was dispersing and the ambulance had already left. Studying the crime scene prior to moving the body should take a lot longer.

Granted, it had taken him a while to get here since he'd been on the other side of town mortgaging his future firstborn child for tickets to January Heat when his beeper had gone off, alerting him to call Steve. Nevertheless, things were moving too fast.

He peered around cautiously, then groaned as he neared the small group that remained. Unfortunately, Allison and her friend with the camera stood only a few feet away from Steve and the two uniforms. He desperately needed to talk to Steve, and carrying through with his role would be a little more difficult under Allison's suspicious gaze.

'Hey, man,' he called, approaching Steve. 'What's going on here?'

The trio turned toward him, and one of the officers replied, 'Nothing that concerns you, buddy. Just keep moving unless you want to sleep in jail tonight.'

'Hey,' Allison protested, clicking over on her designer heels to stand between him and the officer. 'You don't have any reason to talk to this man that way. It so happens, that was a friend of his they just took away.'

'What?' Brad's head jerked toward Steve.

'One of your buddies o.d.'d on something,' Steve explained.

'O.d.'d?' In their brief conversation earlier, Steve had indicated another murder.

'Yeah. Everybody got a little excited when they found him, but there was no homicide. Ambulance just took him to Oklahoma Memorial Hospital. You go on now. Everything's under control.'

'I gotcha, man.' At the official dismissal, he turned around, relieved, and started back the way he'd come, hoping Allison would let him go. He should have known better.

'Bill!' she exclaimed, grabbing his arm to detain him. Her delicate floral scent filled his nostrils, and the touch of her slender fingers tingled his skin all the way through his jacket. It took all his will power to keep his hands off her, to restrain himself from pulling her into his arms and kissing her the way he'd done on her floor . . . and all night long in his dreams.

'It's Dealey,' she blurted out.

'What?'

Her dark eyes were wide and concerned as she gazed up at him. 'Your friend, Dealey. He's the one they just took away. He drank something.'

'Oh, jeez.' It surprised him to discover how upset he was over the news. On a job like this, you couldn't afford to become emotionally involved with any of the people.

'What's going on here?' Steve asked, rejoining them.

'The guy who o.d.'d – this lady knows him,' Brad said. 'Dealey. He's a wino, got a few screws loose. We hang around a little together.' Steve would recognize the name, know this was the person Brad had latched onto in order to facilitate his acceptance into the world of street people.

'How is he?' Brad asked. 'Will he make it?'

'I don't know,' Steve answered, shaking his head. 'He was still alive when they left here. I guess it'll depend on what he drank, how much and how long ago.'

'Allison,' Rick interrupted, consulting his watch, 'we need to get this footage to the station.'

Allison nodded. 'Bill,' she said, 'you wait here, and I'll come back for you and take you to the hospital.'

'How do you know this Dealey?' Steve asked, turning his attention to Allison.

'I met Dealey and Bill while researching a story,' she explained, her haughty tone allowing no room for criticism, and Brad had to bite his lip to keep from smiling.

Steve cut his gaze around to Brad questioningly,

but Brad looked away. Even a moron would be able to figure out that this was the reporter he'd told Steve about.

'I've got to run,' she said, then added in a soft voice, 'Dealey'll be all right, Bill. Try not to worry.' She started up the street, then turned to call over her shoulder, 'I'll pick you up in a couple of hours.'

'No,' he protested. 'I'll get another ride.' He jabbed Steve with an elbow.

'I'll take him, ma'am. Official business. I need him for a positive i.d.'

Allison turned back for a brief instant, searching his face, her eyes asking unspoken questions. He nodded curtly, letting her know he'd still keep their appointment. She tapped away with Rick following close behind, juggling his camera.

He should be glad she'd chosen to keep their future meeting a secret. He'd been terrified she would say something in front of Steve. But he couldn't help a feeling of resentment. If he'd been wearing a suit, she wouldn't have felt the need to hide their plans.

Still, she had defended him.

'Go on,' Steve told the uniforms. 'A false alarm. It's over.'

When they were out of hearing range, he crossed his arms, rocked back on his heels and studied Brad. 'The picture lady, huh?'

'I got the pictures away from her.'

'I'd say the pictures were the least of your worries. That was just too sweet for words when she rushed over to take up for you, protect you from the nasty police.'

'Up yours. Come on, let's go over to the hospital.' Brad started to walk down the street.

'Forget it. You know that was just a ploy to get rid of your girl friend. Go on home.'

Brad stopped and stared at his partner. 'I'd like to see how that man is doing, find out whether he's dead or alive, and it'd look a lot better if you took me officially.'

Steve's expression sobered. 'Man, you've been on the force for, what, thirteen years? You know better than this. You don't get involved. Call and find out about the old wino. And forget about the broad until this assignment's over.' He made a crude suggestion as to what Brad could do with Allison at that point in time.

Brad's fists clenched, and he had to restrain himself from punching out his partner. 'Go to hell, Steve,' he said quietly, then stalked away, gritting his teeth.

Steve had no right to talk about Allison that way. She might be a money-hungry, status-conscious reporter, but everybody had a few faults. She'd certainly flown to his defense tonight and then sympathized with him over his friend's problem, a lot more than his good buddy Steve had done.

Arriving at the truck, he jerked the door open and flopped inside then took a deep breath.

'Calm down, Malone,' he ordered himself. His reaction was all out of proportion.

Maybe Steve's choice of words was bad, but he was right about avoiding Allison as long as he was undercover. Even when the assignment was over, he needed to stay away from her. She was poison, not just because she was a reporter but because her lifestyle was 180 degrees out from his. She'd obviously grown up in, married into and was struggling to get back into a world where name-brand possessions and the right address were essentials. And, to give the devil his – or her – due, she had good reason for her goals. That ex-husband of hers ought to be shot. No, make that hung. With a loose knot.

But the worst part of the whole situation was, in spite of everything, he wanted her – wanted her more than he'd ever wanted any woman. She'd lost that cool, haughty air when he'd kissed her last night. When he'd seen her a few minutes ago, when she'd touched his arm, he'd wanted to kiss her again until those cool, aloof eyes were glazed with passion again, until she melted around him, until neither one of them had sense enough left to stop.

Damn! There was certainly no reason to make things worse by fantasizing about her.

He turned the key in the ignition, and the engine sputtered to life. He'd go straight home, check with the hospital, then call Allison, give her a report on Dealey's progress and tell her he wasn't coming back to finish her floors.

He jerked the wheel sharply as he pulled into traffic, calling himself a few choice names because he knew he'd do nothing of the sort. He'd given her his word that he'd help, and he would. Besides, he had those blasted January Heat tickets.

Okay, he'd go over there this one last time, finish the floors and give her the three tickets. She and the girl could find somebody else to go with them, somebody Allison wouldn't be ashamed of, somebody who drove a BMW and had cute little animals embroidered on his knit shirts.

As he approached an intersection, the car to his right ran the stop sign. Brad slammed on his brakes and jerked the steering wheel, spinning sideways, one front wheel jumping onto the curb. Leaning out the window, he cursed loudly and gestured accordingly.

Evidently the driver was watching in the rearview mirror, because he screeched to a halt and backed up.

Delighted to have a target for his anger other than himself, Brad reached toward the glove box to retrieve his badge and gun. This was going to be fun.

At the last minute, sanity returned, and he rejected the idea.

But it didn't matter. The man got close enough to get a glimpse of Brad's face, then pulled away without so much as a whimper.

Brad leaned back in his seat and burst into hysterical laughter, a release of the anger and tension. This business of being undercover certainly brought out unexpected facets of situations.

The evening had turned cloudy, and darkness was coming down fast as Allison drove home. Appropriate, she thought.

She had finally made the decision to go home, confront Bill and send him on his way. In spite of all the evidence she'd so carefully garnered, she'd forced herself to admit that it was all circumstantial. She had to accept the possibility that he was nothing but a bum, however much she might want him to be something more.

If she'd needed any more proof, he hadn't become upset by the policeman's abusive tone when he'd inquired about the reason for the crowd. Obviously he was accustomed to being treated like that.

Hiring an out-of-work man to do odd jobs around the house was one thing, perfectly acceptable, but kissing him was quite another and not at all acceptable. However, even that wasn't the real problem.

She cringed and felt her face becoming hot as she pulled onto her street. She wanted to kiss him again. That was the real problem.

She liked him, admired – and feared – his strength. Add it all together, and one might say she had a 'thing' for a bearded, penniless, homeless man. That was really what she needed in her life right now.

And there he was, sitting on her front porch, looking forlorn. No, she amended, not forlorn. Shabby, yes, but not forlorn. Rather he looked solid and immovable, like a rock, a part of the earth.

Before she could get out and open the garage door, he was there, raising it easily with one hand. A gentleman.

Even if she seriously doubted that he was the killer, nevertheless, Bill was dangerous.

Parking the car inside, she went out to meet him. A gust of chilly wind greeted her, and she shivered slightly.

'Hello,' he said, white teeth and hazel eyes flashing through the mass of hair and beard.

He looked as though he was glad to see her. She'd better let him know right away that he couldn't stay.

'Let's go in out of the cold,' she said.

She'd tell him he had to leave after he had a chance to get warm.

As they entered the house, he paused, running a thumb down the worn weather stripping around the door. 'Come winter, you're going to need some new . . .'

She tensed, fearful he was going to offer to help, but he didn't. He paused, jerked his hand away from the door as though burned, then turned his attention to the interior.

'Floor's going to look great,' he said. 'Eventually you'll want to refinish, but for now, get an area rug and you're all set.'

'I thought something with blue and cream and maybe just a touch of rose,' she replied, closing the door behind them as she excitedly described the picture in her mind.

'Yeah,' he agreed, surveying the room. 'Brighten up things and bring out the colors in your sofa.' He ran a hand over the faded pattern on its curved back. 'If you decide to get this recovered, let me know. I have a friend who does that sort of thing. He'll cut you a deal.'

She wanted to ask him if his friend did his work on the streets, but decided to refrain. He was relaxed, and his guard was down. She didn't want to alert him.

Then she realized she was doing it again, trying desperately to make him into something beneficial to her career and acceptable to her personal life.

'Thanks. I may take you up on that offer. What do you think about refinishing this table? I bought it at a garage sale.'

He bent over to gently stroke the scratched and

marred surface of her round dining-room table. Allison sucked in her breath. She could almost feel his fingers on her skin rather than the wood.

Whether he heard her intake of breath or whether he suddenly realized he was being too relaxed, she'd never know, but he straightened abruptly, any expression he might have retreating into the shelter of his facial hair.

'I think we'd better leave everything inside tonight and work around it. It looks like rain.'

'Good idea,' she agreed. 'I'll go change and be right back.'

'Mind if I use your phone to call the hospital and check on Dealey?' he asked. 'I didn't get over there after all.'

'Of course. It's in the kitchen.'

She continued up the stairs, changed into blue jeans and came back just as he was hanging up. 'Well?' she asked.

'He's doing better,' Bill replied, smiling up at her. 'They think he's going to make it.'

'I'm glad.'

'Me, too.'

Seeing his expression of relief, there was no doubt in her mind that he really cared about Dealey. Whatever or whoever he was, he was a kind man.

They were just finishing up, moving everything back into place, when the rain hit. The wind shrieked then slammed a sheet of water against the windows. Allison started at the sudden tumult, almost dropping the lamp she was setting back onto its table beside the sofa.

'Rain,' she said, feeling foolish.

He looked at the window, then back to her, and smiled. 'Not even a tornado,' he said, his eyes twinkling.

'Kind of nice, actually.' She straightened the lamp, then stood for a moment staring at the drops of water striking and running down the blackened glass, listening to the rhythmic patter punctuated by howls and sudden bursts against the windows. 'How about I make us some hot chocolate and a couple of ham sandwiches?' she suggested.

'How about you make some hot chocolate and I go pick up a . . .' She turned to look at him when he hesitated, and he immediately dropped his gaze to the floor. 'I'd better get on home.'

'Home?' she queried, hopeful suspicion suddenly rising again at the reference. Had he almost volunteered to pick up a pizza? On the other hand, the man had been gainfully employed at one time; perhaps he was simply falling into old speech patterns.

His head jerked up guiltily, but his eyes met hers, and his voice was calm when he answered. 'Home is where the heart is, even if it's on the street.'

'Well, you're not going anywhere in the middle of

this rain. Forget it.' Springing to her feet, she strode toward the kitchen. 'Anyway, if you won't stay for dinner, I'll have to insist on paying you. I have my pride, too, you know.'

As she prepared thick ham sandwiches with spicy mustard, she listened almost fearfully for the sound of the door opening and closing, but it didn't come. When she set them on the wooden table now covered with a white cloth, he joined her.

'Good,' he approved, taking a bite. 'You're a good cook.'

'It doesn't take much ability to make a ham sandwich,' she said with a laugh.

'I've met women who couldn't make a decent one. Anyway, your pork chops were incredible, and your quiche smelled so wonderful, my mouth watered for days.'

She glowed from the praise and made a mental note to prepare quiche for him again since he hadn't eaten it before.

When she had swallowed her last bite, Allison stood and raised the blinds of the window at the back of the room. As though reading her mind, Bill moved to the wall and turned off the overhead light. With only the glow from the kitchen and living room lights, they could see the raindrops swirling down the dark glass.

Allison brought a pot of steaming hot chocolate from the kitchen and poured two mugs.

'Umm,' Bill approved, sipping his drink then smiling across the table at her. 'Watching the cold outside while we're safe inside.'

Allison nodded, cradling the warm cup in both hands while watching the wet blackness. 'When I was a little girl,' she said, 'my bed was beside a window. I used to love to open it a few inches when it was raining just a little, lay my head on the windowsill and feel the drops on my face while my body was warm under the covers.'

Bill laughed, drawing her attention back to him. 'What did your mother think of that?'

'She didn't share my romanticism. No matter how careful I was, the covers always got wet and gave me away and I got in trouble.'

He nodded, his smile gentle and unfocused. 'We had a back porch that faced the east. I loved to sit out there when it stormed, just inches away but warm and dry. It's such a smug, comfortable feeling.'

'Secure.'

'Secure,' he agreed.

For a moment they gazed at each other, sharing their special moments. Allison felt totally naked, totally vulnerable and totally safe. Never taking her eyes from his, she sipped her chocolate.

'Allis,' he said softly, and reached across the table to stroke her fingers as she lowered her cup. Delicious shivers zipped up and down her spine.

Abruptly he pulled his hand away, scraped his chair across the wooden floor and jumped to his feet. 'Well, thanks for everything, and I'd better be going now.'

Allison felt as though she had been jerked from a warm bed and plunged into a cold shower.

'Go?' she stammered in confusion. 'You'll get wet.'

'I'll probably live,' he assured her, retrieving his worn jacket from the hall closet.

She followed him. 'No,' she protested, suddenly realizing that this weather didn't necessarily mean just a walk in the rain. If Bill truly was homeless – and she must face the fact that he very well might be – he would have to find a place to sleep and would probably be cold and wet all night. 'No, this is crazy. You – you've helped me so much. Let me help you a little.' She hesitated, unsure how to proceed. After the kiss they'd shared the night before and the electricity surging between them tonight, would it sound suggestive if she asked him to spend the night in her house? 'You . . . you can stay in my garage tonight.'

Brad stared at Allison uncomprehendingly for a moment. He'd had women invite him to share their bedrooms, to stay in their guest rooms and even to sleep on their sofas, but no one had ever invited him to stay in a garage.

'I really appreciate the offer, but, no, thanks,' he

said, trying to maintain a straight face.

'I won't take "no" for an answer.' She darted past him and stood in front of the door, blocking his exit. 'I have plenty of blankets, and you'll be warm and dry.'

Brad thought of his heated king-size waterbed waiting at home and bit his lip to keep from laughing. 'Really,' he insisted, 'I have a warm place to sleep tonight.'

'Where?'

'You know I can't tell you that.'

'Then I don't believe you. In fact – ' her chin lifted defiantly ' – there's no reason for you to stay in the garage. I'm not sure why I said that. Since Megan's gone, you can have her room.'

Brad crossed his arms and stared at her in amusement and a little admiration. For someone like her to invite a homeless man to spend the night must be quite a leap. 'I do appreciate the offer, but I assure you, I'll be fine.'

She shook her head stubbornly. 'You're not going out in that storm. I wouldn't sleep a wink tonight for worrying about you.' She blushed, then added, 'After all you've done for me.'

Brad had to admire her concern, however misplaced it might be. 'Okay,' he finally agreed. 'How about a compromise? I stay on the sofa until the rain slacks off.' He'd leave as soon as she had time to get to sleep. For more reasons than one. Knowing she

130

was sleeping under the same roof just a few feet away from him would keep his hormones going full tilt all night.

'All right,' she acquiesced. 'I'll get you some sheets and blankets.'

'Allis.' Catching her arm as she moved past him, he turned her toward him. 'I don't need sheets and blankets.'

Her expression stopped him, took his breath away, in fact. On her face he saw the compassion he'd expected, but he also saw the same desire he felt at her nearness. Her lips were slightly parted, and he knew if he kissed her, she wouldn't protest. He might not have to sleep on the sofa tonight.

He released her and turned away. If he'd wanted her a little bit less, if he could be sure he wouldn't become involved in a no-win situation – but he wanted her so badly, he didn't dare give in. 'I'll just stretch out here. Don't go to so much trouble.'

'I'll be right back with everything.' Her voice faded away as she climbed the stairs.

The sofa didn't compare with his waterbed, but it wasn't horrible. He'd been working unusually hard the last two nights and hadn't slept much last night. He closed his eyes for just a minute while he waited for Allison to go to sleep so he could leave.

Her clock woke him striking two. He sat bolt upright, surprised that he'd slept, even considering how tired he was. He yawned and tried unsuccessfully to push his hair off his forehead. Damn! When this was over, he'd never again complain about having to shave or go to the barber.

He looked at the window and saw that the rain had stopped. Well, his little nap hadn't caused any harm. He had to admit, walking the two blocks to his car would be more comfortable now than it would have been in the downpour. Things had worked out all right after all. He'd kept his hands off her while fulfilling his obligation.

He was turning the doorknob to leave when he remembered his other promise – those damn tickets. Pulling them from his inside jacket pocket, he went back into the kitchen and laid them on the counter where she'd be sure to see them.

On her refrigerator, held in place by magnets, he saw a wipe-off plastic sheet for grocery lists. 'Enjoy,' he wrote. 'A friend gave them to me.' That should do.

He left Allison's house, locking the door behind him. 'Okay, Bradley Malone,' he whispered, 'that's over. Goodbye, Allison Prescott.'

Squaring his shoulders and thrusting his hands into his pockets, he started down her sidewalk.

Relieved, he told himself. That's how he felt to have it over with. Life would be a lot simpler without worrying about her. If he also felt a little sad, well, that was something he'd just have to deal with.

Automatically, from years of training, he scanned the street as he neared the end of the sidewalk. Just a hint of movement in the brown van parked across the street caught his eye, a glint of the streetlight reflecting off something – a camera lens, he was pretty sure.

CHAPTER 7

Losing the van was easy enough. Brad started up the street in the opposite direction from his car and cut through between two houses. When he spotted the vehicle moving slowly down the street, apparently trying to find him as he emerged, he doubled back on his own tracks.

Using an automobile to follow a man on foot was harder than most people realized.

Nevertheless, he scanned the area carefully before getting into his truck and heading home.

Wouldn't everyone, including Allison, be delighted to find a cop leaving her house at two a.m.? Doug would undoubtedly use it to his advantage, and Allison would have her big story.

Arriving home, he headed straight for the refrigerator to grab a beer. Leaning against the cold enamel, he took a long swallow and reveled in the security of being home.

He loved his big old house, every drafty corner of it – the scarred oak floors he still hadn't refinished, the faded furniture, most of it discards from his family and friends, the huge windows with the original, wavy glass – all warm with memories, be they his own or someone else's. But he'd be willing to bet Allison would hate it. Allison would undoubtedly prefer everything shiny and new.

He chugged the last of his beer, crushed the can and threw it into his recycling bag inside the oversized pantry.

Who cared what Allison would think of his house? She'd never get the chance to see it.

As he slid into his warm bed, he smiled at the memory of her insistence that he stay in her garage. She meant well. Give her credit for that.

He sighed and pulled up the covers. He really should call her one more time to warn her about the van and the fact that the man probably had his picture leaving her house at two a.m. He owed her that. She was divorced, the minor child wasn't even on the premises – there was no reason she shouldn't have a man leaving her house at two a.m. He couldn't see any way Dr Doug could use that against her, but he would warn her anyway.

Early the next morning he checked with the police computer and confirmed that the license plates on the van were registered to a private investigator – Homer Sullivan, a sleazy but effective operator.

Since the man specialized in sensational divorces, Brad knew him only by reputation, but it didn't bode well for Allison.

As soon as his coffee finished brewing, he poured a large cup, added two spoons of sugar and, thus fortified, dialed her number.

Her voice when she answered was husky with sleep. He had to push away an image of her emerging from the rosebud comforter he'd seen on her bed, brown eyes half-closed, silky hair in tousled shadows about her face. That image had no place in his life. He brushed it from his mind.

'I think Dr Doug's having you followed again,' he stated bluntly.

'What?' she asked sleepily. 'Bill? Where are you? What are you saying?'

'I left last night when it quit raining and, unfortunately, had my picture taken by a detective named Homer Sullivan.'

Her sigh came distinctly across the line. Her voice was wide awake now, if a bit subdued. 'Here we go again,' she said. 'That's the guy he had before. And you think he got your picture?'

'Best I could tell. But it won't do him much good. I lost him before I left your neighborhood.'

'I appreciate your letting me know. How'd you find out his name?'

Good question and a very bad slip for a professional. 'I've seen him around.' Brad poured himself another cup of caffeine, tossing in three spoons of sugar this time.

'You've seen him around,' she repeated. Her voice was quiet, but he could tell she was mulling over that comment.

'Private detectives are always checking the streets for runaways.' It wasn't totally untrue. Maybe not always, but sometimes.

'I see.' He could almost hear the gears turning in her brain, see the light burning feverishly in her eyes. When she'd asked him to stay in her garage last night, he'd decided she believed his cover story and would back off, but this morning she was getting revved up again. Or maybe he was being paranoid.

'Well – ' he began, preparing to tell her about the concert tickets and end the conversation.

Then his antiquated doorbell chimed. Loudly.

'What was that?' Allison asked.

'That? Oh, church bells. Listen, I left three tickets to January Heat in your kitchen. And I really appreciate your letting me stay last night.'

'You got three tickets to January Heat?'

'I told Megan I would,' Brad replied testily. 'Did you think I'd promise something I couldn't deliver?'

The doorbell called again.

'What an odd church. Why are they ringing their bells so early and not even on the hour?'

'Beats me. Maybe their computer's broken.' Did modern church bells ring from a computer? It sounded feasible to him.

'They have an unusual sound,' she pursued.

Brad moved to the end of the kitchen, stretching the phone cord as far as it would go. He could barely see the window in the living-room door. The smiling face of the teenage boy from next door peered in at him. Brad waved frantically, motioning him away. The kid's smile changed to a disappointed frown, and he left. Well, Brad thought, he'd just have to make it up to the boy later.

'Look, I have to go now,' he told Allison. 'I need to get down to New Hope before breakfast.'

'I understand,' she said. 'If there's ever any way I can repay you for all you've done, please let me know.' She sounded so aloof, as though she knew he was blowing her off.

'Those great meals were more than adequate payment.' He cleared his throat. 'Well . . .'

The doorbell hadn't rung again, no interrupting call had beeped on the line, the television hadn't suddenly come on by some freak accident, he had it made. So why was he hesitating?

'Goodbye,' he forced himself to say, and hung up the receiver.

He poured the remainder of the coffee into his cup and sipped, waiting to feel elation at having completed the call successfully in spite of the odds against it. The only feeling he could locate was a sense of loss. Damn it, that was no good at all. You can't lose what you've never had. Not only had he never had Allison Prescott, he never could, not in this lifetime.

Allison replaced the telephone receiver and burrowed back down under the covers. She knew she was still half-asleep, and the reception in her mind was fuzzy, but there were some things in this conversation that didn't quite focus.

With a sigh, she threw back the warm comforter. Might as well get up and get some caffeine pumping through her system, get ready for work then try to make sense out of Bill the Bum's latest inconsistencies.

And in that connection – she snatched up the phone again and routed Rick out of bed.

'Meet me at the coffee shop in an hour for breakfast,' she ordered him. 'I'll buy.'

She had to find out what he'd uncovered about Bill. She'd refused to listen when he'd mentioned it the day before, had begun to doubt her own motivations in wanting him to be somebody other than a street person. Nevertheless she hadn't stopped wondering. In light of this new evidence, she needed to know.

She might be able to stretch her belief to include his knowledge of the name of Douglas's detective, but she could swear that had been a doorbell, not a church bell, ringing in the background. And there weren't many doorbells on the streets of Oklahoma City.

She dressed hurriedly and drove over to the coffee shop to wait for Rick. She was halfway through her first cup of coffee, trying unsuccessfully to concentrate on the newspaper, when he arrived.

'What did you find out about Bill?' she asked without preamble.

Rick raised an eyebrow as he slid into the vinyl booth across from her. 'I thought that subject was closed,' he said, picking up a menu.

'I'm the one who closed it, so I guess I can reopen it,' Allison snapped.

The waitress approached, and they both ordered. Allison waited impatiently while the woman filled Rick's cup and refilled hers.

Finally Rick leaned back and regarded her with an impish grin. 'Curiosity got to you, huh? And you were worried you wouldn't make a good reporter.'

'That's right,' she agreed. 'I'm a nosy reporter.' That constituted an acceptable reason for her interest in Bill.

Rick set his cup on the table and adjusted his glasses. 'There really isn't a lot to tell. In fact, that's the whole point. I talked to a few sources, including the policemen who routinely patrol that area. This

140

Bill just appeared out of nowhere a few weeks ago with that vague story about being an out-of-work roughneck. He's pretty elusive about concrete details concerning his life, past or present. He comes and goes, he's not around every day, and nobody seems to know where he sleeps.'

'Is that so strange?' Allison asked, unable to keep the disappointment out of her voice. 'All the homeless I've talked to have been vague and elusive.'

Rick nodded. 'That's true, but they usually talk to somebody. Not this guy. He latched onto Dealey, who'd accept a gorilla if it was nice to him and who's too spaced out to ask many questions.'

Allison shrugged. 'Is that it?'

'Pretty much. While he doesn't want to talk about himself, he wants to know everything about everybody else.'

'So he's a nosy bum,' Allison retorted. She'd hoped for something more conclusive. 'You still haven't told me anything to prove he's not just a bum.'

Rick shrugged, wrapping his hands around his cup. 'At least we can eliminate him as the murderer since he didn't show up until after the first two or three.'

'I could have told you he wasn't the murderer,' Allison asserted, though she felt a sense of relief at the logical conclusion. 'He's a kind person.'

Reaching into her purse, she withdrew the tickets

and threw them onto the table. 'A derelict who gave me three tickets to January Heat.'

She crossed her arms and leaned back, enjoying the expression of consternation on Rick's face.

He examined the tickets as closely as she had. 'Where did he get them?'

'Said somebody gave them to him.'

'Oh, sure. Every kid in town and half the adults are trying to get hold of these. Scalpers will be selling them for a fortune.' Rick laid them back on the table and studied Allison. 'You realize, lady, these tickets are probably stolen?'

'No,' she protested, remembering the way he'd taken his picture from her address book but left her money and camera. 'Bill's no thief.'

'Then where did he get the money to buy these?'

'I don't know, but I'm sure he didn't steal them.' Was she sure? Just because he didn't steal from her didn't necessarily exclude the rest of the world from his territory.

Rick shook his head in disbelief. 'Okay, convince me. Let's hear all the gory details of how you came by these tickets.'

Allison shifted uncomfortably and sipped her cooling coffee. At that moment the waitress arrived with heavy plates of eggs and pancakes, and Allison took the opportunity to compose herself. There was no reason for Rick to know everything about her personal life.

'He came by last night – '

'Again? It seems to me you failed to mention this impending visit yesterday.'

'Do you want to hear this or not? He came by last night to finish up the floor. He honors his obligations.' She remembered the irritation in Bill's voice at her suggestion that he wouldn't come through on his promise to Megan. 'Last week he told Megan he'd take her to this concert. Douglas was trying to jack me around, and Bill kind of intervened. At the time, I thought he just said it to help, like when he told Douglas his plumbing company would put us up at the Waterford. But he left these in the kitchen with a note saying someone gave them to him.'

Rick shoved a chunk of syrup-drenched pancake into his mouth, chewed and swallowed. 'Money, food, clothes, even books I can see someone giving as a handout, but tickets to a rock concert?'

'My point exactly,' Allison declared.

'Like I said before, you may be on to something.'

'And that's not all. When he called this morning – '

'He called you this morning?'

'Has no one ever told you it isn't polite to interrupt? Yes, he called. He wanted to tell me Douglas has a detective spying on me again.'

'Oh, jeez. I'm sorry, lady. That man just doesn't give up, does he?'

'I've never known him to,' Allison admitted.

'And I'm afraid he has a picture of Bill leaving the house.'

'Oh, great! That'll look good in court, that you're consorting with derelicts.'

'Consorting? He was doing work around the house for me. Since it's Douglas's fault I live in that dump, he can scarcely begrudge me the cheap labor necessary to keep it semi-liveable.' She speared a piece of egg.

'Seems to me this is the attitude that got you in trouble in the first place, thinking Douglas would play fair.'

'Fair or foul, he's not going to win this time. You know, I ought to let him have Megan. He doesn't want her. He's spent more time with her since the divorce than in all the years before. He'd send her right back rather than have to care for her.'

Rick reached a freckled hand across the table and covered hers. 'No, he wouldn't. He'd just turn her over to Bonnie.'

'Bonnie the Bimbo,' Allison corrected, smiling, touched by her friend's concern.

'Bonnie the Bimbo,' Rick agreed. 'Anyway, you hang in there, stay away from Bill and don't hesitate to ask for my help if you need it.'

'Thanks. I know I can count on you, and that really means a lot to me.' She squeezed his hand. 'But back to the other – I've changed my mind again. I don't think Bill is just a bum.'

Rick rolled his eyes. 'Yesterday you were positive he was.'

'I wasn't really positive. I just thought I needed to look at both sides. But now there's more evidence.' She wrapped both hands around the warm mug. 'He identified Douglas's detective. When I asked him how he knew, he said he'd seen him around.'

'Possible,' Rick said, waving to the waitress for refills.

'And while we were talking, I distinctly heard a doorbell ring, one of those loud, old-fashioned kind. He tried to tell me it was church bells, ringing at ten minutes past the hour because the computer was broken.' She held up a finger to forestall Rick's comment. 'Okay, so it's possible. But there sure are a lot of little things that don't quite add up. A lot of possible-but-improbables.'

'True,' Rick agreed. 'So where do we go from here? Wherever it is, you've got to be damned careful. If Bill isn't a bum, what is he and why is he pretending? And now that Douglas has his picture, what will he do with the information?'

Allison shook her head. 'I don't know, but I have to find out. Like I said, this could be it, Rick, our big story. Do you believe me now?'

'I think there's a possibility your friend isn't what he appears to be, but I'm not sure I believe there's a story there.'

'What if he's hiding from the law? What if he's on the FBI's Most Wanted List?' She didn't believe that about Bill, only wanted to get Rick interested in helping her pursue him. Nevertheless, as she spoke the words, she had to consider the possibility. 'We have to uncover his true identity,' she concluded. 'We have to.'

Rick seemed to be watching her closely. Even though she knew he couldn't read her thoughts, she dropped her eyes to the table.

'To get a story,' he said.

'To get a story,' she agreed. To get a story, she reiterated to herself.

Allison raced home that evening, leaving unfinished work at the station for Tracy to complete. Getting away early had always been a problem, intensified now with the outbreak of rumors about the station being sold.

Everyone was working frantically, and Allison knew she needed to stay to protect her job, but Douglas was scheduled to bring Megan home by seven o'clock. Although he was usually fifteen to thirty minutes late, the one time she'd been late, he'd been early. She sometimes wondered if he sat up the street and watched her house.

However, he'd no longer need to do that, she thought wryly, as she pulled into her driveway. No doubt Homer the Hulk or one of his agents had been skulking around. The black sedan she'd thought she'd noticed a couple of times during the day had settled in across the street and up two houses.

She barely had time to get in the house and survey the living room, picking up stray pieces of carpet padding here and there, before Megan burst through the front door.

'Look at my new jeans!' she exclaimed, pirouetting. 'And this shirt cost fifty dollars! Me and Bonnie went shopping.'

'Bonnie and I,' Allison corrected automatically, glaring at Douglas as he stood in the open doorway. She knew she ought to be grateful that he was always buying clothes for Megan since she couldn't afford to, but all she felt was resentment. It was just another facet of his plan to take Megan away from her.

Douglas fielded her glare with a smug smile, and Allison felt cold inside. 'See you Friday evening,' he called to Megan.

Megan paused halfway up the stairs. 'Okay, Daddy. Wait till you see these dynamite tights, Mom!'

Allison glared at Douglas. 'Friday evening?' she called to Megan. 'Aren't you going to the concert with Bill on Saturday night?'

'Oh, yeah! See you in two weeks, Daddy. These tights will look great for the concert.' She tripped on up the stairs, dragging her bulging bag behind her.

'Two weeks, Daddy,' Allison repeated smugly.

To her chagrin, Douglas didn't look at all defeated. In fact, an unpleasant smirk settled on his face as he folded his arms. 'So you and that raggedy plumber are taking my daughter to a concert. He seems to be spending a lot of time around here. Having plumbing problems again?'

Allison suspected Douglas's question was a crude *double entendre*, especially considering that he had Bill's picture leaving her house in the middle of the night. She bit back an angry retort. 'No,' she said smoothly. 'That's all taken care of now, and much more effectively than the original, I might add.'

She closed the door in his face. Let him think about that for a while.

'Mom!' Megan's voice had a ring of panic – too much panic to be real. She'd probably found a pimple on her chin.

Allison raced upstairs, though, just in case, but wasn't surprised to see her daughter, perfectly safe, standing in the middle of the room gazing upward. 'Look,' she said dramatically and pointed to an oozing water stain on the ceiling.

'It's nothing, dear.' Allison forced herself to appear calm, but she wanted to sit in the corner and cry. She had just dealt with one leak downstairs, and now here was another one.

'Let's see if it's gotten your bed wet.' She ran her hand over the white spread. 'Nope. All dry. It was probably just a fluke caused by that heavy rain last night.'

The heavy rain probably knocked a hole in the roof, and the next shower would flood the entire place.

Megan looked dubious. 'So what are you going to do about it?'

Pray for a long drought, Allison thought. 'We'll get it fixed before it rains again,' she assured her daughter.

'Call Brill. He'll fix it.' Having thus disposed of the problem, Megan lifted her suitcase onto the bed and began rummaging through it, dragging out her new articles of clothing for her mother's inspection.

Allison tried to make appropriate comments about the trendy, expensive items, but she found herself becoming angrier with each designer label – angry at Douglas for putting her in this position and angry at herself for not being financially able to compete with him.

'You know, sweetheart,' she finally said when the bag was empty and the bed covered, 'I'd buy you all these things if I could.'

Megan gathered up a handful of clothes and crossed the room to her closet. 'I know, Mom. Bonnie says you just don't have any marketable skills.'

Allison bit back an angry retort concerning Bonnie's marketable skill. 'How kind of her to make excuses for me,' she murmured, then bit her tongue and changed the subject. 'What do you say to some hot chocolate?'

'Okay, I guess.' With a grunt of effort, Megan shoved the new clothes into her crowded closet.

'And you can tell me what you think about our new hardwood floors downstairs. Did you even notice when you came in?'

'No.' Megan's face brightened. 'Just like at Dad's house?'

'Better. These are antique. Bill helped me uncover them.'

'Brill did the floors? Wow!' She was already halfway down the stairs. 'Cool!' she called over her shoulder, bouncing down the rest of the way. 'Want me to ask Bonnie where she got their rug?'

'I think I'm going to go downstairs and kill my daughter,' Allison muttered to the ceiling.

She took a last look at the ominous water stain. Maybe she ought to crawl up in the attic and have a look around, though she wouldn't know what to do about the problem if she should happen to find it.

With a sigh, she left the room. She suspected Megan was right about one thing. Bill could probably fix it. Maybe he was an out-of-work plumber or even a maintenance man after all. If she was going to be depressed, she might as well go all the way.

* * *

'Mom, you make the greatest blackberry cobbler in the world.' Brad leaned back in the kitchen chair and drained his glass of iced tea.

'That you do, Maggie, for a fact.' Gerald Malone's round face glowed as he smiled at his wife.

Margaret Malone stood, smoothing the fabric of her cotton dress over her spare frame, and began gathering up the empty dishes. 'I think the only reason you two ate everything was so I couldn't recycle it and serve it again.'

Both men laughed.

Brad rose, took a load of dishes across to the sink and began scraping. 'We didn't eat everything. There's some meatloaf left.'

Gerald joined them with a load of dirty dishes, including the meatloaf in question. 'Half a sandwich,' he calculated, looking it over carefully.

'One of you'll eat it before the evening's over.' Maggie's green eyes moved from her husband's beefy frame to her son's baggy jeans. 'And I know which one of you it ought to be.' She plunged her hands into the soapy water and began her ritual of scrubbing.

'Okay,' Brad agreed, 'I've lost a little weight. I can't always eat lunch on this assignment. I wouldn't feel right eating food that could go to someone who needed it.'

'Bad mistake.' His father placed an arm around his shoulders. 'Never tell your mother you've been missing meals.'

Brad accepted a handful of soapy silverware and rinsed it under the faucet. 'I eat a good meal every now and then,' he assured her, remembering the evenings Allison had cooked for him.

He'd enjoyed those times, no doubt about it. However, standing in his mother's cozy but simple kitchen underscored the impossibility of his attraction to a woman like Allison. She'd never be comfortable here.

'How much longer do you think this assignment will last?' Maggie asked casually, but he could hear the worry in her voice.

'We're getting closer all the time,' he assured her. 'Any day now.' Platitudes, and he knew he wasn't fooling her with them. 'What's the matter?' he teased in an effort to lighten her thoughts. 'Don't you like my new look? I have noticed you've stopped introducing me to your friends' daughters.'

'I can't tell how you look with all that hair everywhere.'

'Ah, Maggie, the boy should enjoy it while he can,' Gerald interjected, running a hand over his own bald head.

'To tell you the truth, it drives me crazy,' Brad admitted. 'The beard's hot and itchy and the hair gets in my collar. But it'll soon be over.' He wrapped one arm around his mother's shoulders and patted her cheek with the wet fingers of his other hand.

She pushed away him away and shook her head. 'How many sons go from a nice blue uniform to a suit then to a beard and clothes from the attic?'

'I don't mind the situation at all,' his father assured him, accepting the last pan in the assembly line process. 'I love driving around all day with my pipes and tools in your new truck.'

'Now that gives me an incentive to solve this case. Before long you'll have my truck looking like your old relic.'

'Come on,' Maggie interrupted. 'Let's go see what's on the Sunday night movie. I know you don't have any plans, Brad. No woman in her right mind would go out with you while you look like that.'

That was probably true, Brad thought, settling himself on the sofa, leaning back against one of Maggie's afghans. But he suspected Allison Prescott wouldn't go out with him even if he had on his suit and tie, not if she knew he was a cop, the son of a plumber, and perfectly content to be both.

Not that he had any intention of asking her.

CHAPTER 8

Reverend Pollock greeted Allison with a big smile when she entered New Hope Shelter shortly after noon on Monday, her day off.

'Blessings upon you, my daughter,' he said, grasping her hand gently between his big paws.

'Thank you, Reverend. I brought some spaghetti. I know it isn't much, but – ' She offered the covered plastic bowl with an embarrassed shrug. For some reason she hadn't been able to finish her sandwich at lunch without thinking of these people.

Pollock accepted the spaghetti with a smile as though it were Lobster Newburg. 'You have our undying gratitude. If you will pardon me, I'll put it in the refrigerator in the back room so that we may partake of it for dinner.'

Allison nodded her agreement, then turned to survey the persons sitting in the shelter. Bill was noticeably absent, which didn't surprise her, though she anticipated his arrival soon now that lunch was over. She'd never seen him eat with the others.

If he showed up today, she'd track him to his lair, whatever it took.

Across the room she spotted Jean talking animatedly to one of the men. The big woman was on an eye level with him, and Allison remembered her earlier thoughts that Jean's size made her a possible candidate for the killer.

As she started down the aisle to where the pair sat, the man suddenly rose, snarled at Jean, made an obscene gesture and stalked out.

Allison tried to memorize his face in case he should turn out to be the next deceased.

Jean's smoldering expression warned her away, but her instinct told her this was a good time to find out things the woman might not ordinarily reveal. Squaring her shoulders, she moved between the benches and settled beside her.

Jean gave her a quick glare, then turned her back. Her legs were crossed, and one foot was swinging, just as before, but this time with jerky, angry movements. The red shoes were gone, replaced by worn sneakers.

'I just gave the Rev some spaghetti for tonight,' Allison began, remembering the woman's eagerness when it came to food.

No indication she'd heard.

On an impulse, she unknotted the colorful scarf she'd tied around her neck before leaving the house. She'd given up trying to blend in with the homeless and today wore beige slacks and a matching sweater – not blue jeans, but unobtrusive. However, she hadn't been able to resist adding the splash of rainbow hues. With a pang of regret for the loss of a favorite item, she told herself it was an investment and offered the scarf to Jean.

Big, rawboned hands grasped the piece of silk, and she turned to Allison with a weak smile.

'It's perfect with your coloring,' Allison said. Since Jean's skin and hair were almost the same beige as Allison's outfit, that seemed a safe statement.

Jean tied the scarf about her own neck, then looked down at the ends resting on her faded blue blouse. 'Thank you,' she said, stroking the soft fabric with knotted, reddened fingers.

'Having a little disagreement with your friend?' Allison asked.

Jean's smile disappeared, and she shifted slightly as though ready to turn away again.

'Have you heard how Dealey's doing?' Allison threw out in a desperate attempt to keep her attention.

'Hmph,' she snorted. 'Dealey knows better'n to drink that stuff. Not the first time. He's gonna wake up dead one of these days.' She slapped Allison's leg and laughed at her own joke.

Pollock slid in beside Allison, and Jean's laughter abruptly died. Fingering the new scarf nervously, she looked down at her lap.

Allison turned to Pollock and was surprised to see his perennial smile missing. She thought she detected displeasure and sadness in his gaze, even when he returned the smile to its proper place. But she supposed that was what preachers did, be displeased and sad a lot.

'We were just discussing Dealey,' she told him. 'The last I heard, his condition was improving, and he should be out in a day or two.'

'It's what we pray for,' Pollock replied, then leaned across her and spoke to Jean. 'Is all well with you, sister?'

Without ever looking up, Jean stood and made her way to the end of the bench and out the shelter door.

Allison was torn between following Jean or staying with Pollock. He appeared to know something about the woman's peculiar behavior, and maybe he'd talk more easily than she would.

'Is Jean having problems?' she asked.

Pollock's face was once again a beatific mask. 'Who in this life doesn't?'

She couldn't argue with that. 'Perhaps I could help her in some way, woman to woman.'

He seemed to consider the idea for a moment, then shook his head. 'Like most of us mortals, Jean creates her own hell.'

With his knack for evading questions, the man would have made a great politician.

'That guy she was arguing with, are they romantically involved?'

'Your purity and innocence are like a beacon in the darkness, my child.' He patted her hand, then stood, signifying the questioning was at an end, but Allison stood, too.

'He seemed pretty upset. Do you think he'd harm her?' Or vice versa.

'These earthly bodies are susceptible to earthly pain and destruction, but only we ourselves can harm our eternal spirits.'

'Right,' she said, unable to come up with any other response.

'It's always so good to see you, but my obligations call,' Pollock said, extending an arm to indicate the scattered people. He started down the row away from her.

She grabbed his arm in one last attempt. 'What happened to her shoes? She was so proud of those red shoes.'

Pollock shook his big head slowly. 'Vanity is the devil's favorite tool. Now, if you'll excuse me, I must visit with my flock. Please stay as long as you like.'

'Thanks,' she said, giving up and letting him walk away. The Reverend Pollock might be a little nuts, but that didn't mean he was dumb. She wasn't going to find out anything he didn't want her to know.

She spotted someone else she'd met before and went over to try her luck with him.

Half an hour and several people later, she knew little more than before, but she was convinced something was going on with Jean. No one would talk to her about it, but it wasn't difficult to determine that they were avoiding something, which meant there must be something to avoid. Jean had a secret, though whether it was an affair, kleptomania or something more ominous, Allison couldn't determine.

She was about ready to give up when Bill strolled in. An inexplicable burst of happiness surged through her at the sight of his familiar figure. Happiness due to the fact that she'd been right, that her waiting had paid off, that she had a chance to follow him and learn something, she explained to herself, ordering herself to believe the excuse.

He paused just inside the door, his alert gaze surveying the room. For a moment she stared at him, at the unconscious way he dominated that end of the room. He wasn't subdued or beaten down by life the way most of the people here were. He didn't belong here. And she was going to find out where he did belong.

His stare came to rest on her, and his eyes widened almost imperceptibly. He hesitated, as though he were trying to decide if he should stay or turn around and leave.

She made the decision for him.

'Bill!' Excusing herself from the man she'd been talking to, she rushed up to him. 'I'm so glad you're here. I was afraid I wouldn't see you today.'

He looked at her without expression for a moment, then a sardonic grin split his beard. 'Well,' he said, sounding resigned, 'you've found me. What are you going to do with me?'

'Let's walk while we talk,' she suggested, taking his arm. 'You choose where this time.' Maybe he'd automatically head toward the vicinity of his head-quarters. If he took her in the direction from which he'd been running the night Dealey got sick, she'd know she was on to something.

He didn't.

'So what's up?' he asked, steering down the street the way they'd gone the first night she'd talked to him. 'Something else break in your house?'

With a laugh, Allison looked up at him, but the laugh died at the brightness of his gaze. She was suddenly aware of their closeness, of the fact that she still held his arm, that she liked holding onto his corded arm and walking close to his firm, lanky body, that he appeared to like it, too. She ought to move away from him, but for some reason her body refused to obey the commands of her mind.

They continued to walk down the street in the crisp afternoon air, like a couple of lovers, for all the world to see.

160

For Douglas's detective to see and photograph, she realized, dropping his arm abruptly and moving a couple of inches away. She scanned the area and didn't see anybody familiar, but it could be anyone.

'As a matter of fact,' she said, more sharply than she'd meant to, 'we now have a leak in the roof. However – ' she put up a hand to forestall any protest ' – that's not what I want to talk to you about. Though if you're interested in making some money doing the work, we do need to get it fixed.' Whoever he was, she couldn't let him keep helping her for no pay except meals. She wouldn't be indebted to him, wouldn't give another man even a smidgen of control over her life.

He laughed, but the expression in his eyes had closed to her. 'If not the roof, then what do you want to talk to me about?'

'The concert. Megan is very disappointed you won't be coming with us.' That was true. 'She's been looking forward to meeting all your buddies and maybe even seeing you perform with them.'

He looked at her for a moment, then shook his head. 'Allis, you know I'm not a rock star.'

'I know you promised her she could go with you. You even said these performers were friends of yours.' If he was so damned self-righteous about honoring his promises, let him wiggle out of that.

He jammed his hands in his pockets and strode

161

angrily down the street. Allison was almost running in her effort to keep up.

'I lied,' he grated out. 'How would a homeless bum know anyone in January Heat? I was just trying to – oh, hell! I don't know what I was trying to do.'

He stopped abruptly and turned to her, eyes blazing, looking suddenly like a fierce mountain man.

Maybe – no, he was too educated, too civilized to have spent his life in the backwoods.

'You were trying to help,' she soothed, 'and you did. I can't begin to tell you how grateful I am. Then when you actually produced the tickets, well, that was a duly appreciated bonus.'

'Somebody owed me a favor,' he said, shrugging and resuming the walk.

'I thought you said someone gave them to you.'

'Somebody who owed me a favor gave them to me.'

He was lying. She caught the subtle nuances in his voice and knew he was lying, and that knowledge made her very happy.

They turned another corner, and Allison realized they were making a circle back to the shelter. He wasn't going to inadvertently lead her anywhere he shouldn't.

'Even if you can't take her backstage, she really wants you to go with her to the concert.'

'That's not possible. Think about it, Allis. You've got a tail on you, a private detective! Do you want him to have more pictures of you hanging out with an unemployed bum? Do you want him to have pictures of your daughter going somewhere with me?'

That part did make her a little uncomfortable, especially after Douglas's snide comment about Bill and her, but it wasn't like Bill was a known criminal. At least, he probably wasn't. If he was, she'd have a heck of a story, and she couldn't turn back now. 'If you were to trim your beard a little and – '

'No!' He stopped in front of the New Hope Shelter and glared at her.

'Okay.' She threw up her arms in resignation. 'It's only a little girl's heart we're talking about.'

He'd lied to her, so she figured that entitled her to a little manipulation. Anyway, most of what she'd said was true. The word 'only' that excluded her desire to uncover his identity was the single total inaccuracy.

For an infinite moment they stood rooted to the sidewalk, staring at each other as though the first to look away lost the contest. Allison gritted her teeth and reminded herself she couldn't afford to lose.

She concentrated her entire field of vision on his eyes, clear hazel eyes with flecks of green, eyes that made her feel warm all over, made her tingle as though he were touching her bare skin, eyes that promised an ecstasy of touching and feeling –

'All right!' He whirled away from her and started into New Hope. 'All right! I'll take her!' He slammed the door behind him.

Allison moved shakily to the curb and sat down in undignified exhaustion. Her breath came fast and shallow, and she felt exhilarated and disappointed at the same time. This was crazy. This was awful. How could a bearded, ragged man about whom she knew absolutely nothing make her knees go weak?

She had a sudden vision of taking Bill home to meet her solidly middle-class parents. The picture effectively brought her down from the intoxicated state her encounter with Bill had left her in.

Thank goodness he'd gone into the shelter for the moment, giving her a chance to get her composure back. She had been in no shape to 'tail' him.

And just where, she suddenly wondered, had he come up with that term, 'tail'? It sounded like an old Humphrey Bogart movie. Was Bill a detective? That would explain how he'd known Sullivan's identity.

She shot up from the curb, adrenaline flooding her veins, lending her a new surge of energy.

A detective assigned to infiltrate the ranks of the homeless and solve the murders.

She charged down the sidewalk, seeking a place to hide so she could follow him when he left the shelter.

But private detectives had to be hired. Would the city do that since the police hadn't been able to accomplish anything?

Her step slowed.

No, she didn't think they did that sort of thing.

Her bounce returned.

But maybe he was an undercover cop. That would be quite a story!

Though he seemed awfully kind and gentle, not to mention educated. Douglas had always said cops were big, dumb hulks.

But what did Douglas know?

Brad leaned against the door of the shelter, accomplishing the dual purpose of preventing himself from falling and of keeping Allison Prescott out. Though keeping her out now was like plugging the dam after the flood.

He wasn't sure, but he thought he'd just had mental sex. There was no other way to describe how she'd made him feel, looking at him that way. He'd been afraid if he didn't agree to whatever she wanted, she'd hold him forever with her gaze, until he couldn't control himself and had to take her in his arms and throw her to the sidewalk in front of God, Dr Doug's detective and everybody.

With a lurch, Brad made it to a bench and plopped down on it. 'Hi,' he said to the man sitting next to him – Joe or Frank or somebody.

'Hey, man,' the somebody whispered, 'Preacher's gonna come after you. We better go outside. You got any more?'

The man thought he was drunk, but that was okay. Better the whole world should think he was a lush than know the real reason for his confusion.

Brad shook his head in answer to the man's question. No way was he going outside to face that woman again right now. He had no problem with hauling in drug dealers or disarming murderers or even standing up to the Chief, but Allison Prescott separated him from his common sense.

And now she'd somehow – he wasn't sure how – manipulated him into agreeing to take her daughter to a rock concert while some private detective took pictures of him. Correction, make that mother and daughter. He'd given her three tickets.

'Are you ill today, brother?' Pollock loomed over him, then took a seat and leaned toward him, sniffing unobtrusively.

Brad started to reassure him that he was neither drunk nor on drugs, then decided to let it ride. It wouldn't strengthen his cover to appear too sanctimonious.

'I'm okay, preacher,' he told him.

Of course Pollock didn't believe him. He placed a beefy hand on Brad's shoulder and began one of his cliché-riddled, bombastic monologues.

Brad let his thoughts drift while nodding occasionally. He had to admire Pollock. Though the man was nuttier than one of Maggie Malone's pecan pies, he was a kind man and certainly helped with the physical needs of these people. Maybe even the spiritual needs of a few, he grudgingly admitted.

And that was more than he himself was doing. This was the beginning of his third week, and he had absolutely zilch to show for it. If he didn't produce something soon, the department would pull him in.

He sure wouldn't mind getting off the streets and back into a suit, not to mention out of the field of interest of Allison Prescott, news reporter extraordinaire, but he did mind failing.

'I'm scared, preacher,' he said, breaking into Pollock's discourse. 'I do this – ' best to be non-specific since he wasn't sure what Pollock thought he'd ingested ' – to try to escape my fear about this fruitcake that's wasting our friends.' He leaned forward intently. 'You hear everything. Surely somebody's told you something we can watch out for.'

But Pollock shook his head slowly, sadly. 'You fear the wrong enemy. The one without cannot harm you. You must confront the enemy within.'

'You may have something there, preacher,' Brad agreed, rising from the bench. Allison wasn't hold-ing a gun to his head, forcing him to do all these things for her, to keep coming around her house and

167

risking exposure of his cover. No, it was his own stupid, sappy emotions that kept getting him in trouble, the enemy within.

'See you.' He saluted Pollock and Scott – that was the other man's name.

Stepping cautiously through the door, he checked the area. Allison was gone. Off to harass someone else, no doubt.

He moved out onto the streets, trying to observe everything around him while appearing uninterested. With no real goal in mind, he meandered toward the last crime scene, talking to anyone he met along the way.

Wizened little Chuck sat on one corner, playing sad, off-key tunes on his harmonica. Down the street bug-eyed Mike talked earnestly to a lamp post. Old Raymond meandered along, surveying the world through wretchedly sane eyes.

Feeling thoroughly disgusted with his lack of progress in solving the murders, Brad finally headed out along a circuitous route toward the parking garage where his dad's truck waited.

He stopped at the gate on his way out and paid the attendant, then pulled into traffic.

The worst thing about this day, he thought, facing it at last, wasn't the lack of progress. Police work was always ninety-nine percent unrewarding drudgery. No, the worst thing was that, in spite of everything, some mutant part of his brain was actually looking forward to seeing Allison on Saturday night.

From across the street Allison studied her notepad in awe. She'd done it! She actually had the license number for the truck Bill had driven away in. It wasn't much of a truck, but it was a vehicle, he'd paid parking fees for it, and he was going somewhere in it.

Whatever or whoever the man was, he was not the homeless bum with no material possessions that he claimed to be. She had been right all along! Tomorrow she could wait for him in her car and follow him to his destination.

She wanted to jump up and down and shout. Despite her avowed determination, she was surprised that she had actually been able to do it. And it hadn't been easy. She hoped Sullivan had half as much trouble following her. Of course, she was probably a lot easier since she didn't wander around in circles and keep swiveling her head, watching everything and everybody the way Bill did – if that was really his name, and she doubted it.

She could get a name and address from the license bureau, but right now she had another lead, the kid at the gate who'd taken his money. She strolled over to his little booth.

'That guy who just left, he dropped something. I thought you might know who he is so I could return it.'

The kid smiled slyly. 'What'd he drop?'

With a sigh, Allison extracted a ten-dollar bill from her wallet. Reporters ought to have an expense account for bribes.

'This,' she said, holding the money toward him.

The boy grasped the other side, but she refused to turn loose of hers. 'Who is he?'

'I dunno. He's always here when I come on duty at one. He pays the daily rate and leaves in the evening.'

'Since when?'

'A couple of weeks. I noticed him because he looks like a real loser, but I guess he's got a job.' He tugged gently on the money, but Allison held on firmly.

'What time does he leave?'

'Different times. As early as two, usually around five or six.'

Another car rolled down the ramp, but the boy managed to take the driver's money with his other hand, never loosening his grip on hers.

'Ever talk to him?'

'About the weather, that's all.' He gave a final tug and secured possession of the money. 'I'll sure see he gets this,' he said, smiling.

'I know I can count on you.' Allison returned the phony smile.

As she walked back to her car, her mind whirred frantically, trying to invent a scenario that would best fit the circumstances. He was driving a junker truck that he parked in an expensive garage in order to hang around all day with street people.

If he was on the FBI's Ten Most Wanted list, surely he'd extend his disguise to twenty-four hours a day. His actions made it seem like hanging around with bums was a job.

That would fit if he was a detective or a cop. Or – she stopped in the middle of the sidewalk, earning a dirty look from a man who almost ran into her – maybe he was another reporter, researching a story just like she was, only really going for the in-depth approach.

Damn! She didn't like that idea at all.

Then again, he could be a novelist researching a book. Certainly he seemed more like an intellectual, avant-garde writer than a cop or a reporter. Yes, that seemed the most likely solution that incorporated all the elements – a writer who drove an old truck for superstitious reasons. Creative people did things like that.

As soon as she got home, she called Rick to tell him her findings.

'Well, I'll be damned,' Rick said.

'You had no faith in me, did you? You didn't really believe there was a story.'

'It's not that I didn't believe in you. It's just that . . . well . . . things usually are what they seem. The killer really is the one that all the evidence points to, and bums really are bums. You know I had my doubts about him, though,' he added hastily. 'I even did some checking for you, remember?'

'I do, and now I need your help again. Those friends of yours on the police force, will they check out this license number for you?'

Rick's laughter came happily over the wire. 'You bet they will, lady. By this time tomorrow, we'll know who owns that truck.'

After Allison hung up the phone, she went to the kitchen and poured herself a glass of wine.

'I'm closing in on you, Bill,' she said, lifting the glass in an imaginary toast.

A famous novelist, she thought, sipping the wine. I wonder if I've read any of his books or seen the movies?

Would they be intellectual and thought-provoking or exciting and fast-paced? Definitely the latter, she decided, remembering the energy he exuded, the exciting way he'd made her feel when he kissed her.

She touched her lips, remembering, then lifted the glass for another sip. Let Douglas take all the pictures he wanted. When he found out Bill's real identity, he'd have to eat that stupid smirk of his.

And besides . . .

It was okay to enjoy kissing a novelist.

CHAPTER 9

'I lost him,' Allison complained when Rick answered his phone. 'Did your friend get his name and address from that license plate?'

'Where have you been all day?' The distressed tone in Rick's response frightened her.

'Running errands and chasing our friend, Bill. Why?' She eased into a dining-room chair, not at all sure she wanted to hear the answer.

'Because the news is now official, or it will be at the meeting tomorrow morning. We have new employers.'

'Mo-om, I'm ho-ome!'

'I'm on the phone, Megan, talking to Uncle Rick.'

'Hi, Uncle Rick.' Megan breezed past her mother and into the kitchen. 'How long till dinner?'

'Long enough. Get some fruit.'

Megan reached for the peanut-butter jar, and Allison turned her attention back to the phone.

'Okay, Rick, so what's the percentage of interruption of the status quo?' she asked.

'What? Oh, are we talking in nonsensical phrases for the benefit of those little ears in the background?'

'Megan loves you, too. Now, back to the story at hand?'

Rick sighed, and the clamp around Allison's heart tightened. 'Don't panic yet,' he advised, though he obviously had. 'Nothing has changed officially, but, of course, rumors are flying about everything from the station manager's job to the weatherman's hair piece.'

Allison grabbed Megan's arm as she left the kitchen and inspected her peanut-butter sandwich. Strawberry jam oozed out from all sides, but she let it go with a wave. What was an extra cup of jam at a time like this?

'So what do you think?' she asked Rick. 'You've been through this sort of event before.'

'No way to call it. I've been canned, promoted and left alone. This is a volatile business. But whatever happens, you can't take it personally. If you survive the changes, great. If not, you gird your loins and start again.'

Allison plugged one finger in her ear as the television set blasted forth. 'Turn that down!' The sound decreased by a few decibels.

'I'm just getting started over this time,' she said softly. 'I can't start again already.'

'I know, lady, but you can do it if you have to. And I'm not saying you will have to. I just wanted to let you know what's going on so you'd be prepared for tomorrow.'

'Rick, don't b.s. your old friend. You're worried, and that worries me. But at least we have an ace in the hole. Did your friend run that license plate?'

'I didn't get hold of him yet. He's been out of pocket all day.'

'And I lost Bill today before we even got out of downtown. This "tailing" business isn't as easy as it sounds.'

'Tomorrow. We'll get it for sure tomorrow, and if the new regime tries to run us off, we'll auction our story and our bodies to the highest bidder.'

For several minutes after hanging up, Allison sat with her hand on the phone, searching for the energy to get up and keep trying. For every inch she gained, the opposition seemed to take back a foot.

'Mom, it's supposed to rain tonight. Did you get my roof fixed?'

'Not yet, baby.' If she had a ladder, she'd climb up herself and see if she could spot this hole. Though what she'd do if she found it was a complete mystery.

Her fingers flexed on the phone. She'd call Bill and ask him to fix it.

Stupid reflex. Of course she couldn't call Bill.

Not because he was a street person and didn't have a phone – she'd be willing to bet he had one. But she didn't know his number or even his name.

He might very well have a car phone in that ratty truck. It would be just about right for him to be driving around with a car phone and her sitting here with a leaky roof, unable to reach him.

A leaky roof and the weight of the world on her shoulders.

Not that any of it was his concern.

But he did have a way of making her feel better.

'Take the bucket upstairs, and we'll see if we can get Bill to work on it this weekend,' she told her daughter.

'Malone Plumbing?' Allison stared at the slip of paper Rick had just handed her, waiting for the letters to rearrange themselves into something believable, something acceptable. 'Bill's truck belongs to Malone Plumbing?'

Rick folded his arms and slouched on his editing-room stool. 'I'm afraid so. I had them double check. It's a 1979 Chevrolet truck registered to Malone Plumbing.'

Allison sank onto the stool next to him and sighed heavily. She'd been so excited when she'd walked into the station Friday afternoon and Rick had taken her to the editing room, then handed her the scrap of paper.

Since the announcement of the new ownership of the station on Wednesday, the tension had thickened hourly. To make it worse, Rick's friend on the police force hadn't returned his call until Thursday. Then Allison had been afraid they'd have to wait through the weekend to get the information.

Not that it would have mattered. All she had now was the name of a plumbing company.

'No,' she protested. 'That makes no sense. Why would a plumber be living on the streets? It's a cover. There is no such company.'

'Sorry. I checked. A sole proprietorship, been in business in the same location for nineteen years.'

'I guess that's a little long for a cover.'

Rick nodded agreement. 'And you have to admit, he has the skills of a professional plumber.'

'But nineteen years? I didn't think he was old enough for that.'

'Late thirties, early forties – with all that hair, it's hard to tell. Definitely possible, though.'

She tapped the surface of the editing table with one fingernail – a fingernail noticeably shorter than it had been prior to the big carpet caper. Rick was right. Not many novelists/actors/rock stars/detectives or ordinary people could have repaired her plumbing the way he had.

'I suppose that even rules out the possibility he's a cop,' she sighed.

'I asked my friend. He said he hadn't heard of

anyone going undercover on this case, but that didn't mean anything. The undercover agents are always a secret. Too much of a chance for a leak otherwise.'

'I still say it doesn't make sense,' she protested. 'Why would a plumber be hanging around with the street people?'

'Maybe he's a weirdo – gets his kicks that way. Maybe he's looking for an apprentice plumber and thinks these guys have potential.'

Allison scowled at the attempt at a joke.

'Okay,' Rick agreed, 'so maybe he's the killer.'

Bill was not a murderer. She knew that. She'd bet money she didn't have on that fact. 'But the killings started before he appeared. You said so yourself.'

'He could have killed the first four, then decided to move in a little closer for the next one. Get to know them personally. Who knows how these psychopathic minds operate?'

Allison started to protest, then decided against it. What proof did she have that Bill wasn't a psychopath? Because she liked him? Because he was always going out of his way to help? Because she didn't want him to be? 'But you do believe there's a story here? You will help me?'

'It would seem that something strange is going on when a plumber spends his days cavorting with the homeless.'

At least she had his assistance, even if she found his reasoning faulty.

'Okay, first thing we do is call this Malone Plumbing and try to find out who's been driving that truck.'

Rick glanced at his watch. 'It's after five.'

Allison shrugged. 'So let him bill me for over-time.'

'They may be closed,' Rick explained. 'People with normal jobs frequently leave at five.'

'We won't know until we try, will we?'

She strode out of the editing room and over to her desk. Malone Plumbing was listed in the *Yellow Pages*. Their one-inch in-column ad even boasted that they had been 'serving the people of Oklahoma City since 1977'.

Without a lot of hope, Allison dialed the number listed and got a recording stating their hours were nine to five. However, the female voice continued, in case of an emergency, Gerald Malone, the owner, could be reached at home.

Allison dialed the number given, but hung up with a mumbled apology when a woman answered.

She shrugged at Rick's questioning look. 'The woman who answered Gerald Malone's home phone was the same one who made the recording for his office.'

She tried to keep her voice calm, her face ex-pressionless, but inside she was shivering. Perhaps

Bill only worked for the plumbing company. She had no real reason to assume he was Gerald Malone. But if he was . . .

Why had it never occurred to her before that Bill might be married? If he lied about his occupation, where he lived, where he got concert tickets, why wouldn't he lie about that, too?

Not that he'd ever really lied about it. The subject had never come up. She'd just assumed, after the way he kissed her and looked at her – but married men weren't immune to passion. And he had left before morning the night it rained. Maybe he had to get home to his wife.

'A married plumber,' she mused aloud.

'It happens a lot. These nutty people going around raping and pillaging turn out to be respectable members of the community with pretty wives and bright kids.'

Rick was watching her closely. She couldn't let him see that she was upset. He'd want to know why, and that was a question she didn't want to answer, even to herself, right now.

With a jerk, she pulled her desk drawer open and yanked out the *White Pages*.

'Gerald Malone,' she repeated, running a finger down the listings. 'Here we go. What do you say we drive by as soon as we can get out of here and see who lives at this address, see if he has a beard and curly hair?'

'You got it, lady,' Rick agreed, giving her a thumbs-up.

She picked up the phone again to call Megan and tell her she'd be late, an all-too-common occurrence on this job, especially with everyone tiptoeing around the new owners.

'Do your homework and don't answer the door,' she instructed her daughter.

Megan sighed at the repetition of the familiar orders, but grudgingly agreed.

An hour later, Allison and Rick turned onto Gerald Malone's street. Locating the house was easy, even in the gathering twilight. The dilapidated truck sat directly in front of it. Allison's heart sank even as she felt the excitement of discovery.

She'd been right. Bill had a secret life.

As a plumber. Maybe a married plumber.

Rick pulled over to the curb across the street and up one house.

'One point for you, lady,' he said. 'You had him pegged right from the beginning.'

Allison glanced around the neighborhood. 'Small, old homes,' she commented, talking so Rick wouldn't wonder at her silence.

'Old, but well kept. Kind of reminds me of your neighborhood.'

There was a depressing thought. Bill/Gerald lived in the kind of home she was trying to escape.

No, she thought, peering closer. This house was a little bigger and in immaculate condition. Likely due to his plumbing and carpentry skills.

'Rick, pull up a little. I think I see another vehicle in the driveway.'

She gasped and jerked backward in her seat at the sound of a tapping on her window.

A rotund little man smiled in at her.

With shaking fingers, she hit the window button to lower it.

'Need some help?' the man asked.

'No, uh, thanks, we, uh, we thought we recognized that truck over there,' Allison improvised. 'We used to have a friend named Bill who drove one just like that. You wouldn't happen to know if someone named Bill lives over there, would you?'

'Nope. No Bill. Gerald and Maggie Malone been there a long time. They were here when I moved in eight years ago. And Gerald's had that truck as long as I've known him, though here lately I have seen him driving that new one sitting in the driveway.'

'Well, must be a different old truck. They all look alike. Thanks for the help. I guess we'll be going.' She smiled at the man and waved as Rick, taking her cue, drove slowly down the street.

'Little nervous, are we?' he asked, grinning.

'You're the one who thinks we're on to a killer here,' she mumbled. Gerald and Maggie Malone.

'You get the number on that new truck, and I'll

182

get the car parked next to it,' he ordered as they passed the driveway.

Turning the corner at the end of the block, Rick pulled over and stopped again. He withdrew a small notepad from his shirt pocket and scribbled on it.

'I got the car license. Did you get the truck?'

She reeled off the letters and numbers then frowned. 'No, that's not right. It's – I'm not sure. Can we go back again?'

Rick's face softened. 'Relax, lady. Even if this guy is the killer, he's not going to run out and smash in your head while we're driving down his street.'

'That's not it.' She hesitated, wanting to tell her friend what the problem was but unsure herself. It wasn't like she'd been dating Bill or anything. They'd kissed once in a moment of passion. So it made no sense, this feeling of distress at driving past the house where he lived with his wife.

'Just turn around and go back up the block. I'll get it this time.'

She got it but almost lost it when Bill passed in front of a lighted window just as they drove by. He appeared to be laughing, his posture relaxed and easy, comfortable. There could be no doubt he belonged there.

At least there were no little tricycles in the yard. That would have made it even worse.

Allison tried to put a smile on her face and some bounce in her step when she finally made it home that evening, pizza in hand.

Intermittent bleeps and explosions from the television announced her daughter's presence. Maybe, she counseled herself, all these video games would perfect Megan's eye-hand coordination to such an extent that she'd be able to – what? Teach video games?

'Hi, Mom.' Her attention remained riveted to the exploding colors in front of her. 'Some guy came by a little while ago looking for you. I told him you'd be here soon.'

'Didn't I tell you not to answer the door?' She plopped the cardboard box onto the table.

'The screen was locked.'

'A kidnapper could slash through that screen in a split second. Please don't open the door when I'm not here.'

'Aw, Mom.'

'Megan – ' she started, then bit her tongue. There was no point in taking out her frustrations on her daughter. 'Come on and get some pizza while it's relatively hot.'

'In a minute. I just reached Mars.'

Allison opened the box and inspected the contents. 'Take your time. I think it could stand to be rewarmed.' She slid the soggy concoction onto a cookie sheet and into the oven.

A knock sounded on the door. Probably the salesman who'd come by earlier. Obviously he wasn't a rapist or murderer since Megan had given him every chance to perform and he hadn't.

'Allison C. Prescott?' the rumpled man asked when she opened the door.

She recognized him from all the times before. The process server.

Wordlessly she opened the screen and extended her hand to accept the folded paper he held.

The man left without another word.

Fortunately Megan was still engrossed in Mars.

Allison sat down at the kitchen table and unfolded the petition. Douglas had made good his threat. He was suing for sole custody of Megan, charging, in addition to the standard allegations, that she left the child home alone too much and that she was exposing her to unsavory influences.

Anger flared in her breast. If Douglas the Dork would pay reasonable child support, if he hadn't taken everything they owned, she wouldn't have to work such long hours and leave Megan alone so much.

And as for the 'unsavory influences' – Bill had been much nicer to her and Megan both than Douglas ever had. He'd been there when she needed help, which was more than she could say for Douglas.

She crumpled the paper, making a conscious effort not to scream, throw things or otherwise alarm Megan. Whether or not he had a case no longer mattered. What mattered was that she didn't have the money to hire another lawyer.

The phone rang, and she gasped.

Snatching up the receiver before it could assault her nerves again, she tried to make her voice calm.

'Hello?'

'Allis, this is Bill.'

At the same time she heard his voice, she also heard a woman laugh in the background and she saw the smoke curling out of her own oven.

The smoke detector shrieked.

'Allis!'

'Mom!'

She burst into uncontrollable sobs and slammed the phone onto the cradle.

Allison made a move to climb on a chair and turn off the smoke detector, changed her mind and started toward the oven, then turned back to the smoke detector.

'Mom, what's wrong?'

Only the sight of Megan standing at the kitchen door, her small face puckered in worry, gave her the sanity to do anything. She took care of the smoke detector first, then pulled the black pizza from the oven. A tear dripped onto the rim of the hot pan and sizzled.

'It's okay, Mom.' Megan's skinny arms wrapped around her mother. 'We can eat peanut-butter and jelly sandwiches.'

Allison cuddled her daughter and started to laugh though the tears wouldn't stop.

The phone rang, and Megan moved to answer it.

'No!' Allison protested.

'Don't answer the phone? Why? Who was that you hung up on?'

'Nobody.'

The ringing went on and on.

'Mom, what's the matter?' Megan looked up at her, trying to pull free.

'Nothing.' She saw the crumpled papers still lying on the table. 'Why don't you get out the skillet for me, and we'll have an omelet.'

When Megan moved to obey, Allison snatched up the papers, folded them hurriedly and tucked them into her purse.

The phone finally stopped ringing.

With a worried frown, Brad hung up the phone in his parents' bedroom. Something was wrong. It was hard to imagine proper Allison Prescott crying, but that was definitely what she had been doing. Then someone had broken the connection, and no one had answered when he'd called back.

'Mom, Dad, thanks for dinner,' he said as he charged through the house. 'I hate to run – ' he gave his mother a peck on the cheek and waved to his father ' – but I need to check on a friend of mine. There may be some trouble.'

'I hope everything's all right,' Maggie said, handing him his keys. 'Be careful.'

'It's okay. Not that kind of trouble. Not cop-type trouble.' He hoped. Allison wasn't the hysterical type, though. Something was very wrong, of that he had no doubt.

Pushing the old truck to its limits, he fished his badge out of the glove compartment in case he got stopped for speeding. When he reached Allison's street, his impulse was to drive up, screech to a halt in front of her house and charge in, but his years of training stood him in good stead now.

After parking two blocks away, he took the extra time to strap on his shoulder holster under his jacket. Then he threw caution to the wind and ran the two blocks to her house. He couldn't afford to take the time to slouch cautiously.

The brown van wasn't in evidence tonight, but a dark sedan with someone slumped in the seat looked suspicious.

Brad cursed under his breath as he sprinted up the walk. He'd have liked to check in the windows first, size up the situation, but the man in the dark car would have a great time writing that up in his report to Dr Doug.

He banged imperiously on the door. 'Allis! It's me!'

The door flew back, and he scanned the room, his gaze coming to rest on Megan's smiling face where she stood in front of him.

'Hi, Brill. Come in and have some omelet.'

A movement in his peripheral vision turned his attention to the rear of the room where Allison was emerging from the kitchen. He lunged past Megan, toward her, then stopped short.

Her face, swollen and tear streaked, was nevertheless composed. She was in control, her expression cool. Chilly, in fact.

'I was worried about you,' he said.

'Obviously. You must have been calling from just around the corner to be able to walk here so quickly.'

So that was it. She knew something. Which didn't really explain why she'd been crying or was so obviously upset with him.

'Brill, I've got this really cool outfit to wear tomorrow.' Megan charged over and grabbed his arm. 'Dad and Bonnie got me some great new clothes.'

Reluctantly, Brad focused his attention on the girl. 'New clothes, huh?'

'Yeah. We went to all these cool stores. One place they served us tea.' She pulled out a dining-table chair and sprawled on it. 'We'd have gone to a lot more, but Dad got a parking ticket, so he got mad and we had to go home. He said the policeman was just jealous of his car because policemen don't make very much money and can't buy nice cars.'

Brad stole a peek at Allison. She was scowling,

her expression basically unchanged. He'd expected some reaction when Megan mentioned the police. Maybe she didn't know who he was after all.

'Is Douglas right, Allis?' he prompted.

'I hate to admit it, Megan, but your father's probably right in this instance. Cops don't make a lot of money, and they probably would be jealous of his car. On the other hand – ' she slid her gaze directly to Brad ' – plumbers frequently do quite well.'

Plumbers? She thought he was a plumber? So why did that make her angry since he'd told her that in the beginning as part of his cover?

'Megan, run upstairs and try on your clothes you're wearing to the concert for . . . your friend,' she urged.

'You want to see them?'

Brad nodded. 'Certainly.'

Megan dashed away.

'Excuse me while I salvage my omelet, then we need to talk, Gerald.' She disappeared into the kitchen.

'Gerald?'

She thought he was a plumber named Gerald? For a minute he missed the connection. After all, the man he'd just eaten dinner with was named 'Dad.'

Then he began to laugh.

The look in Allison's eyes when she reappeared in

the kitchen doorway stopped the laughter.

Brad hesitated, uncertain how much she knew, how much he'd have to tell her and how much she could be trusted to know.

'Gerald's my father,' he finally said. 'You want to tell me how you came up with the name?'

She moved a fraction of an inch into the room, her expression a little less angry, a little confused. 'A friend ran the license plate on your truck. I called the shop, then got a home address from the phone book. I saw you there tonight.'

Brad couldn't resist smiling. He had to give her credit for her detective work. 'You drove past Mom and Dad's while I was there? And you thought I was Gerald Malone, a plumber.'

'A married plumber.'

At that, he guffawed, then wrapped his arms around her in delight. To his surprise, she melted against him, returning the embrace, clinging to his waist. Damn, but she felt good, suddenly all soft and molded to him. For a tantalizing moment he couldn't remember why he'd been avoiding this entanglement.

But one of her arms roamed distressingly close to his gun, and he remembered. Finding that would really give her some ideas.

He moved his hands to her arms and pushed her slightly away, looking into her eyes.

'I'm neither married nor a plumber,' he assured

her. 'I'm Brad Malone, the bachelor son of a plumber, driving his dad's old truck.'

Abruptly she jerked away from his grasp, and he saw the tears had started in her eyes again. 'You have to borrow your dad's truck? So you really are just a deadbeat, too lazy to work.'

Snatching her purse from the table, she yanked out a folded paper and handed it to him. Brad flopped into the chair vacated by Megan and read the petition.

'That rotten, no-good – ' Brad stopped himself from using language acceptable in the locker room but not in Allison Prescott's dining room.

Allison sank into a chair beside him. 'You were right. He did get your picture.' Her voice was flat.

'Did you get the information about my truck from him?'

'No! I followed you and got that myself. He just thinks you're a vagrant or a handyman or something unsavory.'

Well, Brad thought, he wasn't too far off.

With a sigh, he took her soft, defenseless hand in both of his.

Not so defenseless, he reminded himself. She had tracked him down and uncovered his dad's identity. She was only one step away from discovering his, and then she'd be in control. It would be to her advantage to expose him, not only for the sake of her blasted story, but now to stop Douglas from taking her daughter. There was no good solution here. He'd have to tell her and try to convince her not to expose him.

'Allis, we have to talk. I'm a cop.'

CHAPTER 10

Allison's mind was spinning. Bill wasn't a plumber, wasn't married, wasn't Bill or even Gerald. Somewhere amidst the chaos, she thought she'd just heard him say he was a cop.

His hands holding hers seemed the only stable thing in the room, maybe in the universe, and that was crazy because he was the cause of the instability.

Megan bounced in room wearing flowered tights and a huge T-shirt tied at one hip. 'Is this cool or what?'

Bill – Brad – turned loose of her hand and faced Megan. 'Too cool for words. I don't know how I'll ever be able to dress cool enough to be seen with you. But right now, can you give me a few minutes alone with your mother? We need to work out some details.'

'Mom, you're not going to do something dumb, like make us leave in the middle of the concert, are you?'

'Stop whining and go blow up Martians or something.'

At Bill's – Brad's – nod, Megan rolled her eyes and left the room. In a few seconds the computerized sounds of a video game cueing up announced her compliance.

Brad turned slowly back to Allison, his expression intense. 'I'm putting my life in your hands,' he said. 'If you expose me, I could be killed. At best, I'm off the case, and we're that much further from solving the murders, that many more people could die.'

'You're an undercover cop?' She was glad he wasn't a bum or a married plumber, but Allison was having a hard time accepting something she'd considered as unlikely as his being a murderer.

'Usually I'm just a plain old detective. Steve Raney and I have been partners for years. But they needed a new face, somebody unknown to the street people.' He grinned wryly through the beard. 'I got picked because I have a forgettable look and lots of curly hair. Makes for a great disguise.'

Not to mention a great story. She'd been right about that! This should tip the balance in her favor at the station.

Except he'd just told her she couldn't expose him.

'Wait a minute. You're saying I can't do a story on this? I have to do a story. You don't understand how important it is to me. The station's been sold. I could lose my job.'

His smile vanished. 'People could lose their lives. I think that may be just a little bit more important.' He took a deep breath, his expression grim. 'If you'll bear with me until this is over, I'll see that you get your story. I promise you'll get an exclusive.'

Damn! Why did he have to put it in those terms? She wanted to argue with him. This was her story; she'd worked hard on it, tracked him down, uncovered the details, and she deserved to get the credit. She deserved to keep her job, maybe – hopefully – get a raise and even a promotion to news anchor instead of just a reporter.

But she couldn't argue with him. She didn't have the right to interfere with his job, to put him and other people in danger.

'How long?' she asked. 'I don't have much time. How much longer are we talking about?'

'I don't know. Until the case is solved.'

'How close are you to that?'

'Not very,' he admitted. 'No one seems to know anything. But I promise, you'll be the first reporter to hear when I do find out something.'

'Great. You're not close to solving the murders, but I am close to losing my job.'

He compressed his lips and looked chagrined. 'I'm sorry.'

'Okay,' she agreed grudgingly. There didn't seem anything else she could do. 'You've got a deal. I get an exclusive in return for keeping your secret for the time being.' The art of losing graciously.

She extended her hand across the table, and he shook it, then slowly, reluctantly, released it. 'Thanks,' he said. The relief in his eyes told her he'd been uncertain of victory.

Surely he couldn't have thought she'd place her needs, great though they were, especially now with Douglas's lawsuit –

'Douglas's lawsuit!' She snatched up the petition and waved it exultantly. 'I can prove you're not an unsavory person!'

Brad shook his head, his expression sad but determined. 'Not until the murders are solved. I'm sorry. You can't tell anybody.'

'But I have to! I can't let him take my daughter!'

'He won't. I promise you, I won't let that happen because of me.'

She heard the sudden hardness in his voice, saw the flint in his hazel eyes, and she believed him. And suddenly it wasn't so hard to believe he was a cop. 'What are you going to do?'

'I don't know exactly. But nobody's perfect, and I've got a lot of friends who specialize in catching those imperfections.'

'Douglas is very determined.'

'I've met your Douglas.' And thus he dismissed

the man – as he had every time they met. 'Have you got a good lawyer?'

For a moment, she considered pointing out to him that her agreement to hold up on her story made hiring a good lawyer a financial impossibility. But her pride kept her quiet. Maybe she could sell blood like the homeless people did.

'I suppose I'll call the one who handled my divorce,' she told him.

Brad shook his head, one corner of his mouth turning up in a sardonic smile. 'Doesn't sound like he did too good a job for you.'

'So what do I do? Get out the *Yellow Pages*? Go visit a few of them and find out who has the meanest look in his eye?' See if she could find one who'd accept the microwave oven as a retainer?

'I have a friend, if you're interested. He owes me. Probably give you a good rate, and I guarantee he'd do a great job.'

'I'm interested.' How many fewer pints of blood would she have to sell for a 'good' rate?

He pulled a pen and a small notepad from his pocket.

'It might be helpful,' she said as he scribbled on the paper, 'for me to have your address and phone number. I presume you do have a home.'

Brad chuckled. 'I have a home. But I did appreciate your offer of shelter the night it rained.'

Allison bristled as his words recalled how he'd let

198

her make a fool of herself, offering him her garage.

He ripped out the two sheets of paper he'd been writing on and handed them to her. She snatched them from him.

'I mean it,' he said softly. 'As far as you knew, you were offering to take in a homeless person. That was very kind.'

'I knew different,' she countered. 'I didn't know who you were, but I knew you weren't a derelict.' At least she'd been pretty sure most of the time. Suspicious all the time.

What she could see of one eyebrow disappeared the rest of the way into his masses of hair.

'I wouldn't have followed you if I'd believed your story, would I?' she persisted.

'No,' he admitted. 'I don't suppose you would have.' But his expression was still dubious.

'You cops don't have a corner on the investigative market. In fact, since it's in both our best interests to get this thing solved as soon as possible, I'll share my information with you if you'll share yours with me.'

Brad shook his head. 'Most of my information is confidential. All I can promise is an exclusive story.' He leaned toward her. 'But any help you give me will get you your story that much sooner.'

She glared at him, considering her alternatives. There didn't seem to be any. She studied his obstinate expression, the stubborn set of his shoulders, and wanted to punch him and hug him at the same time. That strength she so admired was working against her. Once again a man was in control of her life, and things weren't going her way.

'Okay,' she capitulated, spreading her hands. 'I don't have anything definite, just some suspicions. However – ' she allowed herself a smug grin ' – look where that got me with you.'

'*Touché*.' Brad picked up his pen and held it poised over his notepad. 'Go ahead. I'm listening.'

'There's a lady named Jean – '

'Jean Prather. Big lady. Been in and out of the state hospital at Vinita a few times. We've picked her up one time and another for shoplifting, petty thievery and possession of an illegal substance.'

'She takes drugs?' For some reason the idea shocked Allison. Though she knew on an intellectual level that many of the street people did, she had a hard time associating it with someone she knew.

'She's been clean, as far as we know, since her last trip to Vinita,' Brad advised her.

'As far as you know. Well, the other day she was talking to a man, arguing with him. He stormed out, and she was very upset. Maybe they were talking about drugs.'

'What did the man look like?' He was watching her intently, his pen and paper forgotten.

'Tall, thin, brown hair, balding. His forehead

protruded in a funny kind of way.'

'Dwight Miller. He's been known to deal. What were they saying?'

'I couldn't hear. But I did notice her red shoes were missing.' She almost didn't tell him that. As a man, he might not appreciate the significance of pretty shoes to a woman.

Brad grinned. 'For a pseudo-cop, you're not too bad. Jean's nickname is Magpie. She loves bright, colorful things, and she has a habit of trading. The only problem is, she rarely asks the other person's permission for this trade.'

'You think she stole drugs and left the shoes in payment?' Allison asked incredulously.

'It's possible. Maybe Dwight got mad when he found out. There'd have been little doubt who did it.' He spread his hands. 'But that's all conjecture, and even if it's true, how does that relate to the murders? Tell me some concrete facts.'

Allison sighed. She really didn't know anything concrete. 'In order to get her to talk to me, I gave her my scarf. It seemed to make her happy. Maybe it'll turn up some place significant.'

He nodded. 'Could be. I need a description of that scarf.'

She told him, and he wrote it down.

'What else?' he asked.

'Nothing.' Allison rubbed her arms, suddenly chilly. This wasn't as much fun as she'd thought.

'Just that she's big enough to be the killer, and if she's on drugs, that might explain it. You know, going bonkers after getting high or hitting people to steal their money to buy drugs.'

'Could be,' Brad agreed. 'There's a definite correlation between drugs and violent crimes. But you still have nothing but speculation.'

'One more thing, I think Pollock knows about what she's doing. She acted nervous when he came over, practically ran out the door. He seemed disappointed in her but not surprised.'

'That man knows everything about everybody. He just won't tell.'

'I'm not so sure he has a firm grip on reality,' Allison said.

'He doesn't. The man's nuts. But he fills a need. He takes care of his people. Even protects them, as you discovered.'

'If we could only get him to talk.'

'I'm working on it,' Brad assured her.

'If I get there first, I'll let you know.' She waved the piece of paper with his phone number on it and smiled.

'You do that.' He rose from the table. 'I can't emphasize enough that you are not to discuss this with anyone. Not your mother, not your best friend, not another policeman – nobody.'

Allison cringed. Nobody. How could she not tell Rick? Anyway Rick had the license number from the car in Brad's parents' driveway. He'd soon find out for himself.

'That car at your parents' house, was it yours?' she asked abruptly.

'The car's my mom's, but the new truck belongs to me,' Brad answered. 'I borrowed Dad's old one just in case anybody saw me.'

The second truck belonged to him, and Rick had his license number. Soon he'd have Brad's name. Well, she'd just have to deal with Rick. No reason to worry Brad about that.

As she walked beside him into the living room, Allison tried to sort out her tangled feelings for this man. His confession put a whole new perspective on things, a perspective that would take some thinking about. At this point she could only be certain of one thing – she had feelings of some sort for him.

'Brill!' Megan exclaimed, abandoning her game to rush up to him. 'What time are you coming by tomorrow? Are you going to fix the roof?'

'Oh, yeah. The latest catastrophe.'

'It's all right.' Allison wasn't going to ask a policeman to repair her roof. 'It didn't leak the last time it rained.'

'But it didn't rain very hard that time,' Megan protested.

'I've already called someone about it,' Allison stated firmly.

Brad's skeptical gaze told her he knew she was lying.

'I'll see you both tomorrow,' he said.

He paused at the door. Allison followed the direction of his stare and saw the dark car up the street.

'Tomorrow,' he repeated. The word held a promise echoed by his big, solid hand as he took hers and briefly squeezed it.

Allison drove home from work the next day in a state of complete exhaustion. The only thing keeping her awake was the tension that had begun with her drive past Gerald Malone's house then continued through a virtually sleepless night and a long, hectic day at work.

Her first project that morning had been confronting Rick.

'Don't run those license numbers,' she'd requested as they headed to the van to cover an art show.

Rick stopped in his tracks. 'What?'

'I can't tell you why, but it's very important that we not do that right now.'

Unable to come up with a plausible story after tossing, turning and thinking all night, she'd decided to fall back on their years of trust and friendship.

'Are you nuts? That's all I've heard from you for

days, finding out about this Bill or Gerald or whatever. Now we have him, and you don't want to reel him in?'

'I do. We will. Just not right now. Trust me on this,' she implored.

'Uh-uh.' He shook his head. 'I'll trust you when you trust me with the reason for this sudden about-face of yours.'

'I can't tell you. I gave my word. But I can promise you'll be right there with me when the story comes down.'

'That's very reassuring to know. Nevertheless, I think I'll take my chances and run these license numbers.'

Allison crossed her arms and glared at her friend. 'Why can't you trust me?'

'Why can't you trust me?' he echoed.

They stood for a moment in silence.

'Come on. We're going to be late,' Allison grumbled.

'I don't think the sculptures are going to get up and leave before we arrive.' Nevertheless, he followed her to the van.

With a sigh, Allison climbed into the seat and closed the door behind her. Telling Rick the truth seemed the only practical thing to do. She didn't like the idea of breaking her word to Brad, but at least this way she could secure Rick's cooperation before he found out.

'Rick, my dear and trusted friend, put your hand over your heart and swear to keep my secret.'

He had agreed, albeit reluctantly. When she'd told him the story, his reluctance to keep the information confidential had grown to gigantic proportions. The lure of breaking the story immediately, the fear that someone else would somehow beat them to it, had been compelling.

He didn't trust Brad, but she supposed that was understandable. He didn't know Brad the way she did, didn't realize how Brad would go out of his way to keep his word.

In the end, though, their friendship and Rick's sense of fairness, of the harm that could come from breaking the story too soon, had prevailed. Rick had agreed to wait, provided he was involved in all developments.

Allison turned the corner onto her street, her eyes automatically seeking her house.

Parked out front was a large, late-model American car polished a gleaming silver. No sooner had she taken note of that oddity when she noticed movement from the corner of her eye. A man was crouching on her roof! Were there no limits to what Douglas's rats would do?

She wheeled into the driveway, threw open the car door and charged across the lawn.

White teeth flashed down at her from a curly, but subdued brown beard. 'I think I got your leak fixed.'

'You trimmed your hair,' she said, trying to regain her composure.

Brad backed to the ladder and started down. 'I wish I could. I just moussed the hair and beard in place instead of brushing them out. Little tricks I learned from you women.'

He gained the ground and moved toward her, taking her arm. 'All ready for the big blast tonight? Personally, I think I could use a shower.'

As he guided her up the porch steps, toward the front door, Allison felt no lessening of the day's tension, but it did take on a pleasurable aspect.

'Your car door's open,' he said just before they reached the house.

'Oh, yes, I guess I didn't get it closed all the way.' She'd only given it a token shove in her rush to confront the intruder on her roof.

'I'll help you with the garage door,' Brad offered, crossing the lawn with her.

'No need. We'll just leave the car out until we go to the concert.' Surely he wasn't planning to take his dad's old truck.

Brad turned her about so she was facing the large silver car in the street. 'We have adequate transportation,' he assured her.

'Where did you get that?' she demanded, whirling to stare up at him. 'Did you steal – no, of course you didn't. Is that yours?'

'I borrowed it from a friend, the father of a friend,

actually. Considering everyone's preoccupation with license-plate numbers, I thought it would be a good idea.'

'What friend? You realize now Douglas will think you're your friend.'

'Yes, he will, won't he? Assuming, of course, his detective is half as efficient as you are.'

With a huge grin, he took her keys and went over to unlock the garage. Halfway there, he turned back. 'And you don't need to write down the license number to have it traced. I'll tell you when the time is right.'

Allison frowned. 'Now is the right time. I'm not going anywhere in that car until I know who owns it and what you're up to.'

Flecks of green and gold danced in his eyes. 'Be a sport, Allis. Don't spoil my surprise. Trust me. For just a little while.'

He looked so pleased with himself, she didn't push it. But she made a mental note of the license number.

CHAPTER 11

On later reflection, Allison pinpointed the moment Brad emerged from the bathroom as her undoing. Clad in torn, faded blue jeans, with his hair and beard subdued, he looked trendy, fashionable . . . sexy.

'How do you like the latest disguise?' he asked, pausing on the landing when he saw her coming out of her bedroom.

She swallowed hard. 'Disguise?'

When he'd been a shabby bum, she'd found it difficult to deny the attraction. Now tight denim wrapped the muscles of his thighs. Corded arms protruded from the sleeves of a T-shirt that outlined the muscles on his chest, covered his flat stomach and disappeared into his belt. She had to give up any remaining denials.

'I thought I'd blend into the crowd at the concert,' he replied, and his voice sounded husky to her. Maybe because she wanted it to sound husky, to know he found her as compelling as she found him.

'Close,' she assured him, trying to sound normal. 'You need to shave your beard and mousse your hair up instead of down.'

His gaze moved slowly down her body, pausing at her red sweater, moving on to the black slacks then up to her face again. He took a step closer to her, and his voice, when he finally spoke, was a hoarse whisper.

'The only thing you could possibly need – ' he blinked and suddenly stepped back, cleared his throat, then resumed speaking in more normal tones ' – is a coat. It'll be chilly tonight, and we'll probably have to walk a ways from the car.'

'Huh?' Allison blinked rapidly, trying to acclimate herself to the sudden, unexpected change in attitude.

'Cool,' Megan – obviously the reason for Brad's sudden change – approved as she bounced up to study first Brad then her mother. 'Mo-om, you look like you're going to work.'

'Your mom looks great,' Brad disagreed, draping one arm around Megan's shoulders and pulling her over for a hug. 'Let's get our coats and ear plugs and hit the road.'

Brad stepped back into the bathroom, emerging with a denim jacket and a beeper.

'Tool of the trade,' he said with a shrug as he clipped it onto his belt, then hid it with the jacket.

'You see, Mom?' Megan exclaimed triumphantly. 'Are you expecting a call from your agent about a new record contract?'

'If I get a call to do an album, you'll be the first to know.'

'All right!'

When they walked out of the house, Brad took Allison's key from her to lock the door, then wrapped one arm around her and one around Megan as they started down the walk. A glance up the street assured him of a witness, and he wanted the show to be worthwhile.

Allison followed the direction of his gaze, then looked nervously back at him. 'We have company,' she whispered, pulling away slightly.

He held her tighter, brushed a kiss across her smooth cheek and smiled.

As they pulled away from the curb in the big silver car, he watched the van in his rear-view mirror. Half a block behind them, it pulled out.

'Can you lose him?' Allison whispered.

'We don't want to,' Brad murmured. 'Move over a little closer so we can give him a good show.' He reached for her hand and encouraged her to scoot across the seat.

Although he had ulterior motives, he couldn't deny that having her sit next to him was a most pleasurable experience. Perhaps too pleasurable, he thought, reminding himself that, while other aspects of their relationship might have changed, he was still a cop who could never measure up to her financial or societal expectations.

Still, her thigh pressing against his felt awfully nice.

'Are we going to go backstage?' Megan demanded, her head suddenly popping between them from the back seat.

Brad cringed, feeling he'd let the girl down even though he'd been careful not to promise a backstage meeting. 'Not this time, I'm afraid.'

'Oooh,' she started to complain.

'If you're going to whine, we won't go at all,' Allison reprimanded.

Brad sighed. He supposed the next time he'd have to try to figure out a way to get backstage – call in favors, create favors, something.

Oh, jeez, he groaned inwardly. What was he thinking about, contemplating a 'next time'?

Allison shifted, and her leg moved against his. Lightning zinged upward along every one of his nerve endings.

Well, maybe if the next time wasn't too far in the future. He was, after all, tied to Allison for a while, so he might as well relax and enjoy it.

He laid his arm across the back of the seat for the benefit of the brown van, then dropped it to Allison's shoulders for his own.

When they were finally seated inside the Myriad Auditorium, Brad decided the ear-splitting concert might be quite enjoyable after all. In the crush of the crowd, he had no choice but to press his body against Allison's.

For the sake of comfort, he slid his arm around her waist. She leaned closer to tell him something he never did understand, perhaps because her warm lips brushed his ear in the process, and his blood surging through his veins in rhythm to the throbbing beat of the music drowned out her words.

Marijuana smoke hung heavily on the air, assaulting his nose. Maybe he'd inhaled too much. Maybe that would explain his body's hypersensitivity. But that was wishful thinking. He'd never been stoned, but as a cop he knew the symptoms involved more than unbearable arousal. Like it or not, he was going to have to credit Allison and not the marijuana smoke.

He shifted uncomfortably, trying to relieve the pressure and hide the increasingly obvious evidence. Tight jeans had not been a good choice for the evening.

He ventured a glance at Allison and found her watching him. She turned away abruptly but not before he'd seen the smoldering expression in her usually cool eyes. Damn! If she'd been aloof, indignant, angry, haughty – he could have handled that, might have even been able to get himself under control. But seeing a reflection of his own desire only made things worse.

The song being played ended with a crescendo of noises, and the overweight girl on his other side who'd been standing and clapping suddenly plopped onto the bench, almost in Brad's lap. As he reflexively jerked over, pushing against Allison, his hand reached out for balance and fell on her thigh. She didn't move, didn't react. The only change in her profile was a slight parting of her lips. He fancied he could feel her body heat through the fabric of her slacks. Slowly, reluctantly, he withdrew his hand.

Oh boy! Deciding to relax and enjoy the situation was all well and good, but he suspected he'd already let his enjoyment get entirely out of control, and the end was nowhere in sight.

By the time they arrived back at Allison's after the concert, all he could think about was getting into the house, seeing Megan off to bed, then carrying Allison up the stairs and making love to her for at least half the night.

Not that he had any intention of actually doing that, of course.

'We still have company,' Allison said, gazing down the street toward the ever-present van as Megan skipped ahead of them up the walk.

'Good,' Brad assured her. It was good. He couldn't afford to get carried away with all their actions being observed. He'd have to keep his hands off Allison.

214

He again took her key and opened the door.

'Oh, Brill,' Megan exclaimed, grabbing him around the neck as soon as he'd relocked the door from inside. 'I had the most awesome time ever!'

'I'm glad,' he said, returning the embrace and feeling a glow that he'd made the girl happy. She wasn't a bad kid; a little spoiled, but what else could be expected with a father like Douglas.

'It's nearly midnight. You'd better hit the sheets,' Allison advised.

She crinkled up her nose as though to protest, but then shrugged. 'Okay.' After giving her mother a hug, she barreled up the stairs.

'Does she ever walk?' Brad asked, watching her go.

'When she was ten months old, she took three steps before she learned to run.'

'Ah, the energy of youth.'

Megan's door closed with a resounding slam. They were alone. Only willpower and common sense kept his hands in his pockets.

'Interesting evening,' she said, standing scant inches away, well within arm's reach.

He searched her dark eyes for hidden meanings to that simple statement. 'Yes,' he agreed. 'Very interesting. I've never been to a rock concert before. It, uh, had its moments.' Like the feel of her thigh beneath his hand.

'Umm,' she agreed. 'A few. I'm glad we had the ear plugs, though.'

Brad nodded. 'Well, I guess I'd better go.'

He felt foolishly awkward as she moved with him toward the door. He was sixteen again and walking his date from the car to her parents' door, as though he had ten pairs of hands he didn't know what to do with. Then one of those twenty hands reached out of its own volition and touched her shoulder.

She stopped and turned her face to him. As if by mutual assent, following a prearranged agreement, they moved into each other's arms. He gave up every pretense of resistance the moment he felt her soft, rounded body against him. However foolish this might be, whatever the outcome, he had no choice but to continue. This attraction was totally detached from his brain, didn't acknowledge the impossibility of the situation.

His lips touched hers, found them every bit as tantalizing as he'd remembered from that first insane kiss. Her body touching his felt every bit as exciting as in the brief fantasies that had flitted through his mind in unguarded moments.

When she moaned and pressed closer to him, he lost any vestiges of control that might have been left. He tasted the sweetness of her lips, then thrust his tongue between them, into the warm dampness of her mouth. He touched her tongue, savored its silkiness, danced with it, then withdrew and thrust in again, making love to her mouth the way he wanted to make love to her body.

His hands molded her firm buttocks, crushing her against him, wanting her to know his desire for her, challenging her to back out now.

Leaving the soft entanglement of her lips, he raised his face from hers, pulled back enough to look at her. He noted with a surge of delight that he wasn't the only one who'd lost control. Fire danced in her dark eyes, and her lips remained wet and slightly parted, enticing him back.

'Allis?' he whispered, making the word a question, wanting to ask if she was sure, if she knew all the reasons they ought to stop. But he didn't put the questions into words. Like a roller coaster starting on its downward slide, he didn't think they could stop.

'You need to go,' she murmured, her slender hand reaching to the back of his neck, contradicting her own suggestions as she urged him down to her again. Her smoothly curved body pressed against him, her breasts against his chest, her groin against his.

He couldn't resist indulging in one more kiss. After that –

The floor above creaked, and he jumped back, releasing her as he gasped for breath and looked fearfully at the staircase.

'It's just the house settling,' Allison assured him.

'Not Megan?' He'd been so consumed with desire that he'd forgotten the possibility of the child walking in on them.

'She's down for the count. She won't leave that room until I drag her out in the morning.' Allison crossed to the door, turned back to gaze at him for a long moment, then reached for the light switch.

'Wait,' he cautioned, recovering some fragments of his scattered intelligence. 'We can't turn out the lights down here with your friend in the van watching.'

She blinked slowly. 'I guess I forgot about him.'

It would seem they'd both forgotten a lot of things – everything, in fact, except each other. The electric brightness of the room seemed suddenly stark and glaring, offering a heavy dose of reality. Reality reminded him that they were being observed, that her daughter was upstairs, that there could be no future for them.

But there was another reality – the way she looked with her perfect hair mussed and her cool eyes smoky with desire, her lips moist and swollen from their kisses, her rounded breasts rising and falling beneath the clinging sweater. Reality was how much he needed her.

He felt awkward again, unsure of what to say or do. Because it mattered, he realized. What he said and did, how Allison reacted, were important.

She cleared her throat. 'Well,' she said, and it hit him that the moment was slipping away.

In two strides he crossed the room and pulled her

218

into his arms. 'So we leave the lights on down here while we go upstairs.'

He pushed aside the neck of her sweater and kissed her baby-soft skin, running his tongue over the smooth surface. The faint floral fragrance he'd noticed before drifted into his senses. She seemed to taste of summer flowers.

Allison moaned involuntarily when she felt Brad's mouth on her neck. For a minute there, she'd been afraid he was going to leave, and she needed him to stay. Sitting with her body pressed against his at the concert had been excruciating, wonderful agony, and she'd thought she could leave it at that until he kissed her.

As Brad pushed down the turtleneck of her sweater, she cursed her lack of forethought in wearing it. A blouse with buttons would have been a better choice.

'Upstairs,' he whispered, covering her face with soft kisses.

She turned and started across the room in front of him, but he wrapped his arms around her from behind, cupping her breasts and nuzzling the back of her neck.

'I don't think I can turn you loose long enough to climb those stairs,' he growled in her ear.

The idea that he wanted her as passionately, as illogically, as she wanted him, made her knees weak. For an instant she considered sinking to the floor and pulling him with her.

But he urged her onto the first stair. 'Maybe,' he said, lifting her sweater, 'if we make the climb itself rewarding enough – '

She raised her arms and he slid the sweater off, tossing it to the floor below. 'You're crazy,' she gasped, laughing, as they took the next step and he ran his hands over her bare ribs and stomach, skirting maddeningly close to but never touching her breasts. She ached to take his hands and guide them.

As they moved upward, he unhooked her bra and tossed it over the rail, then slid his arms around her from behind to cup her breasts, caressing them, running his thumbs over her nipples.

At the next step she turned to face him, peeled off his jacket and reached for his T-shirt.

'Uh-uh,' he discouraged, leaning over to kiss her again. 'One thing per stair or we'll never make it to the top.'

She leaned her head backward in ecstasy when he trailed kisses down her bare chest, ending with a flick of his tongue across her nipple.

Quickly they moved upward, and she yanked his T-shirt over his head as he leaned forward obligingly. His chest was covered with a mat of light brown, curly hair that failed to conceal his well-defined pectorals.

He pulled her to him, and she reveled in the feel

of his springy hairs tickling her bare breasts and of the solidness of his chest as he held her tighter. His tongue curled inside her ear, and she gasped as the tantalizing waves shot through her body.

'We could stop now,' he teased. 'You could lean forward and hang onto the stair rail. I could – '

Laughing, she reached for his belt buckle.

'Oh, no,' he protested. 'My turn.'

By the time they reached the next step, he was peeling off her slacks. 'A curse on panty hose,' he groaned, caressing her nylon-covered hips. She couldn't have agreed with him more.

Scrambling upward, she reached again for his belt. He had to help her, retrieving his pager and pulling off his shoes so he could slip off the jeans. Laughing, she tossed them to the floor below, then looked back at him, delighting in the sight of the bulging outline of his manhood pulsing beneath red bikini briefs.

'Red?' she teased, stroking him with one finger.

He closed his eyes and groaned but then, when she covered him with her entire hand and squeezed, he grasped her arm and stilled her. 'I don't seem to have much control tonight,' he warned, his voice husky.

Well, that was fine because neither did she. In fact, she was becoming more wanton by the moment, a trait she'd never before noticed in herself. But then, she'd never before known this feeling of imminent explosion if she couldn't have Brad inside her soon to satisfy her needs.

On the landing he peeled off her nylons and finally touched her. 'Oh, Allis,' he groaned, 'do you know how good you feel, how warm and wet?'

She pulled him toward her bedroom, and they collapsed together, not bothering to pull down the comforter. She tried to wrap her legs around him, but he abruptly sat up on the edge of the bed.

'Socks,' he complained, fumbling with them for what seemed an eternity.

At last he returned to her, lying beside her, running his hands along the length of her body, driving her wild. Again she reached for his hardness, but he slid from her grasp and began to kiss her, moving from her throat down her chest, around her breasts. Finally, when she was writhing shamelessly, he slid his tongue upward, settled on her nipple and sucked.

Sensations jolted through her, all the way down to the center of her womanhood. If he didn't love her soon, she would surely die.

'Brad,' she gasped, 'please – '

'I've dreamed about doing this,' he mumbled, switching from one breast to the other. His hand slid down her stomach, caressed her, bringing her to a sudden, unexpected peak of excitation. But it wasn't enough.

Finally he slid over her, and joined his body with

hers in a powerful thrust. She surged upward to meet him, finding a sense of completeness, of wholeness in the union.

'Oh, sweetheart,' he whispered, pausing and leaning down to kiss her again.

Then with a groan he raised his mouth from hers and began to move once more. For an instant she gazed at him, delighting in the combination of passion and softness she could see in his face as the moonlight slanted through the window.

Unable to wait any longer, she closed her eyes, focusing all her senses, matching his frenzied rhythm. Suddenly the ecstasy that centered in one area began to swell, to flow throughout her body – even, she was sure, into Brad's body. The darkness around her exploded into a thousand bursts of light. An instant later when he cried out and pulsed inside her, she knew another kind of ecstasy.

He collapsed on her, and for a while she reveled in the drained feeling of total satisfaction. Gradually her breathing began to slow and her brain to clear, but she still didn't want to let him go. She delighted in his heaviness atop her, the continuation of their joining.

When he rolled off, she missed the weight, but it was okay – he continued to hold her.

'Allis,' he murmured, breathing on the top of her head, fluttering her hair.

'Brad,' she said, tilting her head back and smiling.

'I don't have the energy to say anything else,' he teased, his fingers tracing soft patterns on her back.

'Umm. You can do that as long as you want,' she said, her hypersensitive skin thrilling to his touch.

'As long as I want?' He chuckled. 'I could stroke you forever. But we'd get awfully hungry after the first three days, I suspect.'

She cuddled closer, twining her fingers in his chest hairs, trying to hang onto the glorious feelings. She knew he'd have to leave soon. They'd go downstairs and pick up their clothes then part decorously at the door and go back into their own separate worlds. But for this time their worlds had briefly, miraculously touched, she luxuriated in the delicious feelings.

He kissed the top of her head, nuzzled her hair. 'I've wanted to make love to you for so long.'

'Me, too,' she answered. 'Even when I thought you were a bum. Not that I ever really thought you were a bum.'

He laughed softly. 'You thought I was a plumber, and I thought you were – well, not what you are. Which goes to show, to quote the old adage, appearances can be deceiving.'

His hand moved slowly from her waist to her hip. With one finger he tilted her face up to his and kissed her again, softly, then more urgently. Against her stomach Allison could feel his desire returning, a match for her own.

They both jumped when his beeper shrieked insistently.

'Ignore it,' she whispered against his lips.

'I can't,' he groaned, rolling to the side of the bed to shut it off. 'Where's your phone? This won't take a minute. Save my place.'

But when he returned to her, his mood had changed.

'Dealey's dead,' he told her. 'Murdered.'

CHAPTER 12

Allison pulled herself to a sitting position in bed. Tentatively she laid a comforting hand on Brad's shoulder. In contrast to the intimacy of a moment before, she suddenly felt as though he was a remote stranger.

'I'm sorry,' she said.

He placed his hand over hers, returning some of himself.

'You get used to this sort of thing when you're a cop. It comes with the territory.' He retrieved his 'homeless' clothes from the bathroom and began pulling them on.

She didn't believe he was 'used to this sort of thing', but didn't know how to ease his pain when he wouldn't admit to feeling any. 'Can I make you some coffee to take with you?'

'Yes. No. Do you have any instant?'

'Sure.' She swung out of bed and pulled on her own clothes.

A few minutes later, blue jeans and T-shirt in one

hand and a cup of steaming coffee in the other, he paused just inside the front door. He kissed her briefly, distractedly, his mind obviously elsewhere.

'I'll call you,' he said, and Allison's heart squeezed painfully at the trite words.

'You damn well better,' she said archly. 'We have a deal. If Megan weren't asleep upstairs, I'd be going with you. I guess I'd better at least call Rick and get him over there.'

'You can't call Rick,' Brad pointed out. 'How would you explain your source of information?'

Good question. Unfortunately, Allison didn't have a good answer.

'You told him,' Brad exclaimed when she hesitated. 'After our discussion, after I trusted you with my life, you went right out and told another damned reporter!'

'He had your license number! He'd have found out anyway. This way I was able to swear him to secrecy.'

'Great. And I suppose he'll swear everyone he tells to secrecy, too. Will the story on the ten o'clock news swear all the viewers to secrecy?'

Allison touched his shoulder imploringly. 'Brad, you don't understand.'

He shrugged her hand off. 'I understand we had a deal, and I kept my end, but you didn't. I trusted you.' His hazel eyes that had been smoky with desire only a few minutes earlier were now flinty as he glared down at her. 'I even went out of my way to help you.'

Her head tilted up indignantly. 'I didn't ask you to fix my roof, but I'll be more than happy to pay you for it.'

'That's not what I'm talking about. I'm referring to your Dr Doug. Ah, just forget it.'

Juggling his burdens, he opened the door and stepped out, but then turned back with a phony grin plastered on his face. 'Smile for the nice photographer,' he grated.

She looked up the street at the ever-present watcher and swore softly. Brad waved cheerily. She closed the door, making a real effort not to slam it, then leaned against it.

What a jerk! What an unfair, belligerent jerk. She'd handled the situation with Rick in the only way possible, but he hadn't even tried to understand.

He'd made love to her and then rejected her without even listening to her side of the story. It would serve him right if she did break the damn story. He'd as much as said their deal was off. She desperately needed the story, she'd earned it, and it would seem there was no reason not to run it. If it screwed up his job, that was tough. Not running it was screwing up hers.

But even as the pain she felt at his angry words urged her on, even as she justified the action, she knew she wouldn't betray him. Much as he deserved it and much as she needed the story, she'd given her word.

With a muttered curse at her misplaced sense of honor, she strode across the room, snatched up the phone and punched in Rick's number. The ringing seemed to go on for an eternity before his sleepy voice finally came over the line.

'Grab your equipment and get downtown,' she instructed. 'There's been another murder.'

'Huh? What? Allison?'

'Of course it's me. Who else would call you to talk about murder in the middle of the night? Remember that guy that overdosed? Well, he's the victim. Dealey somebody.'

'Where?' Rick asked, his voice losing its confusion.

'I don't know. The same general area as the others, I suppose. It can't be that hard to find with all the cops there.'

'Where are you? How'd you find this out?'

'I'm at home, and you know how I found out. Just remember, you gave your word to keep quiet about everything. No pictures of Brad and not a word to or about him.'

Rick's sigh came heavily over the wire. 'Yeah, yeah, yeah. I know.'

'Okay, so get on over there, fast. I suppose you'll have to take another reporter with you. I can't leave Megan.'

Rick hesitated. 'Why don't I get as much as possible on film, and you can do an intro and standup later?'

'Thanks, but you know that won't work. Someone needs to be there to ask questions and take notes. Call – call Tracy.' The last word struggled out, barely audible.

'Tracy the Twit? Are you trying to be funny?'

'Hey, she needs all the help she can get to keep her job.'

'Have you been drinking?'

'Not yet, but give me fifteen minutes.'

'I'll call you as soon as I get back.'

'Thanks.'

Allison hung up the phone and poured a glass of wine. A little alcohol couldn't make this evening's confusion any worse.

She flopped into a chair at the dining table and contemplated the ivory-tinted liquid in the dime-store wine glass. A year ago the glass would have been crystal. But what the hell, she'd been hearing lately that the lead in crystal leeched out into the wine.

'To the benefits of being poor,' she muttered, raising the glass in an imaginary toast, taking a healthy slug.

And at the rate she was going, she was likely to stay poor. Not only had she continued to cover for Brad at her own expense when he didn't deserve it, but she'd even given away her scoop on the night's murder to Tracy the Twit of all people.

She wasn't exactly acting in accordance with any known formula for success.

As he drove across town as fast as he dared, Brad tugged at his hair and beard, fluffing them out.

'Stupid,' he muttered, berating himself for his recent actions. He'd trusted Allison, felt sorry for her, tried to help her. And she'd probably blow his cover tomorrow. Not to mention that tonight he'd play hell hiding this bloody car he'd borrowed for her benefit. Stupid, stupid, stupid.

But it sure would have made it easier to be mad at her if she hadn't felt so good in his arms, if their lovemaking hadn't been so incredible that it put his wildest fantasies to shame. He gave his beard an extra hard, painful tug trying to erase the unwelcome memories, trying to keep things in perspective, trying not to get excited again just thinking about her.

By the time he got close enough to check out the murder scene, after parking and running half a mile, the investigation was well underway. Steve's huge frame loomed over the others.

Calling up his role, Brad stuck his hands in his pockets and slouched up the street.

'Hey, you,' Steve called.

'I didn't do nothing,' Brad replied, slowing his walk.

'I know you didn't. But aren't you the guy who identified that overdose last week?'

'Maybe.'

'Come on over here. I think this might be the same man.'

Brad shuffled over, his reluctance no act. He dreaded to see what lay under the sheet. As he knelt down, Steve pulled it back.

Anger rose in Brad's throat as he looked at the still form of the harmless old man, anger that had nothing to do with his 'job'. Dealey's life hadn't been much, but no one had the right to take it from him like this. He'd even been trying to improve himself. Since his last bout in the hospital, he hadn't taken a drink.

Brad's fists clenched. He would get the monster who'd done this.

He stood up and faced Steve. His emotions must have shown, because Steve scowled at him.

'It's the same guy,' Brad said curtly. 'Dealey. I don't know the rest, I don't even know if that's a first or a last name.'

Turning to leave, he was met by a microphone held by a young, blonde girl.

'Did you know the deceased?' she asked.

Lowering his head, Brad pushed past her but not before he'd noticed that her cameraman, from

Channel 7, had red hair. Allison had obviously tipped him off, though at the moment Rick's video camera wasn't pointed in his direction.

Before that could change, he strode rapidly away, not caring if his walk was inconsistent with his character. When Allison blew his cover, it wouldn't matter anyway.

Even though the next day was Sunday, Brad decided, he'd be down here. Time had suddenly become critical. He wanted to do as much as he could before he was exposed, and he wanted to reach the people while their memories were still fresh.

And now he had a legitimate reason to ask leading questions. Everyone knew he and Dealey had been friends.

When he entered the New Hope Shelter the next morning, the place was crowded, and everyone was talking. That was good. He was ready to listen.

Most of the people were clustered on one side, and Jean's head rose from the middle of the group, looking downward, talking to someone. He started toward her since Allison's suspicions of the woman constituted the only lead he had.

As he approached her, however, he saw the person Jean was talking to, the woman whose form had been hidden by Jean's bulk. Holding a microphone between them, Allison looked up at Jean.

Scanning the vicinity, Brad located Rick a couple of rows up, kneeling on one of the benches, video camera trained on the pair.

Trying to get close enough to hear, Brad insinuated himself between two men on the row immediately behind Jean, using her as a shield from the camera. Allison's eyes flicked toward him briefly, but she gave no other indication that she'd seen him.

'I wasn't born on the streets,' Jean was saying. She fiddled with a necklace of gaudy red stones set in goldtone nuggets, and Brad realized Allison had likely bribed her into this interview with a few pieces of colored glass. 'I had a home, a nice home, and then I didn't.'

'I'm sure there was more to it than that,' Allison prompted. 'When did you leave home? Where are your parents now?'

'I don't know. Dead, I guess. I left a long time ago. There was this boy, and we ran away to get married. He paid attention to me. Most men, if you're big, they don't like you. They want little women, like you.' She suddenly glared at Allison, whose average size did look small in comparison.

Allison shrugged casually. 'Not necessarily. My husband left me for a younger, taller woman last year.'

Jean's expression immediately turned compassionate, and she patted Allison's shoulder.

Brad had to hand it to Allison. She'd sacrifice anything, even pride, for the sake of a story.

'Don't you worry. You're short and pretty. You'll find somebody else,' Jean assured her.

'So what happened to your husband?' Allison continued.

'He just took off one day. We was moving up to Kansas, had all our stuff in a pickup, and we pulled into this truck stop. I went to the bathroom, and while I was gone, he just took off.'

'Did you ever see him again?'

'Sure did. Went to his funeral. He couldn't take off from me then.'

Brad could see Allison's knuckles whiten as she clutched the microphone. She cast a quick glance back at him, and he read his own thoughts in her eyes. Her next question echoed the one in his mind.

'How did he die?' she asked.

'I reckon his heart stopped beating.' Jean slapped her thigh and laughed.

Allison laughed weakly with her.

'What was his name?' she asked when Jean regained control.

'What do you care? He's dead,' she snapped.

'So, okay, where did you go from there?'

'I worked,' Jean answered. 'I worked a lot of places. Sometimes I waitressed and sometimes I clerked.'

'Do you ever work now?'

'Sometimes. People don't like big women. I don't care. I get enough to eat. I don't want to talk any more right now. Tell that man to quit taking my picture.'

'Okay, Rick, cut it,' she called to him. Reaching for Jean's hand, she shook it firmly. 'Thanks for talking to me. I hope things get better for you, and – I appreciate the kind words. I'll try not to worry about losing my husband. He wasn't a very good one, anyway.'

She sounded so sincere, Brad had to remind himself it was all part of her act to pry out a story.

Jean beamed at her. 'Maybe we can talk some other time.'

'That would be great.'

Jean's eyes scanned the group, and she motioned to someone a couple of rows away. 'Larry, you talk to my friend for a while. Larry's an inventor.'

A short, bald man with a red-veined nose hesitantly moved through the group, and Jean got up to give him her seat.

'What have you invented?' Allison asked, extending the mike.

Brad moved away to follow Jean, to see what she might know about the murder.

'Too bad about Dealey,' he said, taking a seat next to her in an otherwise empty corner across the room.

She stared at him without expression. 'He quit drinking.'

'I know.'

'It never lasts.'

Brad wasn't sure if she was referring to Dealey's problem with addiction or her own.

'I miss him,' he said, and it was the truth.

She nodded agreement, then turned to face the wall. The conversation was over.

After a couple more questions which were met with silence, Brad gave up and moved on to the others. Sometime, somewhere, somebody must have seen something.

Though Allison had to concentrate to get the most out of her interviews, a portion of her mind and field of vision stubbornly latched onto Brad's every movement. As dedicated as he was to his job, she should have known he'd be here, even on a weekend. With the way things were going, what else could she have expected?

This day, which began with Douglas's calling at seven to arrange to pick up Megan, would not rate a gold star on her calendar. The only bright spot so far was the fact that her in-depth story was going even better than she had dared hope. Jean's endorsement had smoothed her way with the others, and the material she was getting was great.

However, even that had its downside. After learning of Jean's past and her ex-husband's death, she was more suspicious than ever that Jean might be the murderer, and she didn't want her to be. Her heart went out to the large woman. She'd hate to see her stuck in a prison cell for the rest of her life with no pretty things to amuse her.

When Rick signaled that they had to leave, Allison felt she still had potential participants.

'Can I come back tomorrow?' she asked, requesting their permission.

'Maybe we can work you into our schedules,' someone quipped, and everyone laughed.

A good sign, Allison thought.

At the door, her eyes again sought Brad, and she saw that he was watching her. He turned away immediately, and she preceded Rick outside.

'Are you sleeping with that guy?' Rick demanded.

'Why do you ask that? Just because I can see his point about protecting his identity?'

Rick grinned broadly. 'That part I attribute to the fact that you haven't been in this business long enough to toughen up. No, the reason I think you're sleeping with him is because you look at him like you're starving and he's filet mignon, and he looks just as dopey.'

'Speaking of food, want to come over for dinner tonight after we get off?' She changed the subject eagerly, but Rick's description of Brad's expression lifted her spirits minutely in spite of her common sense that told her she hated Brad.

'Sounds good. I'll pick up some steaks. What time?'

'Whenever. I've got to leave the station as early as I can. Douglas came after Megan this morning, and he's bringing her back early, about six. I need to be there.'

But when she got home at five minutes till, Megan was already sprawled in front of the television, munching on a bag of potato chips. Allison switched off the set and snatched the bag as she passed.

'How long have you been home?' She kicked off her heels and made her way into the kitchen on stocking feet.

'A long time,' Megan answered, though that could mean anything from ten minutes to all day. 'I'm hungry.'

'Uncle Rick's coming over with steaks to grill. Why did Daddy bring you back so early?' Allison threw the chips onto the top shelf of the pantry then checked her potatoes to see which ones had the fewest sprouts.

Megan bounced into the kitchen and levered herself onto the counter. 'He lost a book and he thought maybe he'd left it here, so we came over to look.'

Allison laid the potatoes carefully in the sink. Making an effort to breathe, move and speak normally, she asked, 'Your father went through our house looking for something?'

'A book. I did most of the looking. He said I had

to since it wasn't his house anymore, but I told him you wouldn't mind.'

Cautious Douglas. Probably called his lawyer to see just how much he could get away with. 'Did he find the book?'

'Nope.' She swung her feet, thumping the cabinet.

'Don't do that. What was the name of this book?'

'I don't remember. One of those big ones about medicine. Can I have my chips back?'

'Will you settle for an apple?'

'I guess so.'

Allison pulled an apple from the refrigerator and handed it with a trembling hand to her daughter.

She didn't think there was anything in the house that Douglas could use against her, but she'd come to fear his every action.

Then again, maybe he wasn't looking for something in the house, but rather leaving something – something incriminating.

'Hop down and show me everywhere you and Daddy looked.'

'Why? It's not there.'

'Because – because I'll give you back your chips if you do.'

With a martyred sigh that expressed her opinion of adult vagaries, Megan slid off the counter and began opening drawers. Allison checked each one carefully, though she wasn't sure what she was looking for.

Megan then led the way into the living room.

'The sofa, the chair, bookshelves,' she said.

Allison's indignation peaked when Megan pointed upstairs. 'Your bedroom.'

'What!'

'That's where he said it was the last time he saw it. After all, it did used to be his bedroom, too.'

Allison's search turned up nothing until she peered under her bed. A large white sock from Brad's concert disguise, undoubtedly kicked there by him in their excitement last night, was stretched out neatly. There could be little doubt Douglas had seen it. And just when she was sure things couldn't get any worse.

'Come on, sweetheart,' she said, draping one arm around Megan's neck. 'Let's go get your chips.'

'Mom, why are you so upset about Dad being in our house? He used to live here.'

'But he doesn't anymore, and I'd rather he didn't come in. It's sort of like your room. I don't come in there without being invited.'

'It's okay. I invited him.'

Allison ground her teeth and reminded herself that Megan was only a child. 'I'd really appreciate it if you wouldn't do that again. I don't go to his new home while he's not there.'

Megan shrugged. 'Yeah, okay.'

It was probably the best response she could hope for without upsetting her daughter.

Back downstairs Megan climbed onto the counter again, stuffed her mouth with chips and bubbled excitedly about the concert and about her day with Dad and Bonnie.

'Don't talk with your mouth full,' Allison ordered mechanically as she scrubbed the potatoes.

But her mind wasn't on Megan's chatter. She would have loved to be able to call Brad and ask if she had any legal recourse against Douglas, but she couldn't call him, and it probably didn't matter anyway. Douglas always covered his bases.

She was scrutinizing a rusty head of lettuce, trying to determine if she could salvage three salads, when the words 'Dad' and 'Brill' in close proximity caught her attention.

'What did you just say?'

'You never listen to me. Dad wanted me to take him to Brill's house, but I don't know where Brill lives. Then he asked me all kinds of questions.'

'Like what?'

'About the concert and Brill's car and what Brill does for a living. I told him Brill's a rock star.'

'And what did he say?'

Megan shrugged. 'He asked me all sorts of dopey questions about whether Brill smoked cigarettes or a pipe and whether his nose ever bled and did he have a lot of cash. Why do adults think all musicians do drugs?'

'Because a lot of them do,' Allison replied, sud-

242

denly understanding what was going on. The appearance of that expensive silver car driven by a man who looked like a bum, their trip to the rock concert, Megan's insistence that Brad was a musician – Douglas had been searching her house for drugs. He hadn't found that, but he had found a man's sock under her bed. Knowing Douglas, he'd doubtless, somehow, be able to get a lot of mileage out of that.

'Finish tearing up this lettuce,' she instructed her daughter. 'I've got to make a phone call.'

Allison's heart raced as she pounded upstairs to the privacy of her bedroom phone. She had to find out whose car Brad had borrowed.

When he failed to answer at home, she called his parents' house. This was no time to stand on ceremony. His mother answered and immediately put Brad on the line.

'Who does that silver car belong to?' she demanded.

'I told you. The father of a friend of mine. Why?'

'Douglas thinks you're on drugs. He came over here and searched the house today and found your sock under my bed.'

'You let him search the house? Why didn't you call me? He can't do that.'

'I didn't let him. I wasn't here. He conned Megan into helping him.'

Brad swore softly but potently.

'Do you do drugs?' she demanded. 'Do I have

243

something to worry about here? That's all I need, for him to be able to prove my daughter's been exposed to drugs.'

'Of course I don't do drugs. I'm a cop, remember?' His voice was rising, and she knew he was getting angry.

'The cops in movies are always doing drugs,' she defended herself.

'We're not in the movies, and I seldom even take an aspirin.'

'Okay, I'm sorry. I didn't really think you did, I just had to ask. But I've got to know who owns that damned car. Is it a musician? Is it someone who does drugs?'

'No, no. Don't worry about that car. The owner is completely above reproach, trust me.'

Allison ground her teeth again. If the evening kept up at this pace, her dental bills were going to be out of sight. 'Then why won't you tell me?' She knew she sounded frantic. She was frantic.

'Because I want you to be innocent when Douglas finds out. Believe me, he'll drop this drug nonsense as soon as he runs that license plate, and that'll probably be tomorrow or the next day, depending on how efficient his detective is.'

'Don't underestimate Douglas. When he locks onto something, he's like a bulldog. He'll be after you, and I don't think you can count on him to keep your secret.'

Brad's voice turned sarcastic. 'I appreciate your concern, especially since you're my major leak.'

The man was really insufferable! 'I'm keeping your damned secret because you and I have a deal. But you don't have anything Douglas wants, so he's going to be pretty hard to deal with. Not that I care if he blows your cover, except then I wouldn't have an exclusive on the story.'

'I promised you an exclusive, and you'll get it. I keep my promises. And while we're on the subject, what did you find out today? Sharing information is part of the deal, too.'

'You heard what I found out. Jean's past is a little suspect. Beyond that, all I uncovered was a lot of human interest, and we know you're not concerned with something of that nature.'

She could have sworn she heard his teeth grinding now. Good.

'You're doing a human interest story now?'

'That's right. These are real people. They love and hurt and dream dreams, just like us.'

'Not to mention that you didn't get to cover the latest murder, but this little piece will be very timely.'

'Timing is important. So is skill, and so is having something to tell. I think these people have a story worth telling.'

Brad's sigh was clearly audible. 'Whatever. But you didn't pick up anything else to do with the case?'

'No.'

'It might be a good idea if you let me look over your footage. I may be able to spot something you missed. I've been doing this a little longer than you have.'

Much as she wanted to disagree, Allison couldn't. He was right.

'How do you propose to do that? Coming by the station probably wouldn't be a good idea.'

'Bring a tape home with you tomorrow. I'll come by after you get off work and we'll go over it together.'

'All right,' she grudgingly agreed. It was, after all, the only logical way to do it.

The beep of another call interrupted them.

'Hang on a second,' Allison requested, flicking the button.

'Hello?'

'Don't you have any pride?' a vaguely familiar female voice shrieked. 'He's my husband, not yours. Stop dragging on his pants leg and let him come home.'

Allison froze for a brief moment. Did Brad have a wife after all? 'Who are you calling? I think you have the wrong number.'

'Oh, no. I have your number, you pathetic, middle-aged fool. Did you think Douglas wouldn't tell me what you try to do every time he brings Megan home?'

Megan had told Douglas that Allison wanted to kill him? 'I never actually tried to do it. I only fantasized about it and maybe mentioned it a couple of times.' Megan was really going to have to learn not to repeat things.

'You're just using that poor little girl to try to get him back. Let me talk to my husband.'

'Get him back?' Allison started to laugh, then thought better of it. She could reassure Bonnie that she didn't want Douglas back, and he hadn't been at her house for some time, but hearing Bonnie so distraught felt kind of good, especially after the girl's opening insults. 'Eat dirt.' She clicked Brad back onto the line.

'Douglas's new wife,' she explained. 'It would appear he's using me as an excuse for his absences from home.'

'You think he's playing around again?'

'Could be. I guess old habits are hard to break. Then again, he may be up the street watching my house.'

'Probably not. He can pay someone to do that.'

'Which reminds me, whose car will you be in tomorrow night?'

Brad chuckled. 'I don't know. I could probably borrow one from an informant, maybe a drug dealer or a pimp. Give Douglas something to sink his teeth into.'

'That's not funny.' But she laughed anyway.

Bonnie's distress had calmed her down and restored her good humor.

'I'll pick up some barbecue on my way over tomorrow.'

'No, don't do that.'

'You've fed me often enough.'

'And you've done more than enough work around here to justify those meals. Not to mention the concert tickets. I still owe you.'

'I'm bringing barbecue. You can eat it or not. Goodbye.'

She cradled the receiver and stared at the phone for a moment. With every encounter, she was becoming more involved with him, giving him more control of her life. When she released her story was up to Brad. He refused to tell her whose car he'd driven, the name of the person Douglas would now be thinking she'd spent the night with. He'd just made plans for her evening tomorrow, even what they'd have for dinner.

Yet in spite of all that she was looking forward to seeing him. And that, she thought, was the ultimate, most frightening form of control.

CHAPTER 13

Wearing his torn blue jeans and denim jacket, Brad pedaled up to Allison's front porch on a bicycle the next evening.

'Let Dr Doug's friend chew on that for a while,' he said, when she opened the door.

Stepping inside, he pulled a large, crushed white bag from his backpack. The spicy odor of barbecue rose tantalizingly. Brad studied the condition of the sack for a second, then assured her, 'It's ribs. They're sturdy.'

'Did you ride all the way over here?' Allison asked. As she moved past him, closing the door against the chilly evening, she caught a faint woodsy smell separate from the barbecue. Was he wearing cologne?

For the viewing of a video tape, she'd chosen an ivory silk jumpsuit and he was wearing cologne. It should be an interesting evening.

'I confess to being a wimp,' Brad said as she turned back to him. 'My truck's parked about a mile away.'

Megan rushed in to hug him and take the bag. 'It smells terrific! I'll get some plates.'

Allison stared after her daughter in bewilderment. 'She volunteered to do something? This is a first.'

'They usually grow up eventually, or so I hear.'

'You never had any children?' she asked, taking his arm as they ambled toward the dining room.

'Nope. I was only married for six months. My wife couldn't handle my job, and she sure didn't want to subject a kid to it. But that's okay. My brother in Texas has five, so he's taken care of passing along the Malone genes.'

'I didn't know you'd been married.' Or that he had a brother and five nieces and nephews. In fact, she really didn't know much about Brad Malone, which seemed a little odd considering their intimacy – the physical as well as the way their lives had somehow become intertwined.

He shrugged. 'No reason you should. I haven't seen my ex in years.'

'Maybe one day I'll be able to say that about mine,' she said, then immediately regretted bringing the jerk into the conversation. Just thinking about him put a damper on the evening. 'But for now,' she continued brightly, 'we'll forget him and concentrate on solving this crime.'

'What crime?' Megan asked, arranging a huge

slab of barbecued ribs and a sack of French fries on the dining table.

Brad glared at Allison. 'Did you swear her to secrecy, too?' he muttered in her ear.

'The crime of your father sifting through our home, my dear, with you as an accomplice.'

'Aw, Mom.'

Some time later when the rib bones were bare and only a couple of greasy fries remained, Allison sat back with a groan. 'Those were the best ribs I've ever eaten. Where did you get them?'

'A friend. He does this out behind his house in a part of town you'd probably be afraid to go into.'

'Sounds to me like another human interest story.'

'Uh-uh.' Brad shook his head. 'You make him famous and I won't be able to afford to go there any more.'

She pushed her chair back. 'Come on and see my latest work. Megan, would you clean off the table, please?' She braced herself for an argument.

'Okay. But don't start till I get there.'

'It's got to be your influence,' Allison whispered to Brad as they left the dining room. 'Either that or she's up to something with all this obedience.'

Brad grinned, looking pleased but a little embarrassed. 'She's just going through a tough time in her life.'

'Yes,' Allison agreed. 'A long, tough time.

Twelve years so far and, I calculate, about another thirteen to go.'

She popped a tape into the VCR.

Brad laughed, then tugged at his beard. 'I think I'd better wash up before we settle down to watch the show. This damned beard attracts things like barbecue sauce.'

Allison took his hand. 'Come on upstairs, then. I'll get you a towel.'

'I can't wait to get rid of the blasted thing,' he grumbled as they climbed the stairs. 'No wonder the hippies took drugs. It was the only way they could stand to have a beard.'

'I don't even know what you look like without it.' She handed him a towel from the linen closet.

'I make children cry and grown men run in fear. That's why I'm a cop.'

As she started out of the bathroom, Brad took her arm and gently pulled her back. His eyes searched her face, evidently finding the desire she'd thought she was hiding because he smiled and lowered his lips to hers.

She ought to push him away, pay him back for being so nasty to her.

Maybe next time. After all, sex didn't necessarily constitute signing away all rights to your life. Not any more. Not in the nineties.

Her arms wrapped around him, and her body molded itself to his. This kiss was more leisurely,

252

not quite so desperate as the ones they'd shared Saturday night, but the effect was just as consuming.

'Do you think Megan would notice if we stayed in the bathroom for two hours?' he whispered against her lips.

'Using the psychic abilities all children possess, just at the crucial moment, she'd bang on the door demanding we come see her highest video-game score.'

'What time does she go to bed?'

'Right after the news.'

His hands roamed down her back, cupped her hips. 'Maybe I can wait.'

She was almost out the door when his voice stopped her. 'I'm sorry I didn't trust you,' he said softly.

'I'm sorry you didn't, too,' she replied, then relented. 'I'm sorry I had to tell Rick. I really had no choice.'

He nodded and turned on the faucet.

When they were all three congregated in the living room, Allison started her tape. Megan joined them on the sofa, trying to appear blasé, but Brad couldn't miss the obvious delight she expressed at seeing her mother's image on the television screen.

He watched intently as the interviews played out, hoping against hope that somebody would say something to provide a clue. After the third interview, he heard a tiny sniff and looked over to see Megan's face shiny with tears. Allison did have the ability to bring out the individual characters of these people, showing them as something other than stereotypes.

When she finally switched off the tape, he wasn't any closer to solving the murders, but his respect for her work had risen dramatically. She wasn't just a hack reporter, trying to get the most spectacular story on the evening news. She had a talent for this sort of thing.

'Well?' she queried when he didn't speak immediately.

'Those people don't have anywhere to live?' Megan asked quietly. 'No new clothes to wear?'

'Nor any closet to keep them in,' Allison replied. 'So can we hear a little less complaining when you don't get every new item of clothing that hits the department stores?'

'Maybe I could give them some of my old clothes.'

'That's a good idea,' Allison approved, shooting Brad a look that dared him to disagree.

Brad could just see the street people wandering around in Spandex mini-skirts and Madonna T-shirts, but he hid his smile. She was on the right track.

'A very well-done piece,' Brad complimented Allison. If she could reach even a privileged

254

twelve-year-old, she'd done a great job.

'See anything interesting?'

He shook his head. 'But save it. I'd like to study . . . uh – ' At Megan's curious gaze, he decided to reword his thought. 'I'd like to watch it again.'

Megan smiled at him. 'Mom's pretty good, isn't she?'

'Yes,' he agreed. 'Yes, she is.'

Allison pulled the tape from the machine and handed it to him. 'I made this copy for you. We edited the original down to a two-minute segment for the news tonight.' She grimaced. 'Actually, butchered is a better word than edited.'

The doorbell rang and Allison excused herself to answer it.

'I want to see your sleazy boy friend. We know he's in there.'

Recognizing Doug's oily voice, Brad moved quietly up behind Allison.

'Get off my porch and take your sleazy friend with you,' she ordered. 'Go back up the street and sit in your van and live vicariously.'

She started to slam the door, but Brad stepped forward and grabbed it from her.

'Dr Doug, old man! How you been?' He opened the screen and stuck out his hand.

Douglas clasped the proffered hand automatically, then dropped it and wiped his own on his slacks. 'You're not Ethan Jameson,' he sputtered.

'Thanks for the information, but I already knew that.'

Douglas turned to his companion, a stocky man with thin, greasy hair. 'Is that him?' He pointed to Brad.

The man nodded.

'Ethan Jameson is seventy years old,' Douglas declared.

'Actually, he turned sixty-eight last June. But he does look a couple of years older. Too much of the good life, I guess.'

'Just what is your name?'

Megan squeezed between Brad and Allison. 'Daddy, this is Brill. I told you about him.'

'Brill. What kind of name is Brill? What's your last name?'

'Daddy,' Megan replied in disgust, 'Madonna doesn't have a last name, Cher doesn't have a last name, Prince doesn't have a last name. Don't you know anything?'

'Maybe it's Jameson,' Brad replied with a grin.

Douglas glared at him, then turned his attention to Allison. 'I don't know what you're trying to pull, but it won't work. With this information, I'll charge a conflict of interest and ask for a change of venue. I've got you, and I'm not giving up.'

'Have you got me, Douglas? Would you like me to call Bonnie and tell her you're not really hanging around over here after you bring Megan home?

Would you like me to give her a list of all your known excuses for being late coming home?'

'Don't you threaten me, you bitch!'

'Well, Dr Doug,' Brad intervened, clenching his fists at his sides to keep them from punching the man for talking to Allison that way, 'we'd love to stand here and talk all night, but we've got to catch Allison's latest report on the tube.' He nodded to the other man. 'Nice to have met you, sir.' He closed the door in their faces.

'Mom, why are you and Dad fighting?' Megan asked, obviously distressed.

'Because your father is . . .' She paused and took a deep breath. 'Sometimes he's not a very nice person. At least to me. That's why we're divorced. But he's nice to you. He still loves you. He only divorced me, not you.'

She hugged her daughter, and Brad had to admire her restraint. Rather than 'not a very nice person', he would have called the man a rotten, no-good, worthless excuse for a human being.

'It's almost ten,' Allison told her, turning her around and pointing her toward the stairs. 'You need to be in bed. School tomorrow.'

'Ah, Mom, I want to watch you on television.'

'You've already seen the entire tape.'

'Everybody makes video tapes. Being on television is different.'

Allison beamed down at her daughter. 'How can I

say no to that? But go upstairs and get your pajamas on first.'

As soon as Megan had left the room, Allison turned to Brad. 'So will you tell me what's going on? Why did Douglas get so upset because you borrowed some older man's car?'

Brad settled himself on the sofa, and Allison sank down beside him. He draped an arm across her shoulders. He couldn't be that close and not touch her. 'Doesn't the name Ethan Jameson ring any bells?'

'No. Should it?'

'Where are those legal papers Dr Doug served on you?'

'In my purse. Why?'

'You ought to read them a little more carefully. Ethan Jameson is the father of a friend of mine in the DA's office, but he's also your judge.'

'My judge?' She brought both hands to her mouth and burst into laughter. 'You borrowed the judge's car, and Douglas ran a license plate check on it? Oh, that's priceless!'

'I don't know about priceless. A diversion that will buy you a little time if he tries to prove a conflict of interest between you and the judge in order to get the case moved to another court. That's what he meant about the change of venue. About all that will accomplish is to waste his time and give you longer to get prepared. And to prove you're not consorting with an unsavory character.' Despite his cautious words, Brad was delighted he had made her laugh, had given her hope she could best Dr Doug.

'No, it was definitely priceless. Even if it doesn't solve anything, the memory of the look on his face will light up my days for years to come.' She leaned over and kissed his cheek.

'Is that all the gratitude I get?' he teased, his hand caressing her arm.

'Ask me again in thirty minutes,' she whispered, her dark eyes shadowy with desire.

'Don't look at me like that, or I won't be able to wait any thirty minutes.'

Megan brought him back to earth as she bounced downstairs in pajamas and a robe and settled on his other side. He draped an arm around her thin shoulders, too, and she cuddled up to him.

As the newscast came on, he found himself almost purring in contentment. If there was one more kid running around and the television was black and white, this could almost be a family evening in his childhood.

Except he had to keep reminding himself that this family wasn't like his. They'd never be content to live in this kind of a house and spend their evenings watching television. This was temporary, a glitch in time, and it was okay to enjoy it if he didn't expect it to last.

When the news was over and Megan's door had slammed jarringly, he reached for Allison just as she turned into his embrace. Her lips on his sent his blood racing in the now familiar way, but this time their kiss was unhurried, as though they had all the time in the world. And tonight he planned to utilize whatever time they had to the fullest.

Allison could feel her skin warming as Brad slid his hands over the silk of her jumpsuit.

'Soft,' he murmured, nibbling his way down her neck. 'Soft,' he said again, pulling down the zipper of her suit.

She moaned, her mind echoing the word as his tongue traced a pattern across the tops of her breasts, as her head fell back against the well-worn fabric of the sofa. His tongue was soft and warm and tantalizing.

Leisurely, he returned to her lips for another kiss, then stood and offered his hand. Without a word, she joined him, and they climbed the stairs together.

When they reached her room, he opened the curtains to let in the liquid moonlight.

'I want to see you,' he said, standing in front of the window.

Slowly, deliberately, she turned down the comforter, aware of his gaze on the still-open neck of her suit. Even with several feet separating them, even without him touching her, she could feel her desire building. His eyes narrowed as he watched her, and she knew he felt it, too.

Her lips parted involuntarily. Amazed at her own daring, she ran her tongue over them and lazily unzipped her jumpsuit the rest of the way.

'You wanted to see me?' she whispered, peeling off the silk and standing before him in her bra and underpants.

'No pantyhose tonight,' he said, his gaze traveling up and down her body, warming her everywhere it touched.

She blushed as she remembered her deliberate avoidance of the bothersome article when dressing for the evening as well as her careful selection of lacy underwear. 'No pantyhose,' she answered.

He shook his head as though in disbelief. 'You're so beautiful. I never realized you were so beautiful. Do you have any idea what just looking at you does to me?'

'Show me,' she whispered daringly.

He smiled, teeth flashing through the beard. In a moment he had divested himself of all clothing except a pair of bikini briefs that barely contained his bulging desire.

Allison sucked in her breath. She remembered the feel of his firm body with well-defined muscles. The sight of it made her want to feel him again – with her hands, with her body.

He crossed the space between them and took her

in his arms, lowering her to the bed.

But as she tried to pull him down to her, he held himself a few inches above her, looking at her, running his hand over her body, stroking the valley of her waist and the curve of her hip. Under his gentle touch and hungry gaze, she did feel beautiful, desirable.

'Your skin glows,' he said.

She thought he might be right. The fire inside must surely show some evidence on the outside.

'It's the moonlight,' she said, reaching up to trace the muscles in his arms, to tangle her fingers in the crisp hairs on his chest.

Bending over her, he touched his tongue to her stomach. 'You taste like moonlight,' he said as she arched at the unexpected pleasure.

Slowly he kissed his way around her stomach, then over her chest and up her throat, igniting every spot he touched, finally reaching her mouth. She pulled him to her, eagerly devouring him. As his tongue touched her lips, she parted them, inviting him inside.

He slid one hand up her back and began fumbling, pulling on her bra.

She drew back and laughed breathlessly. 'The hook's in front this time,' she said, a little pleased that he wasn't completely slick at this business. She wanted to believe she was special, that she could make him fumble.

With a smile, he unhooked her bra and took her breasts in his hands. He fastened his lips on one nipple, teasing with his tongue, then switched to the other and back again.

In ecstasy, in anguish, Allison rolled her head from side to side as unbearable currents shot through her. She couldn't stand it a moment longer but she didn't ever want him to stop. Blindly she groped for him, pulling the smooth briefs away from his arousal, stroking him, wanting to make him need her as much as she needed him.

His hips began to move in the rhythm of love, and he reached one hand down to push her lacy underwear aside and caress her. She thrust against him and withdrew in imitation of his movements, a preview of what she knew was coming.

When she was sure she couldn't bear the stimulation one moment more, he finally settled between her legs and poised himself, his smooth, rounded flesh pressing against and teasing her body. She pushed upward, but he held her down, his hands massaging her thighs.

'I want to know every inch of your body. Have I missed anything?' he asked, interspersing his words with butterfly kisses over her entire face.

Her feet, she thought, but she wasn't about to tell him now. Instead she pushed again, and this time he joined her.

So intense was her excitement, so ready for him,

she could feel the tension building after only a few thrusts of his body into hers, but he stopped her.

'Not yet,' he whispered, stilling himself for an eternity, then beginning to move again in slow, maddening motions.

She gave herself up to his control of her body, savoring the sweet torture. But then, in spite of his efforts, she felt herself beginning to spiral upwards.

He must have sensed it because his expression changed, and she knew he was losing his restraint and joining her in a wild, uncontrolled rush to rapture. She gasped in surprise at the unexpectedly intense pinnacle of sensation, then lost all conscious thought as his throbbing release touched off further throes of ecstasy.

Later, when she could think again, she lay curled against Brad's warm body, wishing she could stay there for a year or two. It felt so warm and secure. All her problems and worries were somewhere outside that bedroom door.

Brad pulled her closer to him, his chest hairs tickling her back, his beard on her neck.

'I hope you're not planning to shave any lower than the chin,' she teased, wriggling against him.

'Only if you decide you like smooth chests,' he breathed against her hair.

They lay in comfortable silence for a few minutes, then he murmured, 'I can't stay, you know.'

'I know,' she whispered.

He was referring to Douglas's detective, of course, but she wondered if his statement had a deeper meaning, if he was warning her that this was a temporary arrangement. Perhaps policemen weren't as poorly paid as Douglas claimed, but Brad would still be crazy to take on a penniless woman with a teenage daughter and an ex-husband who continued to cause problems and create expenses.

Not that she could afford to get involved with him or anybody else right now. Maybe after she got her own life straightened out, after she was making enough money to support herself and Megan as well as fight off Douglas. Otherwise she could end up right back in the same mess she was in now. How naive she'd been all those years when Douglas had insisted she didn't need to work, that he wanted to take care of her. He took care of her all right. Such care she could only wish on him.

But she wouldn't think about that now. She moved her legs to fit more snugly against Brad's, wanting to have as much of herself as possible touching him, to enjoy the glorious, tingly feeling as fully and as long as possible before she had to face reality again. Bending her head, she kissed the hairy arms that encompassed her.

Against her buttocks, she felt him moving, growing, hardening.

Yes, she thought. That would be a pleasant way to continue feeling glorious. She rolled over to face him, tracing his flat nipple with her tongue.

Sometime later he crawled out of bed.

'I don't think I can ride my bicycle now,' he groaned. 'You've done me in. What if I have to go chase a robber?'

'I guess you'll have to call a cab.' She smiled lazily, enjoying the feeling of total satiety.

'Heartless woman!' Brad smacked her bare bottom, then began to pull on his jeans.

When he was fully dressed, he sat down on the bed beside her. 'Are you ready to head back downtown tomorrow?'

Allison moaned and pulled the covers up. 'My only days off are Monday and Tuesday, and I just spent one of them working. However – ' she pushed herself to a sitting position ' – we can't stop now. What did you have in mind?'

'More of the same. Much as I hate to admit it, you do seem to have developed a sort of rapport with these people.'

'Could I get that in writing?'

He ignored her. 'I'd like you to go in for another round of questioning, only this time you have a goal. Come in by yourself, no camera, just talk to them. Approach them from the side door, so to speak, then work Dealey into the conversation and see what you can find out. You knew him. You have an excuse to talk about him.'

He leaned over and kissed her cheek. 'I'll be there

if you need anything,' he told her, 'but you're the star. I'll listen to anyone who talks to me, but I'm not going to be pushing. Two of us asking questions at the same time would probably seal everyone's lips.'

Allison followed Brad downstairs to see him off, then crawled back into bed and snuggled under the covers. The faintest whiff of his cologne drifted over her bringing a momentarily poignant feeling. Wonderful as things had been, it would have been even better to wake up in his arms.

She plumped the pillow and slammed her head down onto it, trying to dispel all fanciful, potentially destructive thoughts.

When she arrived shortly after one the next afternoon, the New Hope Shelter was again sparsely filled. The people had been fed and no television crew was around to draw a crowd. Things were back to normal.

Brad sat in a corner with a couple of other men, his feet propped up, nodding occasionally at the comments made by one of his companions. He gave her scarcely a glance as she came in. Though she would have liked something warmer, his attitude imbued her with a professional feeling. He was in the background today. This was her show.

Up front the Reverend Pollock was talking to a tall man in a dark suit. They shook hands, Pollock patted him on the back, and the man left, smiling at Allison as he passed.

'Welcome, friend!' Pollock strode toward her with outstretched hands and a wide grin.

'Good afternoon, Reverend.'

He clasped her hand and shook it vigorously. 'Your story has brought many wonderful people to us, just as you promised.'

Allison cringed inside, remembering what she'd told Pollock in the beginning when her real motives had not been entirely altruistic. Nevertheless, she felt a surge of excitement that she had been able to help.

'Have you had contributions?'

'Oh, yes.' He led her to a front row and sat beside her. 'We have had donations of food, clothes, blankets, money – that man who just left gave us fifty dollars and promised to send more every month. The harvest is truly bountiful.'

'That's wonderful! And you think this is all because of my story?'

'We don't have the means to reach the entire city like you do. You were truly sent to us.'

Allison felt embarrassed and thrilled at the same time. 'Really, I didn't – I mean, the story benefited me, too.'

'Blessings are usually double-edged,' he assured her, patting her hand. 'You have the gratitude of everyone here, and all those we will serve in days to come.'

'Thank you,' she whispered, then, catching a glimpse of Brad from the corner of her eye, she recalled her purpose. 'It's too bad Dealey can't be here to share all this.'

She watched Pollock closely for his reaction. It was very possible – likely, even – that he knew something, but she felt sure he'd protect his 'flock', handling matters in his own way.

Pollock's expression, however, gave her no clue. His smile remained beatific. 'Dealey no longer has need of blankets or food. His spirit has been released into eternal glory.'

'Yes, but he was trying so hard to straighten out his life. I hear he'd even given up drinking.'

Pollock's grin became even wider, happier. 'He came to me, and we talked. Mankind wants to be righteous, but the flesh is so weak.'

'At least Dealey doesn't have to worry about being weak any more.'

Pollock nodded, beaming now. 'It's rare to meet another who understands. My sister, you are a saint.'

Allison wasn't too sure of that since she was trying to deceive him even as they spoke.

'Did you see Dealey the night he died?' she asked, approaching the subject more directly since she wasn't getting anywhere by subtlety.

'Oh, yes. He was here.'

'Did you see him leave with anybody?'

'He soared away on wings of love.'

Oh boy. Out in la-la land again.

Nevertheless, his evasive answer solidified Allison's suspicions that he knew more than he was telling.

'This must be very hard for you, seeing people you know murdered. I'm sure you want to see the killer caught and punished more than anybody does.'

His eyes took on a faraway look. 'We are in this world to help others, to be our brother's keeper.' His gaze refocused, and he took Allison's hand again. 'Your help is very much appreciated, my daughter.' He stood and walked away, taking a seat across the room beside one of his people.

Allison glanced briefly over at Brad, but couldn't tell if he was watching her or not. His hair certainly did make a good disguise.

She'd have liked to discuss Pollock's conversation with Brad then and there, but that, of course, wasn't possible. She was more than ever convinced that Pollock knew something but thought he was acting in the right way by hiding it, protecting his friends.

Squaring her shoulders for the job ahead, she wandered around, trying to strike up conversations with people she knew, had met briefly or only seen. The success ratio was about the same with all of them. She had proven herself and been accepted into the group, so most were willing to talk, but none seemed to know anything about Dealey's death.

After four hours, she was exhausted and depressed. Any notions she'd ever had about policemen leading exciting lives were laid to rest. Brad was right about the work being boring and routine.

Then Henry came in.

She'd interviewed the tall, gaunt man the day before, and a few seconds of his story had made it to the ten o'clock news. Henry was, she felt, one of the temporaries. He'd been unemployed for a while, but he signed up every day with the job services.

Henry was smiling shyly as he walked into the room. When he spotted Allison, he headed straight toward her, his long legs taking him across the room in only a few strides.

'I may be getting permanent work,' he told her. 'This guy saw me on television and called the agency.'

'That's wonderful,' she said for the second time that afternoon, and suddenly she didn't feel tired any more. 'Sit down and tell me all about it.'

Allison got so caught up in Henry's excitement, she almost forgot about her duties until, from the corner of her eye, she caught sight of Brad moving around the room.

'You'll make it,' she assured Henry. 'Just be really careful. I understand Dealey was getting his life straight when he was killed.'

Henry eyed her dubiously. 'Dealey had a lot of problems.'

'Maybe he'd never have been able to reenter society,' she agreed, 'but he had stopped drinking. That's a big step.'

'Huh. He never quit for very long.'

'Maybe he would have this time. Pollock was working with him. It's a shame he didn't get the chance to find out.'

'Miz Prescott, I don't like to speak ill of the dead, but Dealey was drunk the night he got killed.'

Allison jumped on the new information. 'Are you sure? Did you talk to him? Did you tell the police about this?'

'Nah. It didn't have anything to do with the murder, and there wudn't any point in telling when it wouldn't help.' He stared down at his work-roughened hands in his lap, then back up to her, his eyes beseeching. 'You won't put this on the news or anything, will you?'

Allison considered her answer carefully. 'I wouldn't do anything to besmirch Dealey's memory,' she assured him. 'Are you positive he was drunk? Sometimes Dealey didn't make a lot of sense when he was sober.'

'Yes, ma'am, I'm real sure he was drunk. The preacher had to help him stand up.'

Allison took a second to allow the full import of Henry's statement to sink in. Maybe it wasn't a lead to the murderer, but it certainly showed Pollock covered up for his people. He'd failed to mention this small fact.

'When did you see him?' she asked.

'It was late Saturday night. I worked all day helping some people move. They paid me extra to arrange the furniture and stuff, then we got a pizza. It was a long walk back here, so it was pretty late. I was real tired and heading straight for this place when I saw them.'

'Outside, you mean? Not in the shelter?'

'Coming around from the back. Dealey couldn't even walk. Preacher was all but dragging him.' Henry shook his head. 'I hated to see that, I tell you, but it didn't surprise me none.'

'Where do you think they were going?'

'Don't know. The preacher dudn't like drinking. Maybe he was trying to help Dealey walk it off, sober him up before he let him in here.'

'But he never made it back inside?'

'No, ma'am. But don't fret too much about it. Drunk as he was, at least he prob'ly never felt a thing.'

Allison nodded, disappointment wrapping around her. How egotistical she'd been to think she could find out something about the murder when Brad, with all his experience, hadn't been able to do so in almost a month. All she'd discovered was that Dealey had lost his brief battle with sobriety, and that Pollock was definitely covering up that fact. Nothing to get very excited about.

She debated whether she ought to confront Pollock with her knowledge and see what he said. The temptation was strong, but if she angered him, he might forbid her to return to the mission. Perhaps she ought to think about that one for a little while, talk to Brad and determine the best way to approach the subject.

She studied Pollock from across the room as he talked to one of the people. His people. He was always talking to them, exhorting them to change their ways . . . protecting them.

Maybe the day wasn't a total waste. Pollock had lied about – or at least hidden his knowledge of – Dealey's last bout with drinking. He'd neglected to mention that he'd seen Dealey on the last night of his life. What other information might he be hiding behind his rhetoric?

CHAPTER 14

Brad waited half an hour after Allison left New Hope before he followed, retrieving his truck and heading for her house. He had to give her credit. She had plugged away all afternoon, talking to everybody who'd talk to her. She hadn't looked particularly happy when she left, so he could only assume she hadn't learned anything of interest . . . at least, nothing world-shattering.

Nevertheless, he was anxious to talk to her. He wasn't really looking for anything world-shattering. That would be nice, but it didn't often happen in real life. If Allison had only one small piece of information to contribute, he'd be thrilled.

He parked several blocks away from Allison's house and walked. He didn't see any suspicious vehicles in the vicinity as he approached, but he had no doubt someone would be there soon. Not for the first time he reflected that he had to be crazy. Associating with – trusting – a reporter was bad enough, but this reporter had someone keeping track of her every movement.

A thrill spread over him when Allison greeted him at the door, a smile on her lips.

Crazy. No doubt about it. Suicidal, even.

'Where's Megan?' he asked as Allison led him toward the dining table. They didn't need a child with an overactive imagination listening in.

'I sent her next door to Mrs Parson's.'

'Good idea.'

As she motioned him to a seat at the table, he noticed with approval that she had been making notes on a pad of paper.

'I made some coffee,' she said, disappearing into the kitchen and returning immediately with two steaming mugs. 'Now,' she continued, settling into a chair, 'before I share my information with you, let's make sure our deal is clear. I'll be right there with you through everything – questioning, what-ever, and I get to bring Rick along to do a videotape when the arrest comes down.'

Brad stared at her in surprise, wanting to wring her soft, white neck. She didn't forget her purpose for one minute . . . and he'd better not forget it either. Making love with her, holding her in his arms, hadn't changed one thing. They were still on opposite sides. 'You can be waiting in the wings, but neither you nor Rick will be allowed to jeopard-ize the arrest or the police procedures.'

She sipped her coffee, her eyes never leaving his

face, then finally nodded. 'But the terms "wings" and "jeopardize" are to be negotiated. You don't get to make an arbitrary judgment.'

Through gritted teeth, he agreed, and she related her conversation with Henry Dawson.

Since Henry was one of the more reliable people he'd met on the streets, Brad gave a great deal of credence to his account of events.

'Okay,' he said when she finished, 'so what we have here is evidence that Dealey was drinking again, that Pollock was possibly the last person to see Dealey alive, and that Pollock lied to us.'

'I've been thinking about it,' Allison continued, 'and I'm positive Pollock knows something. Since Dealey never made it back to the shelter, obviously the preacher took him somewhere to sober up, somewhere he thought was safe, except it wasn't. I think there's a good possibility that Pollock knows who the murderer is.'

Brad nodded slowly, mulling the events over in his own mind. 'It makes sense,' he finally said. 'We ran a background check on Pollock before I went in, and this sort of behavior definitely fits.'

She set her cup down with a thud. 'You didn't say anything about Pollock's background. Is this a one-way deal? I tell you everything, and you tell me nothing? How am I supposed to help if I don't know what's going on?'

'Allison,' he protested, 'I'm a police officer. A lot

of my information is confidential. I'm sorry, but that's just the way things are. But – ' he raised a hand to forestall the complaint he knew was coming ' – but I will tell you about Pollock.'

She nodded, seemingly mollified.

'He used to be a regular pastor in a small town in southeastern Oklahoma. But even then he was something of a fanatic. Soon he started making trips to McAlester to carry on a prison ministry. To make a long story short, he was instrumental in getting several prisoners paroled. One of them was doing yard work for some of the more affluent people in the area, jobs Pollock helped him get. One day the guy had too much to drink, broke into the home where he'd worked the day before and murdered everybody in the family then sat down and drank from their bar until he passed out.'

Allison grimaced at that. Her fingers tightened around her coffee mug until the knuckles whitened. 'How awful,' she said huskily.

He nodded. Obviously she hadn't been a reporter long enough to become immune to the seamier side of life, the side he saw every day. Briefly, irrationally, he wished he could somehow help her maintain that innocence, but a little more time in the media would effectively take it away.

'A lot of what we come across is awful,' he said. 'Anyway, Pollock took what happened very personally. He went into severe depression and was in a mental hospital for a couple of months. When he came out, he was much more subdued than he'd been before, but even more determined to help his fellow man. He testified at the killer's trial, told the court it was his fault, that if he'd been doing his job, the man wouldn't have fallen back into sin. He tried to get him off! That was about a year ago. Pollock disappeared for several months, then re-emerged up here, taking care of the homeless.'

'I see,' Allison murmured, and shivered though the room was warm. 'So everything fits. He knows who the killer is but thinks the man's actions are his fault, so he's duty-bound to protect him, to take care of the situation himself. If you knew this, why weren't you watching Pollock all along?'

'I've been keeping an eye on him and trying to talk to him. Short of sodium pentothal or torture, what would you suggest?'

She shrugged. 'You're right. I wasn't able to get anything out of him, even when I asked him a direct question. He's an expert at avoidance. So, what do we do now?'

He drained his coffee cup. 'Welcome to police work. We beat our heads against the wall some more, meaning we talk to Pollock again. I'd like to get enough evidence to ask for a search warrant and go through that back room of his.'

'Isn't this enough, that he was with Dealey on the night he died, and he lied about it?'

'Maybe, but probably not.'

'So I didn't help much.'

She seemed to droop, looking so disappointed, he reached across the table to take her hand. 'Yes, you did. You've made more progress than I have in three weeks. We rarely solve crimes as a result of a single leading clue or a slip of the tongue, the way it happens in the movies. We accumulate the evidence one tedious piece at a time, and you've just added a pretty big chunk.'

She smiled at him then, her look of disappointment turning to a glow, and he felt an answering glow inside his chest even as the sarcastic side of him marveled that he felt it necessary to comfort her. She'd hunted him down, compromised his cover and blackmailed him into letting her become involved so she could have a story. She ought to be comforting him.

But he didn't release her hand. It felt so fragile and warm and smooth . . . like the rest of her. In spite of the inappropriateness, he responded to touching her just as he always responded.

He wanted to hold her against him, feel her flesh touching his, make love to her again and completely forget about all the reasons he shouldn't and couldn't . . . his undercover assignment, Douglas's detective, Allison's daughter, Allison's job as a reporter, Allison's determination to make a lot of money, the fact that he'd never see her again after she got her story.

As though she could read his mind – or his body – she blinked slowly, her dark eyes becoming smoky. Slowly she shoved back her chair and stood. He did the same, never turning loose of her hand. They moved together, and he pulled her into his arms, his lips descending greedily to hers.

The front door slammed open. 'Mom – oh, wow!'

They sprang apart to see Megan standing in the doorway, grinning happily. 'Don't mind me. I just came over to pick up another game. I can come back later.' She started out the door, looking over her shoulder.

'Don't leave,' Allison protested, darting across the room to her daughter.

Brad cleared his throat. 'Yeah, I was just leaving.'

'You don't have to do that,' Megan protested. 'I think it's really cool that you and Mom are . . . you know. Gosh, wait till I tell the other kids.'

'No!' Brad and Allison exclaimed in unison.

Allison gave Brad a helpless look. He took a deep breath and crossed the room, closing the door so Dr Doug's detective couldn't record the scene, then stood beside Megan.

'Sweetheart, you can't tell anybody. I'm . . . uh . . . hiding.' True enough so far. 'I'm kind of in the middle of a deal, and if word should get to the wrong people, things would be bad. Real bad.'

She looked disappointed, but shrugged philosophically. 'Okay. Can I tell everybody after your deal's closed?'

Now it was his turn to look at Allison helplessly.

'We'll see,' she said, and Brad swallowed a laugh. Mothers hadn't changed much. His own had used that same phrase hundreds of times when she really meant no. And he'd figured that out at a young age. Megan knew it, too. She gave her mother a look of disgust and turned back to Brad expectantly.

'When every part of the deal is wrapped up,' he said, mentally including Allison's struggles with Dr Doug in that 'deal'. Heaven only knew if that would ever be finished. It was a safe promise.

'Okay,' she agreed. 'But you're not really leaving, are you? You can stay for dinner, and we can watch television again.'

It sounded appealing. Much too appealing. He had no permanent place here, and it was dangerous to get too comfortable, too attached to a lifestyle that was a lie. Five years from now Allison wouldn't be spending her evenings in the living room of an old house in front of a television.

'I'm making spaghetti,' Allison said.

Brad shook his head. 'I don't think that's a good idea.' He tilted his head toward the door and mouthed the word 'detective' over Megan's head.

'Sounds like a good idea to me,' the girl protested.

'Megan, run upstairs and wash your hands for dinner,' Allison said.

Megan breathed out an enormous sigh and rolled her eyes. 'Mom, you haven't even started dinner yet. My hands will get dirty again long before then. Why don't you just say, "Megan, go away so I can kiss Brill good-bye"?'

Allison's face flamed a bright red, but her voice was firm. 'Megan, go to your room while I talk to Brill . . . Bill.'

Megan turned back to Brad, raised herself on tiptoe and wrapped a small arm around his neck. The hug was unexpected and disarming. Brad hesitated only briefly before returning the embrace. The child was so small, so fragile . . . so trusting. Whatever happened, he couldn't let Douglas take her.

'Bye,' she said, bounced halfway across the room, then turned toward him again. 'Are you coming back tomorrow?'

'I don't know,' he mumbled. 'We'll see.'

She rolled her eyes again and charged upstairs. 'I'm going in my room now,' she called seconds after she disappeared down the hall. Her door slammed resoundingly.

'Well,' Allison said, wrapping her arms about herself as though she were cold, 'what's next on the agenda? Shall I return to the streets tomorrow?'

'Don't you have to work tomorrow?'

'After work, I meant. I can probably manage to get away a little early.'

'It gets dark earlier every night. I don't think you should be down there after dark.'

She lifted her head a fraction of an inch, her chin thrusting outward. 'Are you trying to get rid of me, to keep me from being a part of all this?'

'No, of course not.'

'Then I'll see you tomorrow after work. I'll try to get down there around four o'clock. Between four and five.'

'I'll look for you.'

She was wrong. He hadn't been trying to get rid of her, though he probably should. He'd been genuinely concerned for her safety downtown after dark. But he decided not to tell her that. The fact he was worried about her was bad enough. He had no intention of letting her know.

'I'll be there,' she said, and he fought the impulse to take her in his arms and kiss her good night, as though they were an ordinary couple. They were neither ordinary nor a couple.

Determinedly he walked out Allison's door and down the street, directly up to the older-model black car parked a few houses away. The man in the front seat watched him approach, his gaze darting from side to side as though looking for a way to escape.

Brad knocked on the window. 'Got the time?' he asked. It wasn't Sullivan. Probably one of his employees. A pair of binoculars and a camera with a telephoto lens lay in the seat beside him.

For a moment the man said nothing, then finally looked at his watch. 'Five-thirty,' he said.

'Appreciate it.' Brad strolled away. Another car, another detective to be on the alert for. He didn't think he'd ever been in such a tangled, no-win mess in all his years on the force.

Allison glanced surreptitiously at her watch. Nearly five o'clock, and this 'brief' meeting of the reporters, cameramen and anchors showed no signs of ending. The new station manager had been admiring the sound of his own voice for almost thirty minutes now. In a way, Allison reflected, he wasn't that much different from Pollock. His topic was 'the good of the station' instead of religion, but he managed to spout meaningless rhetoric as easily and endlessly as the preacher.

She couldn't afford to get up and leave. The best she could make out from what the man was saying, her job – along with everybody else's – was shaky at best. But every passing minute increased the chance Brad wouldn't wait for her. Of course, she could always work on her own. And would if it came to that. However, it would be nice if he was around.

She mentally deleted the word 'nice'. Convenient. Not essential, but convenient.

Finally the station manager wound up. She fully expected him to lead a cheer for good old K-SVN,

285

but he restrained himself, simply urging them, as he thrust his fist into the air, to 'get out there and be your best'.

Allison went to her desk, retrieved her purse and prepared to leave.

Rick walked up to join her. 'We've got some irate tenants picketing the million-dollar home of their slumlord. Want to come along and do the story?'

Allison's first impulse was to agree. It could be a good story, and she needed all the good stories she could get. But she was already working on a good story – and late for her evening's assignment.

'I can't. I – ' She broke off her explanation as Tracy came up behind Rick.

'I'm available, Rick,' the girl said. 'I don't have any kids I have to run home to.'

Allison gritted her teeth and told herself to let it go. 'Thank you, Tracy,' she said, smiling. 'If you ever get a personal life, I'll try to help you out, too.' Okay, so she hadn't been able to let it go. 'Gotta run. See you all later.' She hurried out before Rick could scowl at her for losing her cool or Tracy could figure out she'd just been insulted.

She drove downtown as quickly as she could and parked across the street from the New Hope Shelter. The sun had gone down, and it would soon be dark, but she would be inside the center.

As she left her car and started across the street, she saw Jean emerge from the building and stand for a moment, looking about her uncertainly. Well, it was as good a place to start at any. She never had learned how Jean's husband had died.

'Hi!' she called, waving to the woman.

Jean smiled broadly and lifted her hand in reply. She wore a big sweater over her faded dress, and the scarf Allison had given her was nowhere in evidence. She'd probably traded it for something else, Allison reflected.

'How are you this evening?' Allison asked as she came up beside the big woman.

'Good. Fine. We had pizza for dinner. Lots of different kinds. I like pizza.'

'Me, too,' Allison agreed. Jean must really like pizza. Allison had never heard her so talkative. She continued to smile, and her eyes shone brightly – almost feverishly. If she hadn't seemed so happy, Allison would have thought she might be ill. 'And my daughter could live on it.'

'You got a kid?'

'Yes. A twelve-year-old. Did you have any children?'

Jean frowned in confusion. 'I don't think so.'

'I don't think you'd have forgotten it if you had.'

Jean nodded, smiled briefly, then leaned closer, looking solemn. 'Don't ever let your husband hit your little girl,' she advised.

'I won't,' Allison promised. 'Anyway, he left me for a younger woman, remember?'

Jean patted her clumsily on the shoulder. 'Don't you worry. You're little and pretty. You'll find somebody else. But you be real careful. My daddy left my mama when I was a baby. She got married again, and my stepdaddy was mean.'

Allison saw the avenue of approach to her questions. 'Did he hit you?'

'Who?'

'Your stepfather. You said he was mean.'

Jean shook her head slowly. 'He was. He hit me and Mama both.'

'That's when you left home and ran away with – what did you say your husband's name was?'

Jean scowled down at her. 'What do you care? You can't have him.'

'I know,' Allison soothed. 'I wouldn't try to take your husband. Anyway, you said he was dead.'

Tears started from Jean's eyes. 'Raymond's dead.' She began to sob loudly.

Allison gaped at her in astonishment for a moment. Then she remembered what Brad had said about Jean being on drugs. Was that what had made her eyes shine so brightly? She patted the big woman on her back. 'It'll be okay,' she soothed, unable to come up with anything more specific.

Suddenly something slammed into her stomach, and Allison stumbled backward onto the sidewalk. Fists clenched, Jean leaned over her, screaming. 'You stole him away! You think just because you're little and pretty, you can have my husband!'

'No,' Allison protested breathlessly, scooting away from the hysterical woman as best she could. Jean had punched her! Her stomach ached, and she'd probably have a dilly of a bruise tomorrow. The woman was as strong as a man. 'No, I didn't steal your husband. I lost mine, too. Remember?' An appeal to the sisterhood of deserted wives.

Jean hesitated, blinking uncertainly, but then her lips split in a grimace of hatred, and, with a fierce howl, she threw herself on Allison and began pummeling her. The action and the pain were so unexpected, so foreign to her, it took a moment for the whole thing to register that Jean had attacked her, was beating her! She could die on the sidewalk and then who'd take care of Megan?

Kicking and pushing, Allison tried to roll away, but Jean grabbed her shoulders, lifted her and slammed her head against the concrete sidewalk. Bright lights exploded all around her. She was going to die and be found in an alley with her arms folded over her chest! In desperation, she reached upward, and when her hands touched flesh, she held on tightly.

The painful grip on her shoulders disappeared, and fingers tugged at hers, trying to pry them loose. Allison held on determinedly, doing her best to keep from falling, to keep her head from crashing onto the concrete again. But instead of falling backward, she felt herself rising.

'Allison, turn loose!' Brad's voice. She could see his bushy head above Jean as he tried to pull the woman off her . . . and she suddenly realized her hands were clasped around Jean's throat.

She turned loose, rolling to the side as she fell. Jean, no longer occupied with prying Allison's fingers off her throat, grabbed her hair. Almost screaming in agony, Allison clutched the woman's wrist with both hands, trying to hold it closer, to relieve the painful grip.

In the distance, it seemed, she heard Brad yelling. 'Turn her loose, Jean, or I swear, I'll break your arm!'

And then a siren and flashing lights.

Thank God! The police.

'Break it up, all of you! Up against the wall! You, fellow, turn that woman loose!'

Allison knew the exact moment Brad turned Jean loose. The woman fell on her with a vengeance. Suddenly the three of them were rolling on the pavement together, arms and legs flailing. Then just as suddenly Allison was free. She looked up to see two uniformed police officers holding Brad and Jean. At least, one of them was trying to hold Jean. She was fighting frenziedly. Allison had heard that people on drugs possessed superhuman strength, and she believed it now. The officer was big and obviously trained, but he was unable to subdue Jean.

She struggled to her feet in time to see the first officer shove Brad into the back seat of the patrol car parked at the curb.

'No, wait,' she protested, taking a step in the direction of the car. 'You can't arrest him.'

The man strode over to her and grabbed her, spinning her around and pinning both arms behind her. In disbelieving shock, she felt him slap handcuffs on first one wrist, then the other.

'What are you doing?' she protested. 'I'm a reporter. That woman attacked me.' Wordlessly he propelled her to the car and thrust her into the back seat next to Brad.

'Come back here!' she called, but the man had already slammed the door and was assisting his partner in subduing Jean. Panic-stricken, she turned to Brad. 'What's going on? Tell him.'

Brad heaved a deep sigh. 'Tell him what, Allison? That I'm an undercover cop?'

Allison's mind whirled. This couldn't be happening. 'Brad, that man put handcuffs on me!'

He grinned wryly. 'Yeah, I know. Me, too.'

'Well, what are we going to do?'

'Catch hell, I expect,' he said quietly.

'What?'

'My superiors aren't going to be very pleased about this.'

'I'm not real happy myself.'

The officer who'd handcuffed her slid into the driver's side door, picked up the radio and requested backup.

'Officer,' Brad said as soon as he signed off, 'you can let this lady go. She was just trying to defend herself. That other woman attacked her.'

The man didn't even bother to look back at them. 'Umm-hmm. Did you see this attack?'

Brad hesitated, and Allison knew with a sinking feeling that he wasn't going to lie. 'No. But I came out of the shelter to see Jean – the big woman – on top of her, smashing her head on the sidewalk.'

'Tell it to the judge.' He slid out of the car and closed the door.

'Brad? Are we going to jail?'

'Don't worry. I'll call Steve. He'll get us out.'

'Out,' she repeated as a presentiment of doom overwhelmed her. 'That means we'll be in. In jail.'

'Not for long.'

She strained ineffectually against the handcuffs, not quite able to believe it was all really happening. 'I can't go to jail! I have to get home to Megan.'

'You'll get home. Trust me. It's just going to be a little later than you planned. And don't mention Megan to anyone. If they know you have a minor child alone at home, they'll call the father to go get her. If they don't reach him, they'll call in social services.'

Tears of rage and fear and anguish filled her eyes, and she couldn't even wipe them away. 'How can you be so calm?' she demanded.

'Believe me, I'm not calm right now.'

Maybe not, she thought, but he couldn't possibly be as upset as she was. He didn't have as much at stake as she did.

As they drove to the station, Allison talked almost nonstop to the officers, but to no avail. As the policemen took the three of them in to be booked, Allison thought she had never been so humiliated or so frightened in her life. Jean mumbled incoherently, and Brad kept a grim silence. The only way Allison could maintain her sanity was to hang onto his promise that he would get them out of this nightmare.

'Name?' the man behind the desk asked.

She made an effort to make her voice firm, dignified . . . innocent. 'Allison Prescott.'

'Allison Prescott?' a female voice behind her repeated. 'Don't you work for Channel 7?'

Allison turned to see a reporter from a rival station . . . and a cameraman.

'And I thought this was going to be a dud assignment just hanging around watching the drunks and the hookers come in. What have they got you in here for, Allison?'

The man with her lifted the videocam and started filming.

Allison had only thought she felt humiliated and frightened before. The whole city would know that she had been arrested for street brawling. The station manager would know. Megan would know. Douglas would know.

Beside her Brad groaned softly. She wasn't the only one who would suffer from this public exposure.

CHAPTER 15

'Man, you're thinking with your – '

'Don't say it,' Brad growled, interrupting Steve Raney's tirade. 'You don't know what you're talking about.'

Steve stopped pacing and glared at Brad where he sat slumped at the scarred wooden table in a small, private room at the police station. 'I know you've just compromised your cover for the sake of a reporter.'

Brad shot up from his chair and glared back at his partner, nose to nose. 'You're right, Steve, and you're wrong. And your attitude sucks.'

'My attitude sucks? Well, your actions suck. Getting into a fight and getting yourself arrested is not exactly low-profile behavior. But then, taking a reporter, *a reporter*, for God's sake, into your confidence and letting her help solve your case pretty much takes the cake for stupidity.'

Brad slumped back into the chair. He couldn't deny his partner's accusations. 'It's not exactly like

I suddenly woke up one morning and decided to let Allison Prescott in on things, then invited her to help. I told you how it happened.'

Steve sat down in the chair across from him. 'And I told you to stay away from her in the beginning.'

'It wouldn't have mattered. She's like a bulldog. When she sets her mind to something, she doesn't let up until she gets what she wants.'

'You say that almost like you're proud of her.'

Steve was right, Brad realized. He hadn't been able to keep a note of pride from his voice. For sure, Allison had wreaked havoc on his life, but he had to give her credit for grit and determination. A lot of people in her position would have been so depressed, they'd have given up. But Allison was a fighter. Unfortunately, her single-minded efforts to improve her situation had put him in a bad spot. A real bad spot.

'All right, all right,' Brad said. 'Rag on my butt all you want. But get her out of this place so she can get home to her kid.'

'Kid?'

'Yeah, she's got a twelve-year-old daughter who's home by herself right now.'

'A twelve-year-old daughter who's home alone at this time of night? Why didn't you let somebody know so we could get somebody out there?'

'That's exactly why. She's already in the middle of a custody battle. Bringing in social services would give her ex a pretty major complaint in court.'

'So you just flagrantly ignored the law? How involved are you with this broad? Are you sleeping with her?'

Brad couldn't lie, but he couldn't tell the truth, either. His hesitation was enough for his partner.

Steve leaned back in his chair and swore vociferously. 'I guess that explains a hell of a lot.'

'It doesn't explain diddly-squat. It has nothing to do with anything. Look, how many times have we used an informant to help us find out what we couldn't? This isn't any different. Allison has a rapport with these people. She's discovered some things I didn't.' He hated that Steve was forcing him to defend Allison's actions – actions he himself certainly didn't condone.

Raney shook his head. 'It damn sure is different. You're the one who's supposed to be out there gathering information. Your "informant" is going to inform on you all over the television screen. You'd better get her out of the scene right now. Whatever you do with her in private is your business, I guess, but you keep her out of police business. Got it?'

Brad slammed his fist onto the table. 'Shut up, okay?' he exclaimed. 'I know all the things I shouldn't have done, and I know what I need to do. I'm gonna be hearing it from the lieutenant soon enough. But right now, could you just forget about being a cop for a minute and be a friend and get us both out of jail?'

'Yeah, I guess so,' Steve relented. 'But you've got yourself in a real mess, my friend.'

'Thanks for pointing that out to me. I hadn't noticed,' Brad replied sarcastically.

And Steve didn't even know the worst of it. In spite of everything she'd done, all the problems she'd caused him . . . and was likely to cause him in the future . . . he cared about Allison. When he'd run outside upon hearing Jean's screams and seen Jean slamming Allison's head against the concrete, he'd gone into a complete panic. Allison could have been killed, and that would have left a painful hole somewhere in the vicinity of his heart. It wasn't going to be as easy as he'd thought to turn loose of her when this situation was over.

It was after eleven o'clock that night when Allison finally made it home. Her head and stomach ached, she was embarrassed, depressed and tired . . . and Douglas's car sitting in front of the house didn't improve matters.

She parked in the driveway. Heart thudding painfully against her ribs as she tried not to think about what her ex-husband's appearance meant, she ran toward the front porch. She froze with one foot on the first step when Douglas and Megan emerged, both carrying suitcases. He was trying to steal her daughter, would have whisked Megan away if Allison had arrived home five minutes later.

'Megan!' Her voice came out little more than a whisper.

Megan dropped her bag and ran to embrace her mother. 'You're out of jail! When you called and said you were going to be late, you didn't say you were in jail! I was so worried!'

'So worried you called your dad.' She looked at him over Megan's head.

'Actually, I phoned her,' Douglas replied smoothly. 'You've finally achieved that fame you wanted so desperately, Allison. You made the ten o'clock news on a rival channel.'

'I didn't see it. I was watching your channel, Mom. Dad called and said you'd been in a fight, and you were in jail, and I was so scared. What happened? Are you hurt?' She leaned back to look her mother over anxiously. Even in the dimness of the street light, Allison could see that her daughter's eyes were red and swollen, and dried tears streaked her face.

'I'm fine, baby. It was all a mistake. Let's get you unpacked and go to bed. It's been a long day.' With one arm still wrapped about Megan's shoulders, she started onto the porch, but Douglas grabbed her other arm.

'She's going home with me. I don't think having a brawling jailbird for a mother provides a very healthy atmosphere for a child.'

Allison clenched her teeth, fighting the black fog of fury and fear that threatened to steal her control. Punching Douglas wouldn't solve anything. She'd already determined tonight she had no talent or ability for fighting. And Douglas was bigger than Jean.

'No,' she said simply. 'She's not going with you. She's going upstairs to bed.' She tightened her hold on Megan, praying her daughter wouldn't do anything stupid, like saying she wanted to go home with her dad.

Douglas smiled tightly. 'It's over, Allison. Even if you succeed in keeping her with you tonight, when we go to court and I show the judge a copy of that news tape, I can guarantee you'll lose. It shows you in handcuffs standing between two street people, one of whom is apparently your lover, while my daughter stays home alone until almost midnight.'

'Dad, stop it,' Megan pleaded, her voice cracking as if she might start crying again. 'I told you Brill's not a street person, and Mom already said the police just made a mistake tonight.'

'I'm sorry, Princess,' he said, speaking to Megan but never taking his cold gaze from Allison, 'but sooner or later you've got to face the truth about your mother. She's been consorting with lowlife people and fighting in the streets in front of a shelter for the homeless where your Brill apparently lives. And now she has a criminal record. She's not exactly a candidate for mother-of-the-year.'

'Dad, don't say things like that about Mom!' Her voice cracked as she clung more closely to Allison, wrapping her small arms about her waist.

'Sweetheart, why don't you go on in the house and start getting ready for bed?' Allison said. 'I'll be there in just a minute.'

'Megan, pick up your bag and go on out to the car,' Douglas countered. 'If you want to go to New York with Bonnie and me, you need to come home with me tonight.'

'Douglas, don't do this to her!' Allison protested. Megan was upset enough without having to choose which of her parents to obey, without facing the threat of losing a promised treat.

'She's old enough to know what she wants. Aren't you, Princess?'

'You're old enough not to force her to do that,' Allison snapped. 'Go in the house, Megan. Right now.' Reluctantly she released her hold on her daughter, fearful that Douglas would take the child with him by force.

Megan looked from one to the other indecisively then took a hesitant step forward. Douglas dropped Allison's arm and moved toward Megan, but didn't try to stop her as she ran past him. With tears streaming down her face, she fled into the house, slamming the door behind her.

'If I ever had any remnants of doubt that you don't give a rat's behind about your daughter's welfare, you've just taken them away. How could you do that to her?' Without giving him a chance to answer, she pushed past him and into the house.

She locked the door, then leaned against it, taking deep breaths and trying to calm down before she faced Megan. She could scarcely hope to comfort her daughter if she was in a murderous rage.

'Mom?' The small voice came from the top of the stairs.

'Yes, sweetheart.' Allison moved away from the door and went up to Megan.

The girl stood deliberately erect, her face pale but without tears. She made no move toward her mother.

Nevertheless, Allison wrapped her arms around the unyielding little body.

'Is Dad taking you to court again?'

'I'm afraid so. He – ' She couldn't finish the sentence. She just couldn't force out the words of such an enormous and undeserved lie.

'Why does he keep doing that? You never stop me from going over there. And why did he say such awful things about you?'

Twelve years old was much too young to be torn apart like that, too young to face the reality of her parents' imperfections. Okay, she resolved, for her daughter's sake, she could tell the massive lie after all, had to tell it.

'Your father loves you very much. He's doing what he thinks is right, and I'm doing what I think is right. We both want your happiness. We just have different ideas as to the best way to insure that.'

Megan's tense body lost some of its stiffness. 'Do you think he really won't take me to New York since I didn't go with him tonight?'

Allison smiled, relieved to hear her daughter's materialism take the place of so much pain. 'Of course he'll take you to New York. He'll be in a good mood by tomorrow. You know how people say things they don't mean when they're angry.'

'Yeah, I think he was pretty mad at you for going to jail,' Megan said, pushing away to look into Allison's face. 'What happened? Why were you and Brill fighting that strange woman?'

'I was talking to her, working on a story, when she attacked me. She's a very sick person, probably taking illegal drugs. Bill happened to be close by, and he came to my rescue. A patrol car was passing by, and they took everyone in for . . . uh . . . questioning because they didn't see what happened. As soon as they found out the facts, they let Bill and me go home. Now let's get you in bed. You have to get up for school tomorrow.' She turned Megan and pointed her in the direction of her room.

But Megan wouldn't be satisfied so easily. She turned back, her eyes big with fear. 'What was Brill doing in front of that homeless shelter?' she asked quietly, and Allison knew she was frightened of losing her dream. 'Is Daddy right? Is he just a bum?'

'No, your father's not right. Bill isn't a bum.'

'Is he a rock star?'

'Uh . . . no. But he's a special person.'

Her expression drooped. 'Then who is he?' The disappointment was evident in her voice.

'Somebody special,' Allison assured her. 'And that's all I can tell you right now. It's a secret, a big-time secret. You shouldn't even know that much.' She touched the tip of Megan's nose with her forefinger and smiled at her. 'But I know you can be trusted not to say a word to anybody. You just keep telling them he's a rock star, and when this is all over, I promise you'll be in on the secret.'

That seemed to restore her good humor and bring the sparkle back to her eyes. 'Wow! Is he, like, a spy or something?'

'I won't say another word if you stick splinters under my fingernails.' She was rewarded with a giggle from Megan. 'Now get in bed, and let me do the same.'

Megan gave her a quick kiss and skipped to her room. How mercurial her temperament was, Allison reflected, watching her go. So easily upset, so easily made happy again.

304

Megan turned at the door of her room. 'Are you and Brill lovers?'

Allison opened her mouth to speak, then turned the movement into a cough to buy time. How on earth did she answer a question like that? Should she say they were friends? But she wasn't sure they were. They didn't have what might be termed a friendly agreement.

'Mom, I'm almost thirteen years old,' Megan said when she didn't reply. 'You don't have to be afraid to tell me. I know all about what it means to be lovers.'

'Bill and I are kind of business associates,' Allison finally said.

Megan lifted one eyebrow skeptically, and Allison knew it hadn't escaped the child's attention that she hadn't denied being Brad's lover. Well, she'd just have to be extremely careful, more careful than she'd been before.

'Oh, by the way, Mom, Uncle Rick called and said to call him if you need anything, and somebody from the television station named Cody Hunter called and wants to see you first thing in the morning.' She went into her bedroom and closed the door.

Cody Hunter. The station manager. Great. She was probably going to be fired tomorrow.

The adrenaline stirred up by anger at Douglas left her, and Allison thought she might have to crawl into her bedroom. She dragged herself in and fell onto the bed. She might just sleep in her clothes on top of the covers. She was totally drained.

If she lost her job, she wouldn't even be able to fight Douglas in court. Although after tonight, she wasn't sure that mattered. Douglas was right about one thing. The judge wouldn't look too kindly on her being arrested while fighting with two homeless people and leaving her daughter alone at night.

And to make matters even worse, to put the icing on this poisonous cake, she really wanted to call Brad, to beg him to come over and hold her, to make everything all right. Even if he could fix things – and he couldn't – she didn't dare ask him. If he fixed things, those things would then belong to him, not to her. He could then unfix them just as easily. Just as Douglas had done.

Somehow she had to work the kinks out of her life by herself. And that goal seemed to become more distant and difficult with every effort she put forth.

Would God think it amiss, she wondered, if she prayed for a slow, painful death for Douglas, amnesia for the station manager, a winning lottery ticket for herself, and as for Brad . . . well, she'd have to think about that.

Allison marched into the station manager's office the next morning, head high, determined to go down fighting.

Hunter looked up from his desk as she entered. 'Close the door,' he barked.

She was already in the process of doing so. She had no desire for the rest of the employees to be a witness to her dismissal.

'What the hell happened last night?'

'I was working on a story, and that woman attacked me. The man came to my aid. I was totally innocent. They didn't file any charges against me.'

'Don't they have to let you have one phone call?'

'Well, yes,' she said, confused at the turn the conversation had taken. 'I called my daughter to tell her I was going to be a little late getting home.'

'Damn it! What kind of reporter are you, anyway? Why didn't you call us? You let another station get the story and never said a word to us.'

Even though he hadn't invited her to sit, Allison collapsed into a chair, her legs suddenly weak. 'You wanted me to call you so you could do a story on me going to jail?' she asked in amazement.

'You do remember who you work for, don't you?'

No matter that the man was obviously angry with her; apparently she still had a job. 'Yes, of course. It's just that I . . . well, I didn't intend for anybody to do a story on it. Not yet, anyway. Too much publicity would jeopardize the big story I'm working on.' Please, God, he wouldn't ask her to be more explicit.

'What is this big story?'

'It's about the serial killer who's murdering the homeless.'

'We've done that to death.'

'But I have some new information. I have some clues as to who the killer might be.'

'Tell me.'

'I can't. I can't tell because my source is a secret.'

'I don't care who your source is. I just want to know what your information is. How soon can we go public with it?'

Against her better judgment, she told him what she'd discovered, being careful to edit out Brad's role or any information he'd given her. As she talked, she could almost see the ratings' calculations whizzing around in Hunter's head.

When she finished, he tapped his pencil on the desk thoughtfully for several agonizing moments. 'Okay,' he finally said, 'here's what we do. We tease the viewers. I figure they should all be watching us tonight to see what you're going to say. So you do some kind of story, I don't care what. Then at the end our anchor will ask you about last night. You smile enigmatically and say something like, "I'm not at liberty to say right now, but I have some very interesting information about the murders, and soon I'll be able to give everybody all the details." Every night he asks you, and maybe you even toss out a little tidbit from time to time to whet their appetites. Work up some dialogue and get back to me.' He returned his attention to the papers on his desk, dismissing her.

It could have been a lot worse. At least she still had a job.

'Thank you,' she said. 'I'll do that.' She rose and started out the door.

'Allison.'

She turned back to find him looking at her. He really would be a very attractive man, she thought, if he had any warmth in his expression. Rather like Douglas.

'We can only run this gimmick for a little while. Get your story together and do it soon.'

A little more pressure. Just what she needed.

As she left Hunter's office, she saw Rick across the room waving to her. When she passed Tracy's desk on her way over to Rick, the girl glared at her. That lifted her spirits a little. If Tracy was upset, she must be doing something right.

'What on earth happened to you last night?' Rick demanded.

'It's a long story. Let me make a quick phone call, then we can go chase some ambulances or something interesting while I tell you. It's getting boring with all the repetitions. And while we're at it, we need to talk about how many jewels I need to hock to get you to babysit Megan tonight.'

When she called Brad, his answering machine

picked up. She left a message for him to call her as soon as possible. They hadn't yet agreed on a plan of action for this evening, and she couldn't afford to waste any time.

Allison rushed home and prepared a quick dinner of leftovers. Rick came to the door just as she was taking the bowls of stew from the microwave.

'Uncle Rick!' Megan greeted him at the door. 'Is this too cool or what, Mom and Brill working on a secret deal together? Do you know what they're up to?'

'You'd better say "no",' Allison called, 'or she'll drive you crazy all night trying to drag the secret out of you.'

'Have you heard from the master of disguises yet?' Rick asked, coming into the kitchen.

'Not yet. If he doesn't call by the time we get through eating, I'll just go on down – ' She looked over at Megan's eager face peering around the corner. 'On down there where he probably is.'

'The shelter for homeless people, right?' Megan guessed.

'That was the last assignment. Who knows where we'll go tonight?'

That really was true, Allison thought. Brad might not be at the shelter tonight. He could be pursuing an entirely different line.

But it didn't matter. If he wasn't there, she would

continue her investigation without him. She didn't need his assistance. Okay, she had needed it last night, but if she went inside the shelter, she'd be all right with so many people around.

Nevertheless, she was glad to hear Brad's voice when the phone rang halfway through dinner.

'Are you all right?' he asked.

'I'm fine,' she answered, though she felt anything but fine. 'Are we meeting at the usual place?'

'We need to talk about that.'

'So talk.' She didn't like the apologetic tone of his voice.

'I got a lot of flack about what happened last night.'

'It won't happen again.'

'The whole thing can't happen again. My partner and my lieutenant both read me the riot act about letting you get involved in this case.'

A chill slithered down her spine. 'So what are you saying?'

'I'm not trying to get out of our deal. I'll still see to it that you get first crack at the story when the arrest comes down, but you've got to back off.'

'Back off?'

'Stay away. Let me handle the case. I'm sorry, but I have no choice in the matter. I've been ordered to end your involvement.'

'No. No! Absolutely not.' She lowered her voice, aware that Megan sat only a few feet away in the

311

dining room, straining to hear. 'Because of our deal, I'm in hot water over my head!' she whispered angrily. 'Douglas seems to think he's got the custody battle knocked after what happened last night, and of course I couldn't tell him the truth about you. Then my boss let me know that I'd better produce this story soon or else. Back off? No way. I've got to get into high gear.'

'Be reasonable. We're getting close. I'll have the case solved in no time, thanks to your help.'

'Don't patronize me!' she snapped.

'I'm not! I mean it. What you've discovered has pointed me in the right direction. If I stick close to Pollock, I think he'll lead me right to the killer. And after last night, I wouldn't be at all surprised to find that it's Jean. I'm going to be putting in some night work on this. I promise I'll get it done, and soon. I won't let you down.'

'With or without you, I'm going down there every time I can until I get what I need. I am not about to sit here twiddling my fingers, counting on someone else to take care of things for me!'

'You talk about jeopardizing your job, well, I don't want to jeopardize mine either, especially when it's unnecessary.' His voice had lost its apologetic tone and become firm and determined.

'Fine,' she said. 'You do what you have to do for your job, and I'll do what I have to do for mine.'

'Allis, you can't go down there without me

around. What if Jean attacks you again?'

Allison raised a hand to the back of her head and touched the still-tender area. She really wasn't anxious to meet the big woman again. 'Is she out of jail already?' she asked tentatively.

'Steve got her out, too. She's my prime suspect, and I can't get any evidence on her if she's in jail.'

Allison drew in a deep breath and straightened her shoulders. 'Then I'll have to be very careful around her, but my fear of her doesn't even begin to equal my fear of the consequences of not carrying on with this story.'

'Allison, be reasonable. If you go down there by yourself, especially at night, you're putting yourself in danger. There's a murderer running around loose, and you may have just hit her hot button. What's going to happen to Megan if you get yourself killed? You'll have your story then, all right, and Dr Doug will have your daughter.'

'I don't see that I have any choice. I'll take my chances.'

'Fine,' he said angrily. 'Be that foolish. Risk your life. But I warn you, I won't be around to look out for you.'

'I don't recall ever asking you to. I can take care of myself. So . . . I guess I'll see you around?' She'd intended for the last words to come out as a flip comment, but instead they sounded more like a question, and she hated herself for it. She was

313

practically asking him to at least make plans to see her on a personal basis.

'Allison . . .'

The pleading note in his voice lightened her mood disgustingly. 'Yes?'

'Nothing. Do what you have to do. Goodbye.'

She hung up the phone and stood staring at it for several minutes, unable to go immediately back into the dining room and face Megan and Rick.

She didn't need Brad's help and wasn't really counting on him. But doing this on her own was surprisingly intimidating. And knowing that Brad's job was more important to him than she was, that he could so easily agree not to help her, not to see her at all, left her with an ache that didn't come from the beating she'd taken the night before.

In fact, this ache made the others seem inconsequential by comparison.

And that was really stupid.

CHAPTER 16

Brad went back to the shelter that night, just in case Allison did show up . . . which she did, of course, apparently straight from work, looking totally out of her element in an elegant cream-colored suit with an emerald-green blouse . . . probably silk. Yet she seemed to be able to make the people she talked to forget that her clothes very likely cost more money than they saw in a year, that she was using them for a story to make more money to buy more designer clothes.

She moved easily from one person to the next, smiling and talking as though she were entertaining guests in her living room, and everyone she spoke to smiled in return, greeting her as if she were a good friend. Certainly they'd all heard about the incident the night before, so they were all undoubtedly curious.

Which, he reluctantly admitted, didn't account for all of it. She did have a talent for making people feel comfortable. Just a leftover skill from her days of playing the gracious hostess, he told himself, irritated at the misplaced admiration he felt for her.

He had told her he wouldn't be around to keep an eye on her, but he'd lied. No matter what, he couldn't leave her on her own. She was desperate, and he suspected she'd go to any lengths to get the information she needed. Maybe she wouldn't deliberately put herself in danger, but her judgment would be out of kilter.

Of course, Steve Raney and the lieutenant thought the same thing about his judgment, and they could be right. He was probably all kinds of an idiot for looking out for her – for caring what happened to her. For caring about her. But she wasn't just a reporter any more. He understood her motivations. True, she had her eye on the dollar sign, but with good reason. Still, that meant when she got her big story and he got his killer, she'd be out of his life forever.

Nevertheless, right now he'd do his best to see that she survived long enough to get that story.

He tensed as he watched Jean approach Allison. When Allison looked up and saw the woman barreling down on her, her eyes widened, and he fancied he could feel her fear from across the room. But she stood her ground and waited. Allison never backed down. He could almost hear Raney's voice: 'You say that almost like you're proud of her.' Well, along with her faults, she

316

did have some good points. Some damn good points, and courage was certainly one of them.

After a few moments Allison relaxed and smiled, and Brad felt himself relax.

When he'd talked to Jean earlier, she'd seemed to have no memory, or at least no anger, about the night before. Apparently she was reacting the same way to Allison.

He jumped when Pollock slid onto the bench beside him. Damn! He had to quit letting himself get so wrapped up in Allison that he wasn't paying attention to what was going on around him, to his job.

'That was a brave and good thing you did last night,' he said, then looked in Allison's direction. 'But I fear, my son, you are now reaching for that which is outside your realm and can only bring you heartache.'

It took a moment for Pollock's words to register. He'd noticed Brad's obsession with Allison's activities, and was warning him that she wasn't right for him, that a homeless man shouldn't aspire to a relationship with someone like her.

'I know that, preacher.' He smiled at the irony. He might not be a street person, but Pollock had hit the nail on the head anyway. 'I was just worried about her. You know, afraid Jean might try to hurt her again.'

Pollock's face lit up, and a smile stretched from

ear to ear. 'You can relax your vigilance. Our sister, Jean, has seen the light. She has repented and will indulge no more in the halls of evil.'

It was just the opportunity Brad had been waiting for. He'd talked to Henry Dawson last night and confirmed what Allison had told him; Henry had seen Pollock and Dealey leaving the shelter by the rear door the night of Dealey's murder. Dealey had been 'dead drunk', he'd said, unable to walk, supported and dragged along by Pollock. If Henry was telling the truth – and he'd never known the man to lie or be mistaken – the situation had suddenly become very interesting.

A check of the autopsy report showed no traces of alcohol or drugs in Dealey's blood.

Which left a big question in Brad's mind. Was Dealey unconscious or even already dead when Pollock was dragging him? Was the preacher trying to hide the evidence and protect the killer, blaming himself for the evil perpetrated by the people he was trying to save from themselves?

Brad snorted. 'So Jean says today, but what about tomorrow? Tell me, preacher, does anybody ever really make it, really stick with it?'

'Certainly, my son. Your friend, Dealey, made it.'

'Huh!' he grunted. 'That's not what I hear. There's a rumor going around that he was seen drunk the night he died. I hear he was so drunk, you had to drag him out of here.'

Pollock flinched as if he'd been hit, and his big features drooped sadly . . . though only for an instant. He recovered his usual cheerful expression almost immediately. 'I'm afraid, my son, this world is far from perfect. There are always those who would cause trouble and besmirch the names of the innocent. If you pay heed to such viciousness, you are only damaging your own soul.'

'Are you telling me Dealey didn't fall off the wagon, that he really was going straight?' he asked as if Dealey's sobriety were his only consideration.

'Dealey rests in the bosom of the angels. We should all rejoice to be as he is.'

Brad shook his head, watching Pollock closely. 'Somebody killed him, somebody very evil, and that somebody deserves to be punished.'

'Judge not that you be not judged. Only God can discern the hearts of men.'

Rhetorical and nonspecific though Pollock's speech might be, it sounded pretty damning, pretty much like the man was covering up for somebody. But it was a lead-pipe cinch he'd never get any straight facts out of Pollock.

'You must learn to look to your own life,' Pollock continued, 'and keep yourself centered on goodness and purity.'

'I'll keep that in mind,' Brad mumbled. *While I try to figure out some way to convince the judge to give me a search warrant for that back room that you carried*

Dealey out of. Or Dealey's body.

From the corner of his eye he saw Allison moving toward the entrance, leaving. Without thinking, he was on his feet, heading in her direction.

'Bill, I fear you're creating trouble for yourself!' Pollock called.

Brad looked back toward him. Great. The preacher thought he had the hots for Allison and was going to pursue a woman he had no chance of attaining.

And wasn't that exactly what was happening?

No, damn it! Not entirely, anyway. He and Allison had a deal, and he needed to talk to her.

She was already in the parking lot across the street, unlocking her car door when he caught up to her. Well, he'd just have to take his chances on being seen in public talking to her. They did have a connection after their joint trip to jail, so anyone watching shouldn't be unduly suspicious.

'Hi.'

She turned around and saw him and gave him her phony made-for-television smile. 'Hello.'

He clenched his hands into painful fists to keep them from reaching for her, from pulling her to him so he could kiss away that phony smile and replace it with a real one. He knew she had a real one, along with real feelings. She could maintain her pretense of alabaster for the rest of the world, but he knew better.

Not that it did him one bit of good.

'We need to talk,' he said. 'I have some new evidence.'

'What?'

He bit his lip. 'You know I can't tell you right now. But it may be enough to get me a search warrant.'

She maintained her cool façade, but her eyes lit up at that information, becoming the rich color of brandy in front of firelight. He'd rather have seen them light up that way again with desire . . .

On the other hand, he reflected wryly, this was desire. Desire for her goal if not for him.

'We need to meet somewhere we can discuss this,' he said.

She leaned back against her car and folded her arms, aloof and self-contained. 'All right. Where? Do you want to come by my house?'

'Not with Dr Doug's boys on the job. How about if you come by my parents' house tomorrow evening?'

She stood up straight, her arms dropping to her sides. 'Your parents' house?'

She looked and sounded as shocked as he felt. He hadn't known he was going to say that. Even so, he understood immediately why he had said it and knew the idea must have been fermenting in his subconscious for a while now.

It was the ideal place for two reasons. He'd have to keep his hands off her, something he couldn't guarantee if they met at her house or his. Certainly not his without even Megan around to worry about.

But secondly, and probably most important, seeing her in the setting of his parents' middle-class home, a setting very similar to the one from which she was so desperate to escape, should help him keep things in their proper perspective until this venture was over. Until his exposure to Allison was ended.

'Yes, my parents' house. I think you know where it is. I need to check with them first, of course. I'll call you later tonight. If that's all right.' Good grief. How had he let his voice go all soft on that last comment, making it sound like he was asking permission for a friendly call?

'Of course it's all right,' she said with just a whisper of her genuine smile. It was enough to almost do him in.

What were they doing, he wondered, acting like strangers when they'd been so close so recently? On the same side, in the same bed . . . sharing the same bodies.

'Allison . . .' He took a step closer to her before he stopped himself. Raney and the lieutenant were right. He was letting his emotions get the best of his judgment. Do anything with her you want after the case is closed, they'd warned him. But he knew there would be no connection between them after the case was closed. So that pretty well shut off things at both ends.

'I'll talk to you later,' he mumbled, looking downward and taking refuge behind the beard he so despised.

'Right.' She started to get into her car, then hesitated, one shapely leg, shiny in its nylon stocking, still extended out, slim foot arched into the high-heeled shoe resting on the pavement. He felt like a schoolboy, getting aroused over nothing more than a woman's leg . . . and the lower half of it at that.

'Douglas is picking Megan up at six tomorrow,' she said.

It took him several seconds to figure out what she was talking about, what they'd been discussing before he'd fixated on her leg. 'No problem. We'll make it six-thirty or seven.'

She nodded, slid the rest of the way into her car, and he watched her drive away, the red tail lights growing smaller and smaller.

Maybe he hadn't exactly planned on a future together with her, but, he realized as she drove out of his field of vision, it would seem he'd somehow lost sight of a future apart from her. Facing that picture head-on was a lot tougher than he'd ever have thought. But her last words should serve to remind him of the status of her life, a status that could never include him.

Meeting her at his parents' house would be good.

Allison felt cold as she drove home. She turned on the car's heater, but the chill was inside her and couldn't be warmed so easily. Brad had caused it, so perhaps only he could take it away. She certainly hoped not; it could be a long, cold winter if that were the case.

She shivered as she thought of how radically he'd changed overnight. Okay, so he'd been forced to back away from her assistance on his case. She didn't like that or agree with it, but she could accept it. However, there was no reason for him to act like she'd recently developed leprosy.

She pulled into her driveway and stopped.

She might as well have leprosy. Brad had every reason in the world for avoiding her. An ex-husband bent on keeping her in court for the rest of her life or her money, whichever came to an end first, private detectives swarming around taking pictures, and a station manager who grilled her for information. She didn't blame him for not wanting to be a part of her life. She didn't much want to be a part of it either.

The front door flew open, and Rick bounded out, coming over to open the garage door and motion her inside. Megan stood on the porch, her small body outlined by the light from the living room.

Allison smiled. Her life wasn't so bad after all. She had the best friend and the greatest daughter in the world, and, no matter what, she wasn't going to lose either one of them. What could she possibly need Brad for?

Yeah, okay, sex, maybe.

Then again, she could always buy a vibrator.

She eased the car into the garage.

So why was she looking forward to his phone call, to meeting his parents, even when it was strictly a business deal?

Allison broke every speed limit and a few other traffic laws on the way home the next day. The station manager had sent her on a late-breaking story, and she'd seen no option other than to do it. Now it was almost six-thirty on Friday night, she was late, and Douglas would probably be early. Douglas would certainly be early.

Sure enough, the Mercedes that angered her by its very existence sat in front of her house when she screeched into the driveway.

Charging inside, she saw that Douglas had made himself comfortable. He sat on the sofa reading a magazine while Megan sprawled entirely too close to the television, shooting down alien space ships, absorbing homespun gamma rays or whatever the television set exuded.

'Hi, Mom,' she called without looking away from the screen.

Douglas studied his watch pointedly. 'Well, Allison, I assumed you'd make it home eventually since your clothes are still here.'

'I was working. You didn't need to wait. You could have taken Megan and left me a note.'

Douglas stood and picked up his jacket. 'But I wanted to see for myself just how long you'd leave my daughter alone after dark.'

'Mrs Parsons is right next door.' Her feet ached, and she longed to kick off her shoes, but right now she needed every advantage, and an extra couple of inches helped a little.

'Mrs Parsons is an old woman. What could she do if Megan needed help? How would she even know if Megan needed help?'

'I don't need any help,' Megan advised her father. 'I can take care of myself.'

'So you've been telling me, Princess,' he said, his eyes never leaving Allison's, 'but you should have an adult in the house, especially at night.'

Allison couldn't argue with that, not that it ever did any good to argue with Douglas anyway.

'What time are you bringing her back on Sunday?'

'Six o'clock. I'd appreciate it if you could manage to be here. I don't want to leave my twelve-year-old daughter alone for God knows how long.'

'If you could bring her back at seven, as our divorce stipulates, it would make it easier for me to get away from work.'

He smiled – a bad sign. 'Does my daughter interfere with your work?'

'I'll be here at six.' She exhaled slowly to keep it from coming out as a sigh of defeat.

'Come on, Megan. We're going to be late for our dinner reservations.'

Reluctantly the girl abandoned her game, hugged her mother and bounced outside. 'Don't forget to record your show every night in case we don't get home in time to watch it!' she called from halfway down the walk.

Douglas followed her out but turned back at the door. 'Where's your homeless buddy tonight? Still in jail? Where'd he get Judge Jameson's car? Steal it for the night? And why is he trying so hard to hide his identity? Don't worry. I'll have all the information on him I need before the trial.' He smiled again, even wider, and closed the door behind himself.

'Damn you to poverty and sudden baldness!' She kicked the door ineffectually. 'And damn me for letting him upset me every time he comes around.'

But he had. Her adrenaline was gushing as anger and fear raged chaotically. A great way to start the evening.

She took a deep breath, ordering herself to calm

down, and headed for the bathroom to freshen up before she went to Brad's parents' house.

The doorbell rang. Had Megan forgotten some article of clothing? Or had Douglas forgotten some threat or insult he'd been saving for her?

She went back and threw open the door, then wished she'd followed her advice to Megan about not answering after dark. Bonnie the Bimbo stood there in all her blonde glory, wearing a full-length mink coat. The weather really wasn't cold enough to justify the fur, so she must be bent on intimidation.

'He just left,' Allison assured her, starting to close the door.

Bonnie opened the screen then grasped the edge of the wooden door with a gloved hand. 'I saw him pulling away as I drove up.'

Allison looked pointedly at the hand intruding into her house. If she slammed the door hard and fast enough . . .

'You and I need to talk,' Bonnie said smoothly. 'May I come in?'

Allison hesitated. A lifetime of correct manners died hard. 'No,' she said, proving they could, however, be momentarily sidestepped.

The perfect oval face framed by the perfect blonde hair suddenly became ugly. No amount of surgery could disguise that hatred. 'We have bent over backward to get along with you, but you insist on ruining everything. Well, it's almost over. It's only a matter of time before we have full custody of Megan.'

Allison's heart clenched at the thought of losing Megan, of this creature raising her daughter. Her distress must have shown because Bonnie smiled maliciously.

'You don't like that idea, do you? When that happens, you won't be able to lure Douglas over here with all the leaky faucets and broken windows and imaginary prowlers in the world. You'll be out of our lives. We'll never have to see your aging face again.'

With that, she whirled around and stalked down the walk. Her spike heel caught in one of the cracks, and she teetered, spoiling her perfect exit.

If there's any justice in the world, she'll fall, Allison thought heatedly. Come on, Lord, just a little fall, a little humiliation. I'm not even asking for any blood. But Bonnie righted herself and continued on out to her red Mercedes parked at the curb.

As she drove away, Allison checked the license plate from force of recently acquired habits. 'MRS-DOUG.' If she wasn't so upset, she'd gag.

'Calm down,' she ordered herself through clenched teeth as she closed and bolted the door, then leaned against it.

She had an appointment with Brad's attorney

friend on Monday, and, if he was half as resourceful as Brad, she needn't worry, she reassured herself. Except, of course, about paying his bill.

And therein lay the kicker. She'd won the last custody fight. She might win this one, might even be able to hock her rhinestones and pay the bill. But what about the next one and the one after that? Douglas wasn't going to quit, and obviously Bonnie, for her own reasons, supported him in his efforts.

As Bonnie's words came back to her, she managed a half-smile. Calling Douglas about the leaky faucet, she'd plead guilty to. At least, Megan had called him. But where did she get that business about the broken window and the prowler?

'Ah, Douglas, what will you use for an excuse to get out of the house when I'm out of the picture?' she asked the empty room. Then the implications of her being 'out of the picture' hit, and depression settled in again.

But she couldn't afford to indulge the emotion. She had a meeting with Brad tonight. He was going to tell her they were ready to break the case and give her the exclusive story. That had to be what he wanted to talk about.

She couldn't bear to think it might be anything else.

Maybe he even wanted to apologize for being so cold to her lately.

Or maybe not. That part didn't matter. All that mattered was getting her career off the ground, getting back in control of her life and staying there.

She plodded upstairs to the bathroom, forcing herself to concentrate on the possibility of soon being able to air her big story.

If she thought about anything else, she'd never be able to make it to Brad's. She'd sink down on the bathroom floor and cry and never even make it out of the house.

CHAPTER 17

'Mom,' Brad protested, 'this isn't a social event. You don't need to serve coffee to this woman. She's only an informant in a case I'm working on. I just need to be able to talk to her for maybe ten minutes.'

'I don't recall ever hearing a separate set of manners for informants,' Maggie replied, measuring grounds into the coffee maker.

Gerald pulled Brad aside. 'You're sure this Ms Prescott isn't dangerous? Maybe we ought to send your mother to the store or something.'

Brad smiled at the thought of Allison's being dangerous. 'I'm sure. Trust me, you'll like her. She's a very nice lady. I apologize for using your house, but I didn't want to take her to mine, and we can't go meeting out in public.'

Gerald waved aside the apology. 'Your mother's all excited about meeting a real-life informant. When this undercover thing is over, she'll retell this story at her bridge club for the next twenty years.'

The doorbell rang and all three people dashed in to answer it. Brad got there first.

Allison didn't disappoint him. In her royal blue suit, white silk blouse, shiny hair swinging about her perfect face, and her regal bearing she would allay any fears his parents had about entertaining an informant.

And she looked far too elegant to be comfortable in such a simple place with such down-to-earth people. He'd always known that, and seeing it for a fact should make it easier to let go of his persistent thoughts of her, his persistent need for her.

He'd been right about what this visit would accomplish. So how come he felt so disappointed? How come he still had to resist the impulse to take her hand, stroke her hair, touch her in some way?

'Come in, Allison,' he invited, stepping back to allow her entrance – to get out of touching distance of her.

'Allison Prescott,' Maggie exclaimed from close behind him. 'I watch you every night!' She pushed past Brad and grasped Allison's hand. 'I'm Maggie Malone, Brad's mother. And this is Gerald, his father. Brad, you didn't tell us you were working with Allison Prescott. Come in, dear, and have a seat. I'm just making fresh coffee. Do you take cream and sugar?'

'Uh, no.' She looked to Brad in confusion, but he

could only shrug. She was on her own now.

He hadn't considered that, while he found her occupation an annoyance, her quasi-celebrity status might impress his mother. In fact, it hadn't even occurred to him that either his mom or his dad would recognize her. He watched his mother escort Allison to the sofa as though she were an honored guest.

'I'll be right back with that coffee.' Maggie disappeared into the kitchen.

Brad looked toward his father. Gerald advanced on the now-seated Allison with his hand out-stretched.

'It's a real pleasure to meet you, Ms Prescott. Your work is very impressive. You make all your stories sound interesting, no matter if it's a cat show or a drug raid.'

'Why, thank you, Mr Malone.' Allison smiled and blushed becomingly as she shook Gerald's hand.

'Call me Gerald.' He sat down across from her.

'And please call me Allison.'

Maggie arrived with a tray holding four cups of coffee. Obviously she didn't plan to let Allison get away without a visit.

'Mom, Allison may be in a hurry. We just planned on a brief meeting.'

Allison accepted a steaming cup. 'No, I'm in no hurry.'

Brad glared at her but she was looking at his mother, so the glare fizzled in mid-air. Damn it, what was the matter with her? This wasn't a social occasion! She was here to make business arrangements with him, not to have a party with his parents.

'Brad?' His mother held a cup out to him. With a sigh, he sat down on the sofa beside Allison – the only seat available since his mom and dad were in both the chairs.

'You have a lovely home,' he heard Allison say.

'Thank you, dear. We've been here a lot of years.'

Allison sounded so sincere, Brad looked around the place, checking things out to see if he'd missed something. Nope. Except for being more cluttered, the little house wasn't that much different from the one Allison lived in . . . and hated.

Framed family pictures, including many of himself through the years, perched on all flat surfaces from the coffee table to the top of the upright piano. Cabbage roses on the area rug faded from the original pink under the lamp tables to muted mauve in front of the sofa, and he suddenly wondered why his parents had never replaced the rug. They had the money. Perhaps they, like he, hadn't noticed its gradual demise – until tonight. Until he tried to see the place through Allison's eyes.

Okay, he should have known she'd be polite. She was as big on 'manners' as his mom was. That didn't mean she fit in. He'd be willing to bet that suit she was wearing cost more than the sofa she was sitting on. She did look out of place, just as he'd known she would. But it didn't matter. He still wanted her. Like a man on a diet would still crave rich desserts, he still craved Allison Prescott, no matter how impossible their relationship might be.

'Isn't that an Oehrke rug?' she asked, and he cringed, knowing his mother wouldn't have any idea what Allison was talking about, would likely be embarrassed. This hadn't been such a good idea after all.

'Why, yes, it is,' Maggie answered, beaming. 'We got it new when the boys were young. It's had to survive a lot of abuse.'

Allison smiled knowingly, then set her cup on the coffee table and picked up one of the framed photographs from the lamp table beside the sofa. 'Is this a picture of your boys? They look like they could ruin a few carpets. Definitely mischievous.'

'That's them. Brad's on the right, in the jeans with the torn knee – he hasn't changed much – and the one beside him is his brother, Dennis, fourteen months younger. They should look mischievous in that picture. It was taken just before we found out they'd been up the street in the big oak tree water-bombing cars.' She paused and gave Brad a scathing look. 'Even convertibles.'

'Mother!' Brad protested. Next thing he knew,

she'd be dragging out baby pictures that showed his bare butt. He looked to his father for support, but Gerald was leaning forward, obviously enthralled with Allison.

'Girls aren't any better,' Allison said. 'When my daughter was seven, she and the neighbor girl had a contest to see who could flush the biggest roll of toilet paper. The plumber was the only winner.'

'You have a daughter! How old is she?'

'Twelve going on twenty.'

'Mom, Allison, do you suppose we could get down to business?'

All eyes turned to him, and he realized he'd sounded querulous. Well, damn it, he hadn't asked Allison over here to chit-chat with his mother. He needed to discuss a little case of murder with her.

But in all honesty, he had to admit that wasn't what was making him irritable. He'd expected to prove a point tonight, and the only point she'd proved was that she had impeccable manners. That wasn't something that would keep her out of his thoughts.

'Well, Maggie, let's go finish up in the kitchen and let the young people talk,' Gerald said, rising from his chair. 'Allison, it's been a real pleasure meeting you.'

'Yes, it certainly has been,' Maggie echoed. 'We're having pot roast for dinner, and we'd be thrilled if you'd join us.'

A look of longing flitted across Allison's face, then vanished. For a moment, Brad thought she was going to accept the invitation. For a moment he wanted her to, wanted to forget everything but this cozy family scene where she seemed to fit so well. Letting her come here had been a big mistake. He'd accomplished the opposite of what he set out to do.

'Thank you so much,' she said. 'I'd love to stay, but I have to get home and fix dinner for my daughter.'

Maggie looked at Brad as though she somehow knew Allison's reluctance was his doing. 'Of course. Maybe next time.'

'I'd like that.'

His parents went into the kitchen, closing the door behind themselves, and Brad was left sitting on the sofa with one cushion separating him from Allison. One small cushion the width of the ocean.

'Brad, what's going on?' she asked, her dark eyes sad, confused and a little fearful.

He felt like seven kinds of a jerk. He didn't want to answer her question honestly. Surely he could evade the issue. Just say, Dealey wasn't drunk, he ordered himself. The words were on the tip of his tongue. Distract her and avoid the subject she was really questioning him about.

But even he couldn't be that insensitive. He'd arranged the situation, now he had to face up to the outcome.

'My folks like you,' he said.

'They're nice people. I like them. But that's not what we're talking about. Why are you acting so strangely to me?'

He drained his coffee cup, buying time, even though it was only a few seconds.

Allison watched Brad squirm. She understood that he'd been warned by his superiors to stay away from her right now, but that didn't explain the nervous, fidgety way he'd been acting this evening, his rude outburst. She got the idea he didn't like her getting on so well with his parents. Had he wanted them to dislike her?

She tried to tell herself it didn't matter. She knew it shouldn't matter. They'd had their moments, and those moments had been pretty incredible. She could no more afford to get involved with him than he could with her. She had to get her life in order, get things under control before she dared let anyone share that life. Still, she couldn't deny that his attitude hurt.

He set his empty cup down then leaned backward, into the corner of the sofa, laying his arm along the back. When he spoke, his tone was defensive. 'Allison, this is where I grew up.'

'I gathered that.' Did he think she'd been asleep or that she had short-term memory loss?

'My own home isn't very much different. A little bigger, a little less well-decorated.' He gave a faint smile. 'Especially the kitchen. I keep my record collection in one of the cabinets.'

'So?

He drew in a deep breath and sat up straighter, as if determined to get an unpleasant matter out of the way. Allison took another sip of coffee and braced herself. She didn't think she was going to like this.

'I'm a cop. For the most part, I love my job. I get a real charge out of thinking I'm improving the world by helping people and by locking up criminals, even if a lot of them get out the next day. I'll never be anything but a cop. And that means I'll never be rich.'

He paused and looked at her, his gaze piercing.

'Good,' she said. 'Everybody needs a goal in life.' It was probably one of the most inane things she'd ever uttered, but she wasn't sure what he wanted her to say.

He pounced on her comment. 'And your goal in life is to make a lot of money, to return to your former lifestyle.'

She could feel the angry blood rushing to her face. 'That's not fair. You know why I need to make money. To keep Megan. To fight Douglas.'

'Yeah,' he admitted, looking down, his attention apparently riveted to the embossed pattern of the dark blue sofa. 'I know that. But the fact remains that you and I live in different worlds, and we always will.'

'Different worlds.' She repeated the clichéd expression, letting it sink sharply into her heart, ripping with its jagged edges. She knew her world was insecure, terrifying, costly, in constant upheaval, and his was relatively stable . . . except for putting his life on the line in his job. So he couldn't stand any more excitement. She'd always known that just as she'd always known she couldn't get involved with him. But hearing it expressed so baldly, so finally, was like having a knife plunged into her guts.

He lifted his gaze to hers again, and she saw a weary sadness in his eyes. 'Allison, you're the most exciting woman I've ever met.' Suddenly his words came tumbling out as though the dam had broken. 'I think I could make love to you twenty-four hours a day. Okay, maybe twenty-three. But more than that, I've come to admire and respect you. And care about you. I don't know how it happened, but you've become important to me. And you and I both know that once this case is solved and you get your story, we'll never see each other again.'

Allison sat for a moment staring at him, trying to absorb everything he was saying. On the one hand, he'd admitted that he cared for her, a confession that should give wings to her soul. But the admission was only a part of goodbye. And in spite of understanding the reality of the situation, she didn't want to say goodbye.

She stood and picked up her purse with trembling hands. 'Very well,' she said, trying to keep her voice from cracking. 'I misunderstood the purpose of this meeting. I thought you had news concerning the murders. You will let me know when you do? I presume we still have a deal.'

He jumped up with her and took her hands in his, restraining her from leaving. For a moment, as they stood so close, as his gaze held hers, she thought maybe . . .

He released her hands abruptly and sat back down. 'I do have news. That's why I wanted to talk to you tonight.'

'So talk,' she said brusquely, determined not to let him know how much he'd upset and hurt her, glad to have another topic to focus on.

'To begin with, the coroner's report showed no trace of alcohol or drugs in Dealey's blood.'

She sank onto the sofa again. That was news. 'What about Henry Dawson's story?'

'He's sticking by it. I questioned him myself. So we can only conclude that Dealey was either unconscious or even dead when Pollock dragged him out the night he died.'

'Pollock does know something! He was hiding the body! He's hiding the killer.'

'Probably. I talked the judge into giving me a search warrant for that back room of Pollock's since that's where he was coming from with Dealey. We plan to go in tomorrow afternoon.'

'Brad, this could be it!' Her excitement at the idea of finally getting her big story almost took away the pain of Brad's hurtful words a few minutes before. Almost. 'I want to be there! I'm the one who talked to Henry first. I'm entitled to be there! We have an agreement.'

'I knew you'd feel that way, but, remember, this is only a search. It may produce nothing. You may have to hold onto whatever you get until we're ready to release the story.'

So much for her burst of excitement. 'All right,' she agreed. 'But Rick and I get to be there for all of it.'

'Rick?'

'Footage. Pictures. Television is a visual medium. Remember?'

He nodded curtly. 'I remember. Okay. Here's the plan. Steve's going in through the front door with a couple of uniforms. They'll keep Pollock occupied while Steve lets me in the back way. If we turn up anything, my cover's going to be more important than ever in getting Pollock to talk, so you don't say anything to me. In fact, you and Rick will have to stay out of the way and not say anything to anyone. You'll be nothing more than observers. No questions, no comments. Not even a sneeze. You can't interfere in any way. Think you can do that?'

'I've done all right so far.' His implied criticism

added to the unhappiness she already felt.

They talked for a few more minutes, ironing out details. When the conversation dwindled to a halt, Allison again stood and Brad rose with her.

'Tell your parents goodnight for me,' she requested.

'Will do. I'll call you tomorrow as soon as I have a definite time.'

As she approached the door, he reached around her to grasp the knob but froze in place, making no move to turn it. His arm touched her hip, and she stood still, too, not wanting to break the contact. The touch was accidental and buffered by several layers of clothes, his and hers. But none of that mattered. It felt wonderful, and she wanted to savor every drop of the pleasure it brought . . . for what might be the last time.

When he still didn't move, she turned to look at him. She barely had time to catch a glimpse of the desire smoldering in his eyes before his lips descended. With a sigh, she tilted her head and offered her lips to his. His beard tickled her nose in a way that had somehow become as familiar as if she'd known the feel for years. He tasted of his mother's coffee, and his lips were soft and warm as they caressed hers, sending spikes of electricity all through her body.

He wrapped his arms about her and pulled her close, so close, as if he'd never let her go. She surrendered herself to the moment and tried not to think beyond it.

'Brad – oh, excuse me!'

They jumped apart at the sound of his mother's voice, but she had immediately retreated into the kitchen, closing the door behind her.

'I'll be in the office tomorrow, waiting for your call, ready to spring into action.' Allison tried to sound flippant as she turned away from Brad, opening the door for herself this time.

'I'll call as soon as I have a definite time.'

She hurried down the sidewalk and out to her car, anxious to get away from Brad, from the way he made her feel, to go home . . . to her empty house. Well, she could always watch television. Maybe she'd rent a videotape of *She Devil*.

Allison's biggest fear the next day was that she'd be out on an assignment when Brad called. Though she'd gone out during the morning, she was determined to stick close to the phone that afternoon, and to keep Rick and his camera with her. Getting this story had always been important, but now it seemed doubly so, as if expanding that segment of her life could compensate for the hole Brad had left in another part.

Rick groaned when she gave away the second assignment. 'What if your friend lets you down and doesn't call?' he asked, laying his video camera on her desk and leaning toward her anxiously, balancing on both hands. 'What if they change their plans and don't go in until tomorrow? Giving away stories to people already trying to stab us in the back isn't a good plan for employment longevity.'

'He'll call. And they're going in today. He'd have let me know if the plans had changed.' She knew that for a certainty. Brad wouldn't let her down. No matter if their love life was in the toilet, she knew she could trust him.

Her phone rang, and they both jumped.

'We're going in thirty minutes from now.' Brad's voice was tight, curt. If she had to guess, she'd say his superiors weren't too happy about the arrangement he'd made with her. Well, that was tough. They had their job, and she had hers. She couldn't afford to worry about irritating people.

'We'll be there. And . . . thanks.'

When she and Rick arrived at the shelter, the search was apparently already underway. The shelter was deserted except for two uniformed officers who flanked an unsmiling but calm Pollock. The lack of his usual grin was the only evidence that anything was wrong.

'You folks can't come in here right now,' one of the officers said.

For a brief instant Allison experienced a shot of panic. What if –?

No, there were no what if's. She would get in. She strode toward the men, extending her identification. 'I believe arrangements have been made for us to be here.'

The officer gave her a disgusted look, but nodded his assent.

Rick raised his camera and began filming, and Allison flinched at the betrayed look in Pollock's eyes. She searched for something to say, but couldn't think of anything that wasn't deceitful. She lowered her eyes and sat down a few rows back.

Rick soon turned off his camera and joined her.

Time seemed to stretch forever, though the hands of Allison's watch showed a lapse of only ten minutes when Steve Raney appeared at the door to the back room.

'Bring him in, boys,' he ordered.

Allison and Rick started after them, but one of the uniforms barred their way, holding out his arm and giving Raney a questioning look.

'It's okay,' Steve growled reluctantly. 'Let them come, and that guy just walking in. Get him back here, then one of you stand guard at the door and keep everybody else out.'

Allison turned, surprised to see Brad hesitating halfway through the door. Insanely, she felt a surge of happiness at the sight of him.

'Come on, come on.' One of the uniformed policemen started toward him.

'I didn't do nothing,' Brad protested, and Allison suddenly realized it was all part of the act. He must have gone out the back door and come around to the front so he could confront Pollock without blowing his cover.

'Nobody's accusing you. Just get on back there with the others.'

Allison entered the small room, very much aware from Steve Raney's expression that he didn't want her there. However, she glared right back at him. He wouldn't be there if not for her.

She and Rick stood at one end in front of an old electric stove and a table, both covered with pots and pans and various other cooking paraphernalia. Raney and the other uniformed officer were standing across the room on either side of an old ladderback chair. On a shelf next to Raney sat a Bible and a large iron skillet. The pan struck Allison as being a little out of place since the others were on or near the stove.

'What do you want with me?' Brad asked. 'What's coming down here, preacher?'

'Do not be afraid, my son. These people cannot harm us. The pure in heart have nothing to fear, not even the dark of night.' He turned to Raney. 'Why are you detaining this man?'

Steve shrugged. 'Maybe he knows something. He did come in during the middle of our little project.'

'Purely accidentally,' Pollock argued. 'Please release him.'

'When we're done.'

'It's okay, preacher,' Brad said. 'It's not the first time I've been around cops.'

Pollock shook his head sadly. 'It'll soon be over. If you gentlemen will tell me what you're looking for, perhaps I can help you find it.'

Using a handkerchief, Raney picked up the out-of-place iron skillet while he watched Pollock.

'Have a seat, Reverend,' he instructed.

Pollock turned to look at Brad and managed a reassuring smile. Although he obeyed Raney's order, Pollock gave the impression that he was in control. This was, after all, his territory.

Raney turned the pan over and studied it carefully. 'Rust,' he said. 'Don't you cook in this one?'

'I have plenty of pans, thanks to the generosity of our friends who follow the admonition to do unto the least of creatures.'

'I see some scratches. It's been used for something recently.'

Pollock was silent.

Raney returned the pan to the shelf and leaned over to study the chair back, tapping the wood Pollock leaned against. 'Some odd stains on the wood. Even worse ones on the seat. That hemp absorbs real good, but it doesn't clean easily.' He paused, then walked around in front of Pollock.

'I'm going to take the pan and the chair into our lab, and I'd be willing to bet you we find traces of blood, flesh and hair. Are you a betting man, Reverend? Want to take me up on this?'

Allison stifled a gasp as she realized what Raney was suggesting. Nausea rose in her throat as Raney waved the skillet around, a skillet that might have been used to kill people. From behind her she heard the soft whir of Rick's video camera, but somehow she was unable to feel any elation that they were indeed getting their story.

'Take the pan and the chair and anything else you desire. Worldly possessions are of no value. Only the spiritual treasures we store are lasting.'

Raney slammed a fist down on the shelf, making everyone but Pollock jump. 'Do you know what an accomplice is? Do you know how long you could spend in prison as an accomplice?' Raney leaned over the sitting man, his face only inches away from Pollock's. 'Don't you have something you want to tell me? Like who you're protecting, for instance. You were seen leaving here with Dealey's body. It's all over. You don't have any choice but to tell us what you know.'

Allison couldn't see the expression on Pollock's face since Raney was between them, but the Reverend seemed to tense. His voice, when he spoke, echoed that tension.

'The strong must care for the weak.'

Muttering a few choice words, Raney stood erect, then strode around behind Pollock. 'Reverend,' he said into the man's ear, 'one of these people that you feed and care for is a murderer. He's taking the precious gift of life from his friends, from your friends. If you really care about these people, you'll tell us so we can help him stop.'

Pollock wagged his head slowly from side to side in a negative response. His eyes were full of sadness.

Allison bit her lip and resisted an urge to comfort him. He might be crazy, but he meant well.

'Man wants to be good, but the forces of evil constantly assail him, try to drag him from the path of righteousness. I am here to fight evil, to drag man back from eternal damnation.'

'Like you're trying to drag Jean?'

'Jean cannot fight the wickedness of the world. She needs to be guided through this life.'

'Come on, Pollock. We know she's getting drugs from Dwight. Did she kill these people while she was wasted, or did they have a little money and she wanted it?'

Pollock didn't answer, only shook his head.

Allison thought he might be going to cry.

'Maybe we better go find this Jean and question her.' He nodded to the uniformed officer. 'Logan, go get Collins and check around until you find this woman, then we'll take her and Pollock both down to the station.'

'Jean killed no one!' Pollock burst out, losing his control at last.

'Then who did?'

Allison almost missed the barely perceptible nod Raney gave Brad. Even seeing it, she nevertheless gasped aloud when Brad suddenly burst into action. Covering the space between Raney and himself in a few long strides, he grabbed Raney's collar.

'Leave him alone. I'm the one you want,' Brad shouted. 'I killed them all.'

Logan grabbed Brad's arms and pulled him off, wrestling him to a face-down position on the floor in front of Pollock, who was now standing in shocked horror. The officer snapped handcuffs on Brad and yanked him to his feet.

'You have the right to remain silent,' he began and proceeded to Mirandize him.

'No,' the Reverend protested, trying to push Logan away from Brad. 'This man has done no wrong. Don't you know that you invite burning coals on your head when you harm the innocent?'

'Innocent? We got a confession from him,' Raney growled. 'We should be able to put him away for the rest of his life, maybe get the death sentence.'

Pollock turned to him, hands outstretched. 'There's been no murder. Our bodies come from dust and return to dust. Dust has no life. It cannot die. Only the spirit lives and can never be extinguished.'

Brad struggled against Officer Logan. 'I bashed in their heads! I killed them! Punish me!'

Logan wrestled him to the floor again, and Pollock threw himself across Brad's body. Tears rolled down his big cheeks as he looked up to Raney.

Allison wiped a tear away from her own eyes. She didn't want to watch this. Surely they could have handled this differently, caused Pollock less pain.

'Stop,' the preacher begged. 'Know you not that you invite the fires of hell by persecuting the innocent?'

Raney bent over Pollock, scant inches away from his face. 'This man's a murderer,' he grated. 'He's evil. He deserves to suffer, and I'm going to see to it that he does.'

Pollock pushed at Logan, trying vainly to free Brad.

Allison felt Rick's hand on her arm, restraining her, and she realized she'd taken a step forward.

'No death,' Pollock exclaimed. 'I released them while they were in a state of light before they could fall into darkness again. I gave them life, not death!'

No one moved. Pollock's sobs sounded loudly in the silence.

As the meaning of what she'd just heard penetrated, Allison raised a hand to cover her mouth. It wasn't possible. The man was too kind, too caring.

'Come off it. You're covering for somebody,' Raney huffed, but to Allison's ears he sounded only half-convinced.

'I want no more souls on my conscience,' Pollock cried. 'So many times I have failed. Even now one man I was sent to help languishes in sin, in prison for the rest of this life. He was given into my keeping, but I failed him.' Abruptly the tears stopped, and his familiar smile appeared. 'I helped Dealey and the others, though. I was not too late for them. With my help, they escaped.'

'Unlock the cuffs,' Raney ordered Logan.

As soon as he was released, Brad took Pollock's arm and helped him to his feet, then guided him back into his chair.

'Can you tell me how you were able to help these people?' he asked quietly, kindly.

'When their spirit was right, I brought them back here to pray. They sat in this chair and I picked up the skillet and released them into everlasting peace.' He looked up at Brad, his eyes suddenly sad again. 'I tried so hard, always I tried, but sometimes they slipped back so fast, before I could help them. I must try harder. The fields are ripe for harvest, but the workers are few.'

It was true, then. Pollock of the gentle hands and perpetual smile, of the ceaseless ranting against sin, had murdered six people. Pollock was more than a little nuts. He was completely insane. In the last few minutes, he seemed to have lost what little touch with reality had remained to him.

Brad nodded reassuringly. 'I'm afraid you're going to have to go with the police. Do you understand why?'

Pollock's smile reasserted itself. 'Police struggle with evil, also.'

Logan stepped forward with his handcuffs, but Brad shook his head. 'Don't do that to him. He's not going to cause any trouble.'

Raney nodded agreement. 'Officer Logan,' he said in a tired voice, 'have you met my partner, Detective Bradley Malone?'

Logan studied Brad closely, then grinned. 'I've met him before, but he sure didn't look like this.'

'He won't look like that for much longer,' Raney said. 'Come on, Pollock. Let's go for a ride.'

Brad took the Reverend's arm, and the four of them, with Allison and Rick close behind, walked out to the street. When Pollock was settled in the squad car, Raney turned to Brad.

'Want to ride down with me? We can come back for your truck later.'

'Hold it,' Allison exclaimed, stepping forward. She'd become so involved in the unfolding drama, she'd almost forgotten her job. 'I need an interview.'

Raney glared at Brad, but Brad didn't flinch. 'I'll be along in a few minutes,' he assured Raney, then steered Allison and Rick back into the shelter.

CHAPTER 18

When she and Rick charged into the station half an hour later, Tracy and another cameraman were on their way out the door to cover the capture of the serial murderer.

'Got it right here,' Allison assured them, patting Rick's camera. 'We'll have it edited in time for the six o'clock news.'

Tracy scowled. 'How'd you do that? We just now heard about it.'

'Oh,' Allison said airily, 'I have an "in" at police headquarters.' Okay, so she didn't really have an 'in' any more. It didn't hurt to worry Tracy a little, maybe give the girl a few wrinkles.

As she and Rick worked together to get the story ready to air, Allison was amazed and impressed. It was a great story, no doubt about it.

Without a minute to spare, they got it on the six o'clock news.

And then it was over. The camera was off, neckties were loosened, perpetual smiles relaxed.

Allison's co-workers turned back into real people.

'Great story!'

'Way to go, you two!'

She and Rick accepted the congratulations, some sincere, some forced.

'Telephone, Allison.'

Allison dashed to pick up the phone. Only when she heard Cody Hunter's voice did she realize with a flash of irritation at herself that she'd been hoping it would be Brad.

'Good job,' the station manager enthused. 'It was well worth the wait. Come in on Monday, and let's have a chat. Bring your cameraman.'

'Right. We'll be there.'

Allison hung up the phone in a glowing daze.

'Who was that?' Rick asked. 'Your hairy friend?'

That dulled the glow a little.

'No, that was the omnipotent Cody Hunter. He wants to have a little chat with both of us on Monday.'

'All right! Do I smell raises?'

Allison sniffed the air. 'Raises and promotions.'

Rick chuckled. 'Why not? If you're going to dream, go for the Neiman–Marcus variety.'

'You bet. Doesn't cost a penny more.'

Another co-worker stopped by to congratulate them.

'So are you celebrating with the bearded wonder?' Rick asked when the co-worker moved on.

'I told you my relationship with Brad was strictly business,' she snapped. And stop bringing him up, she added silently. How the hell was she supposed to forget about him if Rick kept reminding her?

'Great! Then you're free to go celebrate with me. I owe you a dinner. After all, you had to practically drag me into fame and fortune.'

'Sounds like a terrific idea.' Much better than going home to an empty house, and that, she realized, was her alternative option.

Damn Brad! This should be a time of pure ecstasy for her, and he was diluting it. Against her better judgment, she wanted him to be here to share the moment. And that knowledge only made things worse. Her happiness couldn't depend on him. She'd learned the hard way that was guaranteed disaster.

Not that she'd been really happy with Douglas, at least not in recent years. But she had counted on him to be there, to take care of Megan and her, and he'd turned that dependency against her.

She wasn't going to repeat her mistake with Brad. Even if he were willing to let her, which he wasn't. And that was good. Made it easier for her to let go and go on.

'Let's go all the way,' Rick was saying in a mock-dramatic voice. 'Dinner at some restaurant where we can get a juicy, rare steak, then a movie at some theater where they still put coconut oil on their popcorn.'

'Why not? We've only got one life to live, so let's live it on the edge! Laugh at danger.'

Some joke. She'd been doing just that, letting Brad into her life, into her bed . . . into her heart. Thank goodness her association with him was ended, and none too soon.

It was only a little after ten o'clock when Allison arrived home, but it felt much later. Probably because of starting the evening so early.

She smiled to herself as she put her car in the garage and closed the door. They'd had fun. Rick was a good friend. That was what she needed. Friends. That was all she needed. Friends and her daughter. That was safe.

The evening was chilly, a promise of the cold winter ahead. But cold wasn't so bad, she thought. The air felt cleaner, more invigorating than the heat of summer.

Overhead the sky seemed to spread out more, the stars farther away.

Cold. No matter what she told herself, she didn't like the cold. She dashed up the porch steps, anxious to get inside to the warm.

Unlocking the front door, she let herself in just as the phone rang. She lifted the receiver, half-expecting to hear from another well-wisher.

'Didn't you get my messages?' She barely recognized the near-hysterical voice as Bonnie's.

Her heart began to pound wildly. Had something happened to Megan?

'Messages?' Whirling, she looked at the answering machine. The red light blinked madly, indicating numerous calls. 'No. I just walked in. What's the matter? Is Megan all right?'

'You need to come and get her. Right now.'

'What's wrong? Is she sick? Is she hurt?' She realized her own voice was becoming as hysterical as Bonnie's.

'Nothing's wrong with Megan. Your ex-husband is in jail, and I'm divorcing him. I hope you're happy now. Get over here and get your daughter.'

The first statement was so important, it took a minute for the second to sink in.

'Douglas is in jail? What happened?'

'Don't pull that innocent crap with me. Just take his car down there and bail him out.'

'Me? I don't have his car, and I have no intention of bailing him out. Why doesn't he call his lawyer?'

'He's not home. Your daughter's dressed and waiting for you.'

The line went dead.

She stared at the phone in total confusion. Douglas was in jail, and Bonnie wanted her to come get Megan, then bail Douglas out. Bonnie was divorcing Douglas. Apparently they'd had a fight. Had Douglas hit Bonnie? That seemed the obvious answer, though Allison couldn't imagine Douglas indulging in physical violence. He wouldn't want to damage his surgeon's hands for one thing, but mainly he was too skilled at the emotional variety.

She didn't suppose it mattered. Right now all that mattered was to get her daughter out of whatever sordid mess Douglas and Bonnie had created.

She smiled as it dawned on her that Douglas's little indiscretion – whatever it was – might very well work in her favor. He was so anxious to tell the judge she'd been to jail. Now she could use that same threat against him.

She hurried out the door to retrieve her daughter.

A few minutes later she pulled up in front of the large house Douglas had built for Bonnie, a house located in the same neighborhood where she had once lived with the man. He really was a creature of habit.

She parked in the circle drive and ran down the walk. Just before she reached the door, it opened and Megan rushed out.

'Are you all right?' Allison demanded, trying to hug her and examine her at the same time.

Though the girl seemed to be making an effort to appear unaffected, her eyes were red. 'I'm okay, Mom, but Daddy's in jail.'

'Take this with you!' Bonnie's voice suddenly cut into her consciousness, and she looked up to see the woman, blonde hair and makeup in disarray, lugging a suitcase out the door. 'Anything else he wants, he'll have to talk to my lawyer.'

Allison shook her head, more to clear it than in negation of Bonnie's statement. 'Let's go,' she said, wrapping an arm around Megan and ignoring the suitcase as they started down the walk.

'You take his damned clothes,' Bonnie shouted. 'I don't ever want to see him again except in court!'

Allison turned back to face the screeching harpy. She ought to feel triumphant, but all she felt was relieved that Megan was all right and with her again. 'Bonnie, I'm sorry, but I see no reason for me to go down and bail out your husband. If he doesn't reach his lawyer soon, he can find another one. He has the money.'

'Mo-om!' Megan protested.

'Don't act innocent with me!' Bonnie interrupted. 'When I went down there to get that no-good jerk out of jail, the police told me the woman he'd been caught with, his wife, Mrs Prescott, was sober enough to drive the car on home.' She kicked at the suitcase. 'You've got the rotten jerk, Mrs Prescott. Take his clothes with you.'

She turned and stormed into the house, her exit much less dignified than the day before, even taking into consideration her near fall.

Megan reached for the suitcase.

'Leave it,' Allison directed. 'What would we do with it? He and Bonnie will make up.'

Megan hesitated, her small face filled with uncertainty and hope. 'Were you with Dad tonight?'

'No, sweetheart, I wasn't. I spent the evening with Uncle Rick.'

'Truly?'

Allison nodded, feeling Megan's regret that her parents weren't together again after all. 'Truly.'

'Then who was Daddy with?'

'Who knows? Come on, let's get home.' She urged Megan toward the car.

'Don't forget Daddy's bag.'

'Right.' She'd have to take the damned suitcase. Megan was upset enough already. Dutifully she lugged it into the back seat.

As she slid into the driver's side, she looked over at Megan. The child seemed to have shrunk. She slouched in the seat with none of her usual buoyancy.

Allison pulled her close for a hug and stroked her long hair. 'Don't worry about Daddy. He's got enough money to buy himself out of trouble. What happened anyway? What did he do to get sent to jail?' She started the car and pulled out of the circle drive, away from the big house she'd once envied.

'He got a D.U.I. That means he was driving while he was drunk. Him and Bonnie had a fight, and he left and was gone a long time, then he called and told her he was in jail. She was going to get him out, but she came back without him, and she was really mad then. That's when she started calling you.'

'I see. Well, don't worry. Your dad can buy himself out of a D.U.I. Hey, I've got news about Brill. He closed his big case today, so I can tell you his secret identity, if you're interested.'

'Sure I'm interested.' It wasn't the enthusiastic response she'd have liked, but Megan's tone was marginally improved.

'To begin with, his name is really Brad, and he's an undercover cop.'

'Cool!'

Allison related the events of the last couple of weeks, concluding with her story and the future meeting with Cody Hunter. As she spoke, Megan became more and more excited. The distraction had worked better than she'd dared hope. She finished just as they arrived back home.

Megan leaned over the gear shift and wrapped her arms around her mother's neck. 'That's wonderful, Mom! You're finally going to be rich and famous.'

Allison laughed. 'I'll settle for a promotion to weekend anchor and a small raise. Make that a substantial raise.'

'Since Brill's a policeman, he can get Daddy out of jail!'

So much for the success of her distraction.

Megan stayed with her while she put the car into the garage for the second time that night.

She had to drag Douglas's suitcase across the yard. It was too heavy to carry, so there was really nothing she could do about the scratches it would likely sustain from being dragged. The thought gave her a small uplift.

'Are Daddy and Bonnie going to get a divorce?' Megan asked.

'Probably not.'

'Bonnie's pretty mad.'

'She'll get over it.'

'Somebody was watching your house, and he told Daddy that Bonnie came over here last night. Did she?'

Allison hauled Douglas's suitcase onto the front porch. Bonnie must have filled the damned thing with his medical books just so she'd get a hernia lugging it around. 'Yes, Bonnie came over, but just for a little while. She couldn't stay.'

'Then she accused Daddy of messing around with you. That's what they were fighting about.'

Allison flinched at the hopeful tone in Megan's voice. 'Bonnie's mistaken,' she said firmly, unlocking the door and flipping on the light. 'Ah, home at last. How about a little hot chocolate before we go to bed?'

'Mom, we have to call Brill to help Daddy.' She made a beeline for the telephone.

'Sweetheart, it's late. We can't call anybody at this hour.'

'He won't mind. Wow, look at all the messages.' She hit the play button on the recorder.

Allison sank onto the sofa, wondering how she was going to get around this latest crisis. The tape whirred softly as the answering machine rewound.

Douglas's voice came through first, desperate but controlled, requesting that Allison come down immediately and get him out of 'this awful place'. Four more messages followed, alternating between Douglas and Bonnie, with each one a little more frantic.

Then in the midst of all the discordance, Brad's voice, deep and strong and filling her with thoroughly disgusting happiness.

'I guess you're out celebrating. And with good cause. I caught the repeat of your story on the ten o'clock news. Congratulations. It was good. You're good.'

Silence. The end of the message. She hated herself for being disappointed, for wanting more.

Megan shot her a triumphant glance. 'See? He couldn't have called very long ago if he saw you on the ten o'clock news. It's okay if we call him now.'

Before Allison could think of a reason to protest, the next message began to play.

'These fools have put me in here with the scum of the earth,' Douglas proclaimed. 'These people are drunk, on drugs, they're filth. They're throwing up and snoring and they smell. Allison, I fear for my life. You have to come get me out. I promise I'll make it worth your while.' He paused, then went on. 'Megan, Princess, Daddy needs your help. Talk to your mother.'

That was just like the slimeball, using his daughter to get what he wanted.

The last call was from Brad. 'Allison, please call me as soon as you get home, no matter what time it is.'

The words she'd wanted to hear, but the tone was curt, professional – his 'cop' voice. She couldn't imagine what he wanted that was so urgent. However, she could only handle one crisis at a time.

'Mom,' Megan begged, 'please help Daddy. What's Brill's number? I'll call him.'

There seemed to be no way to get out of it. Douglas was Megan's father, and for that reason she couldn't allow him to rot in jail . . . no matter how much the prospect appealed to her personally.

'All right,' she said with a resigned sigh, 'bring me the *Yellow Pages*, and we'll find a bail bondsman and try to get your father out, though I don't know what you think we're going to use for money to post bond.'

'Mom!' Megan came over to stand indignantly in front of Allison, her small hands fisted on her narrow hips. 'You don't know anything about bail bondsmen and stuff like that. Brill can take care of it. Policemen know all about that kind of stuff. He got you out of jail, didn't he?'

'I really appreciate your vote of confidence,' Allison snapped, then immediately regretted her angry comment as Megan's face crumpled. The girl sank down beside her mother and laid her head on her shoulder. Allison wrapped her arms around her daughter. 'I'm sorry,' she said. 'I know you're upset about your father and Bonnie and everything.'

'I know you can do it, Mom. I just wanted Brill to be here right now. He always makes things better. Wouldn't it be easier to ask him for help? He does everything so good. He fixed the leak under the sink and the floor and the roof.'

Megan's words hit Allison between the eyes. Like it or not, she had been depending on Brad for some time now. And Megan was right. Asking him to help tonight would be easier than dealing with a system she really knew nothing about. She could do it, though. If she chose to, she could do it. So that made it all right to ask.

Besides, he'd left a message asking her to call him.

The phone rang, interrupting her rationalizations of why it was okay to call Brad, rationalizations that ignored the fact that she desperately wanted to talk to him. Like her daughter, she wanted to be with him, to let him make things better, as he always did.

She raced Megan to answer the phone. It was probably Douglas again.

'Hello?'

Brad drank in the sound of Allison's voice like a man dying of thirst who suddenly gets a glass of ice water. It seemed much longer than a few hours since he'd heard that voice. 'Allison, it's Brad. I'm glad you're home.'

'Brad. How are you?' Her tone was soft, breathless, almost a purr. Or did he just imagine what he wanted to hear?

'Ask him, Mom! Ask him!' Megan's voice in the background.

'Ask me what?'

'Well, it seems her father got himself in a little trouble – '

'You mean the D.U.I.'

'How'd you know that?'

'I got a phone call from a friend of mine on the force. That's what I was calling you about. But if you already know, I guess I'm not in time to warn you.'

He'd just told her a lie. True, he had wanted to tell her about Dr Doug. But he'd grabbed onto the incident as an excuse to call her. Ever since last night he'd been kicking himself for the things he'd said to her at his parents' house. It was all true, but he'd failed to tell her or himself the important part . . . that he loved her. That realization had come when she'd walked away from the New Hope Shelter after her interview with him . . . walked away and out of his life forever.

He wanted to ask her to forget everything he'd said last night, to tell her how much he missed her already, how much he cared about her, how much he loved her . . . to ask her if they couldn't find some common meeting ground for their different worlds.

'Yes, you're too late to warn me,' she said. 'However, I don't know any of the details. I just know he was arrested. I'd appreciate it if you could kind of fill me in.'

So he wasn't going to say any of the things he wanted to say. He was going to talk to her about her ex-husband. 'It seems Dr Doug slid through a stop sign. No big deal, but it is Saturday night, a lot of drinking and driving going on. Anyway, my friend witnessed the incident, and he recognized the license plate – I told a few people to keep an eye out for it – so my friend pulled Dr Doug over. The doc got belligerent right away, and he reeked of alcohol. He flunked the breathalyzer test, so my friend had no choice but to haul him in.'

He held his breath as he waited to see how she would take the information that he was responsible for her ex being in jail. She professed to hate the man, but one never knew where loyalties might lie in these matters.

'That's very interesting. Tell me more.'

He relaxed back in his arm chair. She sounded

happy. Restrained, naturally, with Megan there, but definitely not upset. 'The passenger, a woman who identified herself as his wife, passed the test and took the car. I knew from my friend's description that it wasn't you.'

'I can't believe you would have even considered that possibility. However, that does explain why Bonnie thinks I was with him.'

'Yeah, while she was waiting for a bail bondsman to meet her at the station, she asked about the car. The officer on duty looked at the report and, since Bonnie had identified herself as Mrs Prescott, he thought she was nuts. He told her she'd already taken the car home. Needless to say, she left poor Dr Doug in the slammer.'

'An action I would love to repeat, but Megan has different ideas.'

'Wants her father out, huh?'

'Oh, yes.'

'That's too bad. This could be a real learning experience for him.'

'I agree. However, I suppose I'd better find a good bail bondsman. Can you recommend anyone?'

'Sure. Want me to get things set up, then come by and take you down to the station?' He amazed himself with his desire to see her, even under less than romantic circumstances, with how much he wanted to be there when she rescued Dr Doug . . . how important it was to him to be sure that

Dr Doug didn't go home with her now that his wife had deserted him.

'I couldn't ask you to do all that,' Allison protested. 'If you can just give me a name, I can do the rest.'

There she went, assuring him she didn't need him again. Well, damn it, she did need him, and he needed her. If he could admit it, she could, too. 'You didn't ask me. I volunteered. I'll be there in half an hour.'

He hung up before she could protest again.

Of course, she could always call back.

But she didn't.

That was good. However, getting a woman's ex-husband out of jail wasn't exactly his idea of a perfect date.

CHAPTER 19

'He's here!' Megan called when the doorbell rang.

'I'll be right down!' Allison checked her reflection in her bedroom dresser mirror. She'd changed from the crumpled suit she'd worn to work into black slacks and a black and white sweater, then combed her hair and freshened her make-up. She needed to look like she was in control of the situation, even if she weren't.

'Hi, Megan.' Brad's voice drifted up the stairs as she started down.

'Brill?' A surprised squeak.

'Yep, it's me.'

'You look so funny.'

What on earth must he look like now if Megan thought he looked funny? Allison hurried on down the stairs.

A tall, clean-shaven man with a square jaw and short, curly hair dressed in a maroon sweater and stone-washed blue jeans stood in her doorway.

373

He grinned a little sheepishly. 'I forgot to mention that I got a hair cut and shave.'

'You look . . . different.' Unrecognizable. Had she really made love with this man, explored the hidden parts of his body? His body, yes, but not his face. This man was a stranger. She knew nothing about him. Where was the familiar man she'd come to trust, to care about? She felt absurdly deserted and alone.

He rubbed his hand over his bare chin. 'It's still me. I was always here, under the hair.'

She laughed nervously at her own silliness. 'You look nice,' she said inanely. He did. He was gorgeous, actually. 'It'll just take a little getting used to.'

'Are we ready to go get Daddy?' Megan asked.

'Everything's been arranged. All we have to do is go down and pick him up.'

'Then let's go!' Megan dashed out onto the porch.

'Could you get this suitcase? It belongs to Douglas,' Allison requested.

Brad picked it up and toted it out easily. Allison followed, pausing to lock up behind them.

'Wow, is that your truck? Cool.'

Allison turned to see the new white truck parked in front of the house.

'It's mine.' He smiled down at Allison. 'Really.'

'I recognize it. Rick and I took down the license

plate when it was parked at your dad's.'

His smile widened. 'I remember. You tracked me down. I was really angry with you, but even then I had to admire your ingenuity.'

He admired her ingenuity. She liked the sound of that.

He placed his free hand at the small of her back as they started down the steps, and finally Allison recognized him. She'd recognize that touch in total darkness. It was warm and comfortable, exciting and electric and seemed to meld his body with hers.

She stopped abruptly and turned to look up at him. This time she saw only his eyes, and they were Brad's eyes – clear and hazel and intelligent and caring. The first time she'd seen him, she'd known he wasn't a street person because of those eyes. She lifted a hand to touch his face, ridiculously happy as though she'd just recovered something she'd feared lost forever.

She loved him. It was that simple and that complex. If loving him meant she depended on him, left herself open to possible hurt – well, that was just the way it had to be. She didn't seem to have any choice in the matter.

Anyway, she couldn't judge him by the standards she'd used for Douglas. Brad would never hurt her in the ways Douglas had. He'd never try to take her daughter, her home, her self-esteem. And she had her own career now. He could only hurt her by taking himself away, as he'd done at his parents' house last night.

But tonight he was with her, and she wasn't about to let him get away with any more of that 'different worlds' garbage. If he didn't love her, she'd have to live with that. But he wasn't getting away until they'd had a chance to talk – really talk.

'Mom! Brill! Come on!'

Megan was standing beside the white truck, motioning impatiently for them to hurry.

'Don't you think we'd better take my car?' Allison asked. 'There won't be room for everybody in your truck.'

'Dr Doug could always ride in the back,' Brad said. 'Sober him up.'

Allison laughed giddily at the mental image of that. Actually, she was laughing because she felt good. Any excuse would have done.

After what seemed an eternity of tense waiting, Douglas finally walked through the door. His cotton shirt and usually immaculate slacks were wrinkled and stained, and his face was drawn. For a brief instant, Allison felt sorry for him.

'Daddy!' Megan ran to him and threw her arms around him.

'My sweet little Princess, I was afraid I'd never see you again!'

Allison lowered her head to hide her expression

of disgust. To her consternation, he kept one arm around Megan but turned his attentions to her.

'And there's my sweet wife.'

'Ex-wife,' she reminded him, dodging his embrace and moving over to stand beside Brad. 'Bonnie's your wife now, and I think you'd better trot out your best excuses for her benefit. She's a little irritated with you right now.'

'That bimbo!' he exploded, using the term he'd criticized Allison for using. His gaze shifted to Brad, and he frowned, seeming to notice him for the first time. 'Who's this?'

Allison started to remind him of his previous meetings with Brad, then realized Douglas didn't recognize him out of his disguise. 'Detective Bradley Malone,' she replied.

Douglas's eyes narrowed. 'Detective? What did you hire a detective for? Where'd you get the money?'

Allison started to protest, but Brad beat her to it.

'I'm with the Oklahoma City Police Department,' he said stiffly.

'Oh, that kind of detective. Well, Officer, I really appreciate your helping Allison with the ugly details tonight. She's led a pretty sheltered life, being married to a doctor.' He released Megan and held out his hand as though to shake Brad's. 'Nice to have met you. Be sure to call us for a donation to the fund.'

Brad ignored the hand, and Allison remembered the way Douglas had wiped his off after shaking with Brad last week. Brad's action was justified.

'We've met before,' Brad said. 'Maybe your flunky needs a new picture.' He rubbed his jaw. 'One without the beard.'

Douglas looked uncomfortable, then uncertain – the effect Brad always seemed to have on him.

Megan, however, apparently sensing the tension, was also starting to look uncomfortable, her gaze shifting from one to the other of the two men she adored.

'Let's get out of here,' Allison said firmly. 'Douglas, would you prefer to go home or to a motel? Bonnie sent you a suitcase. We've got it in the car.'

'Let's go home,' Douglas said, sending Brad a scorching glance. 'To our house,' he amended, beaming down at Megan. 'I could sure use a cup of coffee and a little friendly conversation after all this,' he appealed to Allison before she had a chance to refuse his first request. Order was actually more like it.

'You can have a cup of coffee while you visit with your daughter at my house, but then you call a cab and break down Bonnie's door or go to a motel. I don't care which, but Megan needs her sleep, as do we all.'

Douglas glared at Brad, who returned his look

dagger for dagger. As the four of them left, only Megan was chattering happily.

When they reached the house, Brad walked to the front door with them, then said goodbye.

'Nonsense,' Allison exclaimed, trying to sound light and keep the panic out of her voice – panic that he'd leave her before they got a chance to talk and panic that he'd leave her alone with Douglas. She had to admit that she needed his help getting rid of her ex. He always did it so well, while Douglas still managed to take control of the situation away from her. 'You've got to come in and have some coffee before you try to drive this late at night.'

'Don't leave, Brill,' Megan begged, momentarily deserting her father to cuddle up to Brad.

'Actually, we could use a little privacy,' Douglas contributed, pointedly setting his suitcase inside.

Brad's jaw tightened ever so slightly at Douglas's comment, and Allison knew then he'd stay. She took his arm and led him into the house. He made no protest.

The first thing Douglas did when he walked inside was to take off his suit jacket and hang it in the hall closet. Not a good sign. But Brad could handle him.

Going straight to the kitchen, Allison started a pot of coffee then returned to find Brad in one of the chairs, Megan and Douglas on the sofa, the cushion beside Douglas empty. She took the other chair.

Douglas smiled at her, and her defenses went up. 'I can't tell you how good it felt to see your pretty face waiting for me after my ordeal,' he said to her. 'You know I still think of you as my wife, the mother of my child.' He hugged Megan tighter for emphasis.

'Then I guess you'd better do some rethinking. I'm the mother of my child, and Bonnie's your wife.'

'You were right about her, you know.' He looked at Allison beseechingly, a look she recognized and had fallen victim to many times in the past. 'I'm sorry I hurt you. That thing with Bonnie was nothing. Mid-life crisis.'

'What about the thing with the lady you got caught with tonight? Post-mid-life crisis? Excuse me. I think the coffee's ready.'

When she returned with steaming cups for everybody, including cocoa for Megan, she decided a change of subject was in order.

'My special on the homeless went over great with the new station manager,' she said. 'I hope to get a raise and maybe a promotion out of the deal.'

Douglas caught her wrist as she leaned over to hand him his coffee. 'That's wonderful,' he said in an intimate voice. 'But you don't have to worry about working any more. I'll take care of you just like I used to. Surely all the happiness I gave you, all those wonderful years we had together, outweigh these past few horrible months. Maybe we could even have another child. You always wanted that.'

He held her wrist firmly, forcing her to look at him, and for a moment she considered his words. Megan would have her father back, and she herself could stop working so hard and worrying about every penny, every future penny. Her comfortable life would resume where it had left off. It would be as though nothing had changed.

But everything had changed. She'd changed. None of those things he promised mattered any more. She had a roof over her head, even if it was a little leaky. She had a job she enjoyed. With Douglas's indiscretion tonight, she could probably stop worrying about his trying to take Megan away. And, most importantly, she didn't want to live with this man before her. If she'd found it difficult for a few minutes to comprehend that Brad was the same person she loved after his physical change, she now found it impossible to believe she'd ever cared for Douglas with the changes they'd both undergone.

Brad's voice startled her out of her reverie. 'Thanks for the coffee,' he said, and she shot him a nervous glance, noting the coldness in his eyes. What was wrong with him? 'I've got to be going now. It's getting late.'

She tugged her wrist away from Douglas, not

caring that she was spilling coffee all over him and her sofa.

'No!' she said, her exclamation drowned by Douglas's bellow as the hot liquid ran between his legs.

At least the clamor halted Brad's exit.

Douglas marched upstairs to sponge off, and Allison took Brad's arm, leading him across the room, away from Megan. 'Get rid of him for me,' she whispered.

He'd always done such a good job of it before, but this time he wasn't helping at all. In fact, he gazed down at her almost coldly as she made the request.

'I can't,' he said. 'This is something you have to do. You're always so eager to do everything for yourself. Now's your chance. The wisest thing for me would be to get out of here and leave it with you.'

He was throwing her to the wolves – wolf, anyway. He didn't love her, didn't want her. If she'd been alone, she'd have burst into tears. But she wasn't alone, and she had no intention of letting him see her cry.

'Fine,' she snapped, taking refuge in anger. 'Leave. I can handle it myself.'

'You're the only one who can.'

'Mom,' Megan said, rushing up to stand between them. 'Mom, Brill doesn't have to leave just because Dad's moving back, does he?'

382

'Brad does have to leave even though your dad's not moving back.' And she couldn't get rid of the two of them fast enough. They both talked a good line, but when the chips were down, when she needed them, they pulled a vanishing act. She knew that. Why had she let herself get sucked into thinking Brad was any different?

'Don't make a hasty decision, Allison.' She looked up to see Douglas coming down the stairs. Later, she could laugh at the memory of him trying to be so dignified with a wet crotch. But right now she didn't feel like laughing. 'Give yourself a little time,' he said, oozing what she once thought of as charm. Now it seemed phony and slimy. 'We'll talk some more after your friend gets out of here.'

She yanked open the closet door, pulled out Douglas's jacket and threw it across the room. It only went a few feet, but she felt she'd made her point.

'You had your cup of coffee,' she said. 'Now say your goodbyes.'

She stalked over, snatched up the coat from the floor, marched to where he stood at the foot of the stairs and shoved it at him. He grabbed it in an automatic gesture.

'I didn't get to drink any coffee,' he protested, his expression startled. 'It spilled.'

'What you did with your coffee isn't my concern. You had it, and now you're leaving. I'm going to count to one hundred while you tell Megan good-bye. Then, if you ever hope to have more children, you'd better be gone before I get a carving knife from the kitchen.' With any sort of luck, he wouldn't leave, and she could carry out her threat. The thought gave her the most pleasant feeling she'd had since this mess began.

He backed up a step. 'I'll go if that's what you want, but you need to think about giving us a chance. Just promise me you'll consider it. This decision is too important to make on the spur of the moment.'

Turning her back, Allison stomped across the room, snatched the handle of his suitcase and dragged it onto the porch. She stepped back inside and folded her arms. 'One, two – '

Douglas edged toward her tentatively. 'You do want me to drop the custody suit, don't you?'

Before he said it, Allison would have sworn she couldn't possibly get any angrier, but a fresh wave of ire surged through her. She shot a glance at her wide-eyed daughter.

Brad moved over to Megan, wrapping his arms around her protectively.

'I'd just as soon you didn't dismiss it,' she answered Douglas. 'I was rather looking forward to telling Judge Jameson how you ran off and got drunk while Megan was in your custody, how you were thrown in jail for driving under the influence.

Yes, I anticipate this should be a very interesting trial.' She moved toward the kitchen. 'Thirteen, fourteen – '

'Be reasonable. I don't even have a car! Do you expect me to walk?'

'I'm sure your friend in the van will take you wherever you want to go. If not, walk down to the corner convenience store and call a cab. Seventy-five, seventy-six – ' So she was skipping a few numbers. He'd never played fair with her.

Douglas's expression became ugly as he backed toward the front door. At least, she thought, now he's being honest.

'You're going to regret this,' he told her. 'I can make your life miserable.'

'Only if I take you back. Eighty-seven, eighty-eight – '

'I won't pay any child support!' He opened the door.

'It always comes down to money with you, doesn't it, Douglas? Well, my child is going to be raised with different values, important values. Ninety-eight, ninety-nine – '

Douglas slammed the door behind him.

'Mom?'

Allison whirled around to face the room again. Her heart was racing, her adrenaline surging. Why hadn't she done this a long time ago? Douglas was a pompous phony, not someone to be feared.

Advancing on Brad, she retrieved her daughter and cuddled her close. 'It's all right, baby.' She forced herself to calm down, to avoid frightening Megan.

Megan gazed up, her eyes sad but accepting. 'You and Dad aren't ever going to live together again, are you?'

'No. I'm sorry.' She pushed the stray hair back from her daughter's forehead. 'Maybe you and I should talk about this.' She glanced at Brad. 'Alone.'

Megan stood with a sigh. 'I think I just want to go to bed now. I'm awful tired. If you need to talk, we can do that tomorrow.'

If you need to talk? Her daughter would never cease to amaze her.

Megan hugged her mother, then Brad.

With the resiliency of youth, she bounced halfway up the stairs, then stopped and looked back at Brad. 'When Madonna comes to town, do you think your friends could get us tickets?'

'Er, um – '

'We'll see,' Allison interjected for him. 'Goodnight.'

When she heard Megan's door slam, she turned to Brad and said sarcastically, 'Thanks for all the help. It's good to know I can count on you to be there when I need you. Goodnight.'

He grabbed her shoulders as she whirled away

and turned her back to face him. 'You thought about it,' he accused. 'You actually thought about taking that slime back.'

'What if I did? Is that any of your concern?'

'Yes, damn it,' he barked, 'it is my concern. I love you, and that makes it my concern.'

'You love me? Oh, that's rich.' She shrugged off his hands. 'If you loved me, you'd have helped me.'

'On the other hand, if you loved me, you would never have considered Dr Doug's proposition.'

'For one split second – ' she held up a hand, thumb and index finger a hair's breadth apart ' – the idea went in and out of my head. How could I not give it a thought? We were married, Megan's his daughter. But I rejected it.' She poked him in the chest with one finger. 'Remember that. I had a choice, and I made it. And so did you. You chose not to help me. When I needed you, you wimped out.'

'I chose to let you make that choice. You're not a cave woman who belongs to the strongest male. I can only help you so far. You're the only one who can get your life together, the only one who could get your ex out of your life.'

They stood scant inches apart, glaring at each other. Allison remembered she was angry at him and wanted him to leave, but she was having trouble hanging onto that anger. Especially since she knew he was telling the truth. Since he'd just forced her to do what she'd needed to do all along, take control of her life.

'I guess I'd better go,' he said.

'Yes,' she agreed, 'unless, of course, you'd rather stay.' There. Let him make a few choices.

He grinned. 'Yes, I'd rather.'

He reached for her, and she slipped into his strong arms, lifting her lips to his. It was a little strange to feel short, prickly stubble against her face rather than the tickly beard. But his lips hadn't changed. Soft and warm and strong, they seemed to pull all the intensity and emotion from the last few hours and channel it into the fire igniting between their bodies.

'If the custody case is over,' he whispered, lifting his mouth from hers, 'does that mean –?'

'It means you have to get up at six in the morning, reappear at the door thirty minutes later with doughnuts and convince Megan you just dropped by.'

He frowned. 'Sounds like you've done this before.'

'No, but I've fantasized about it a lot.'

His frown changed to a smile. 'I guess if I don't want doughnuts for breakfast every morning, we'll have to make this legal.'

'Whenever you're ready for eggs and bacon,' she agreed.

He kissed her again, his hands sliding over then under her sweater, stroking her bare skin.

'I put clean sheets on the bed,' she told him.

'You have been fantasizing.'

They started for the stairs, but he pulled her back. 'I'll never make a lot of money, you know,' he said.

'What are you, obsessed with money or something? There are more important things in life.'

He pulled her to him again. 'Like what?' he whispered.

'Come upstairs with me,' she invited, taking his hand. 'We'll have show and tell.'

THE EXCITING NEW NAME IN WOMEN'S FICTION!

PLEASE HELP ME TO HELP YOU!

Dear *Scarlet* Reader,

As Editor of *Scarlet* Books I want to make sure that the books I offer you every month are up to the high standards *Scarlet* readers expect. And to do that I need to know a little more about you and your reading likes and dislikes. So please spare a few minutes to fill in the short questionnaire on the following pages and send it to me. I'll send *you* a surprise gift as a thank you!

Looking forward to hearing from you,

Sally Cooper

Editor-in-Chief, *Scarlet*

P.S. Only one offer per household.

QUESTIONNAIRE

Please tick the appropriate boxes to indicate your answers

1 Where did you get this Scarlet title?

Bought in Supermarket ☐

Bought at W H Smith ☐

Bought at book exchange or second-hand shop ☐

Borrowed from a friend ☐

Other _____

2 Did you enjoy reading it?

A lot ☐   A little ☐   Not at all ☐

3 What did you particularly like about this book?

Believable characters ☐   Easy to read ☐

Good value for money ☐   Enjoyable locations ☐

Interesting story ☐   Modern setting ☐

Other _____

4 What did you particularly dislike about this book?

_____

5 Would you buy another Scarlet book?

Yes ☐   No ☐

6 What other kinds of book do you enjoy reading?

Horror ☐   Puzzle books ☐   Historical fiction ☐

General fiction ☐   Crime/Detective ☐   Cookery ☐

Other _____

7 Which magazines do you enjoy most?

Bella ☐   Best ☐   Woman's Weekly ☐

Woman and Home ☐   Hello ☐   Cosmopolitan ☐

Good Housekeeping ☐

Other _____

cont.

And now a little about you –

8 How old are you?
Under 25 ☐   25–34 ☐   35–44 ☐
45–54 ☐   55–64 ☐   over 65 ☐

9 What is your marital status?
Single ☐   Married/living with partner ☐
Widowed ☐   Separated/divorced ☐

10 What is your current occupation?
Employed full-time ☐   Employed part-time ☐
Student ☐   Housewife full-time ☐
Unemployed ☐   Retired ☐

11 Do you have children? If so, how many and how old are they?
_____
_____

12 What is your annual household income?
under £10,000 ☐   £10–20,000 ☐   £20–30,000 ☐
£30–40,000 ☐   over £40,000 ☐

Miss/Mrs/Ms _____
Address _____
_____
_____
_____

Thank you for completing this questionnaire. Now tear it out – put it in an envelope and send it before 31 March 1997, to:

Sally Cooper, Editor-in-Chief

SCARLET
FREEPOST LON 3335
LONDON W8 4BR
Please use block capitals for address.
No stamp is required!   UNLOV/9/96

***Scarlet* titles coming next month:**

SUMMER OF FIRE – Jill Sheldon
When Noah Taylor and Annie Laverty meet again, they are
instantly attracted to each other. Unfortunately, because of
his insecure childhood, Noah doesn't believe in love, while
Annie has trouble coming to terms with her terrifying past.
It takes a 'summer of fire' to finally bring Annie and Noah
together . . . forever.

DEVLIN'S DESIRE – Margaret Callaghan
Devlin Winter might *think* he can stroll back into Holly
Scott's life and take up where he left off – but Holly has
other ideas! No longer the fragile innocent Dev seduced
with his charm and sexual expertise, Holly is a woman to be
reckoned with. Dev, though, won't take 'no' for an answer,
and he tells Holly: 'You're mine. You've always been mine
and you'll always *be* mine!'

INTOXICATING LADY – Barbara Stewart
Happy in her work and determined never to fall in love,
Danielle can't understand what Kingsley Hunter wants
from her. One minute, he is trying to entice her into his
bed . . . the next he seems to hate her! 'Revenge is sweet'
they say . . . but Danielle, Kingsley's 'intoxicating lady', has
to convince him that passionate love is even sweeter.

STARSTRUCK – Lianne Conway
'Even ice-cold with indifference, Fergus Hann's eyes de-
mand attention' and they make Layne Denham realize an
awful truth! To be starstruck as a film fan is fun . . . but to
be starstruck in real life is asking for trouble . . . with a
capital 'T' for Temptation.